A GAME OF DECEIT

BY K. A. DAVIS

A Game of Deceit

Cover Design by Karen Phillips
Edited by Chandler Groover
Interior Formatting by SheridanINK

ISBN-13: 978-0-9990688-1-6
ISBN-10: 0-9990688-1-4

First Edition

Printed in the U.S.A

DEDICATION

For my husband, Dan, who gave me the support and encouragement
needed to believe in myself and create this book.

And for my granddaughters, Jaidyn, who bravely fights
the Rett Syndrome monster every day,
and for Emory, for being tenderhearted and caring for her sister.
They both inspire me to
find joy in the simple things in life.

I will donate 10% of the net proceeds from each sale of
this book to https://www.rettsyndrome.org/
with the hope that a cure will be found one day!

ACKNOWLEDGEMENTS

This book has been a long, long time in the making. Without the gentle nudging (and sometimes a downright push), support, and maybe even bribery from my husband, Dan, I never would have finished the book. His patience at reading it multiple times, answering my questions, and calming my fears have made me realize, multiple times over, just how lucky I am to have met him.

A huge thank you to my early readers, Mary Karnes, Briana Warner, Kathy Keith, and Janet Clause. You put up with my rough drafts and gave me good insight on how to make my story better.

A special thanks to authors, H.Y. Hanna and Daryl Wood Gerber for taking time out of your busy schedules to answer my questions about publishing and giving me vendor recommendations. I also am grateful for authors Paige Shelton, Jenny Kales, Catherine Bruns, and Daryl Wood Gerber for reading my book and giving me encouragement to see it brought to publication!

I so appreciate the cover design by talented Karen Phillips. She brought my story to life and until I saw her vision for my book I hated all my working titles. But seeing it put together in one cohesive package helped me find the perfect one.

Thank you too, to my editor Chandler Groover. He worked tirelessly to eradicate the endless commas liberally sprinkled throughout my manuscript and I now realize I should probably disable the comma key!

I must also thank all of the lovely people who follow my blog, Cinnamon, Sugar, and a Little Bit of Murder, for sharing my love for mysteries and food! While traditional mysteries and suspense don't typically have recipes, I've chosen to include several that my protagonist enjoys. Food speaks to the heart and helps people find a common ground. My baking and sharing food with friends and family expresses the love I have for each one of them and as a result, I want to share those special recipes with you as well.

A Game

of

Deceit

Newport Beach, California

The watcher lifted binoculars to his eyes, staying hidden behind sheer flowing curtains. The sun broke free of the morning clouds and its rays penetrated the mirrored glass of the high rise apartment just opposite him. As the sunlight became more intense, the outlines of the nude woman began coming into focus.

Six months before, the watcher had been pacing this room when he noticed that the mirrored glass in the building opposite was becoming transparent in the morning sunlight. That morning, a stunning blonde woman met an older man and entertained him.

Week after week the watcher became a hidden part of the woman's encounters with the man. The increasing use of violence, leaving cuts and bruises on the woman's perfect body, titillated him almost as much as the sexual acts.

Today, though, when the woman began dancing, her guest walked up behind her, remaining fully clothed. He traced his fingers along the outlines of her curves, starting from her slender thighs, to her taut derrière, to her flat stomach, around her full breasts and slowly encircled her neck. She was gently swaying, as if to music, with her eyes closed, when suddenly her eyes snapped wide open. She twisted and tried turning, her hands going to the fingers grasping her neck, her mouth open in a scream. With each passing moment her attempts to free herself became weaker, until there was no movement at all. Slowly the limp body was lowered to the floor.

When the woman's body was out of sight, the man walked to the window and smiled. His cold, piercing blue eyes seemed to penetrate the watcher's brain. With that the mesmerizing spell was broken. The watcher heard a click and turned to glimpse a tall, blond man standing behind him, just before everything went dark.

Chapter One

Kathryn Landry closed her laptop with a snap and snatched the flash stick out of the computer. Tucking the tiny device into her light pink backpack, she headed for her office door. The ringing phone slowed her stride, and with a sigh, she walked back to her cherrywood desk and sank into the cushioned black leather chair. Waiting to see who had interrupted her escape, she gazed out the windows and saw palm trees swaying, their fronds snapping briskly in the stiff winds that had started early that afternoon.

"Landry Designs, how may I help you?" Marianne Patton, her assistant, answered. "Just a moment, Mr. Selton, I'll see if she's available."

Kathryn sighed again when Marianne poked her head into the office.

"Mr. Selton says it's important. Do you want to take the call?" Marianne asked.

"Guess I have to," she answered, reaching for the phone. "After all, he's the one paying our bills at the moment."

The Selton Investigative Firm had contracted Kathryn to redecorate their luxurious office in Newport Beach, California. John had been impressed with Kathryn's style and extended the contract to include his mini-mansion in Newport Coast.

"Hi John, what can I do for you?" she asked.

"Promises, promises." He laughed, his deep velvet voice filling the phone. "Have you found out if my artwork has cleared Customs yet?"

"No, I'm afraid it hasn't. I've called them several times today but I can't get anyone to give me a definite time frame. The most they'll say is hopefully before the weekend."

"That's perfect, as long as you promise you'll have the paintings installed Saturday. I have Trieste this weekend and I would like her to spend some time watching you work."

"I think I can manage that," she answered. "I'd better warn you though, I'll have to charge extra for the moving van and installers."

"No problem. Whatever it takes to see you."

Kathryn cleared her throat. "By the way, how does Trieste like her new bedroom decor?"

"Actually, she hasn't seen it yet. I was busy last weekend so she stayed with her mother. I was thinking it would be a nice surprise if you were the one to show her the room since you put so much care into designing it."

"John, I would love to. Thanks for including me!"

"I'm glad it makes you happy. I'll see you Saturday then, around nine o'clock?"

"That'll be fine unless I run into any more problems with Customs. Either way, I'll have Marianne confirm with you on Friday."

Kathryn hung up the phone and stretched her tense shoulder and jaw muscles.

How am I going to explain this to Neil? He's never going to believe I need to be there on Saturday to hang paintings. I can already hear him complaining that's what he pays Marianne for.

Kathryn grabbed her backpack and headed for the cozy reception area. Marianne's silvery head was bent low over an invoice.

"Marianne, what are you still doing here? You didn't need to wait for me," she said.

"It's okay. I was trying to tally the invoices we need to pay next week," Marianne answered, pushing her reading glasses to perch on top of her head. "I wanted to give you the amount so that Neil can deposit money into the company account before Friday."

"You can do that tomorrow. Grab your things and we can walk out together."

"Okey-dokey." Marianne picked up her tote and followed Kathryn out the door after setting the security alarm. "Cute running outfit. Is it new?"

"Yes it is! I saw it at Athleta a few weeks ago and just had to have it," she said, while admiring the peach-colored tank top, which she knew made her green eyes sparkle and complemented her shoulder-length auburn hair, now pulled into a ponytail. The matching skort showed off her long, tanned legs.

"I can't believe you're going to jog home, Kathryn. This heat will kill you!"

"I know, but I need to train for my half marathon," Kathryn said, stretching her hamstrings while waiting for the elevator. "It's only a month away and I'm not sure I'm going to be ready for it."

"Have you told Neil why you're running in it yet?" Marianne punched the elevator button again.

"No, I never seem to find a way to bring it up. He gets so upset when anything reminds him of his little sister." She exhaled deeply. "Thank you again for your donation for Rett Syndrome research. I wasn't sure I could raise the money to meet the race's charity requirements."

"Richard and I are happy to help out all those little girls. And I'm proud of you raising money despite Neil's attitude." Marianne followed Kathryn into the elevator when the door slid open, then punched the button for the ground floor. "Is he home for dinner tonight?"

"I'm not sure," she answered. "He always seems to have a dinner scheduled with some editor or publisher, or someone with a good story. I have a hard time remembering his schedule."

Kathryn tried not to grimace at her lie. There wasn't anything wrong with her memory. Instead, her husband of eleven years never bothered to tell her when or where he was going.

"In that case, could I interest you in taking home this last piece of lasagna for yourself?" Marianne's voice intruded into Kathryn's thoughts. "*Cooking Light*, healthy for you. Really!"

"Thanks, Marianne, I'd love it." Kathryn knew she'd dispose of it before she arrived home. It was too difficult explaining to her grandmotherly assistant why Neil wouldn't allow her to eat it and why he forced her to weigh twice a day.

Kathryn started her slow jog up the hilly Newport Beach street. Even though it was just after five o'clock, the blazing sun blasted her skin and the buzzing rush hour traffic added to the heat. Hot Santa Ana winds blowing from the east parched her nose and mouth, making her sneeze. She slowed to a walk and retrieved a cold water bottle from her backpack. Turning around, she saw Catalina Island in the distant Pacific surrounded by an ugly brown haze of smog being blown in from the desert.

She arrived at her apartment building thirty minutes later with perspiring red cheeks and limp, sticky hair. She and Neil had purchased their unit five years ago and hoped that one day it would be a good investment. In the meantime, they were upside down on their mortgage and she dreaded having to ask Neil for more money to pay her company's bills.

"Mrs. Landry, you really shouldn't be running in this heat!" Tommy, her doorman, said as he held open the door and handed her mail.

"I know, I know," Kathryn answered, punching the elevator button. "I didn't realize it was so hot until it was too late. I'll be fine as soon as I get something cold to drink."

Entering her apartment, she was grateful that Neil had the air conditioning turned on. They rarely needed it living in coastal Southern California, but it was nice to have, especially when heat and dust were blown in on the wild winds from the desert each fall. Grabbing a huge glass of ice water from her spacious kitchen and leaving the pile of mail on the granite counter, Kathryn went to Neil's office. She quietly knocked on his closed door, and when he didn't answer, opened it. He wasn't there, but she could picture his intense hazel eyes and handsome chiseled face framed by short, curly golden hair. Sometimes he let his beard grow for a few days and there were traces of red highlights when he was in the sun.

Neil's laptop was shut and secured with an anti-theft device and his file drawers were locked tight which meant he was out for the evening. Carefully closing the door, she headed to their bedroom suite for a cool shower.

Stripping off her damp running clothes, she walked to the glass-enclosed shower and let double shower heads send cold water cascading over her head and down her body. When goose bumps covered her limbs, she warmed the water and shampooed her hair. After a final cold water rinse, she dried off with a thick Turkish cotton towel then padded to their walk-in closet to dress.

Kathryn pulled the double mahogany door open, snapped on the hanging crystal chandelier light and gasped. Neil's side of the closet was bare. Not one pair of pants, not one shoe, not one necktie. She flung open his bureau drawer where he kept underwear, socks and t-shirts and found it empty as well. Running to the bathroom, she found his toiletries had also vanished.

"Dammit, Neil, how could you do this to me?" Kathryn screeched. She grabbed a sea-green silk robe and stumbled to her bed. She sat and massaged her temples as she felt her heart start palpitating, her scalp tingle, and her hands turn clammy.

Kathryn dashed through their large apartment looking for a note Neil might have left for her, but found nothing. She ended the search in the kitchen and tried to calm herself by pouring a chilled glass of her favorite Cakebread Cellars Chardonnay. Her hands trembled and pale golden wine splashed down the front of the silk robe. When her knees began quivering, she stumbled to the kitchen chair and sank into its upholstered cushioned seat.

She took a sip of wine but the taste turned sour in her mouth and her stomach revolted. Clutching her midriff, she rocked back and forth while tears stung her eyes. She tried to visualize that morning with Neil. Had he done or said anything out of the ordinary? She couldn't think of anything. It was like all other mornings. He read the *Orange County Register* over breakfast while covertly observing as she measured cereal and fruit. Once she sat down to eat, he finished the sports section, then asked about her schedule and clients before she left for work. He typically called four or five times a day to see what she was doing. She realized Neil had only called once that morning and felt guilty for not noticing the lack of his usual calls.

"History repeats itself," she whispered, remembering her father disappearing the same way when she was fourteen years old…

Chapter Two

Returning home from an afternoon of shopping with her mother, fourteen-year-old Kathryn was eager to listen to her new favorite boy band CD. Slamming her bedroom door shut, she grabbed her father's portable player, jumped onto her pink canopied bed and inserted the shiny disk. Just as she pushed the play button she heard her mother's high-pitched scream.

Kathryn dropped her player and ran to the living room, where she found her mother slumped on a dusty-rose-colored wingchair, the cushions sagging from age.

"Mom, what's wrong? What happened?"

Her mother didn't answer, but instead wailed and pointed towards the master bedroom.

"Is it Dad? What's wrong?"

Kathryn ran towards her parents' bedroom and found the scratched wooden closet doors flung open, exposing bare gray metal racks and empty bureau drawers dumped on the floor.

"Mom, what happened? Where's Dad's stuff?" Kathryn pleaded.

"He's gone," Evelyn Muir answered in between sobs. "He took everything and he's gone."

***

Using the sleeve of her green silk robe, Kathryn wiped tears from her face, not sure if she was crying about losing her father or losing Neil. Neil knew that her father had abandoned her when she was a child and she couldn't believe that he would be so cruel to leave in the same way. Especially when she had remarked on her last birthday that this was the age her mother had been when her father left.

Maybe he just needed some space for a while and he'll come back home. Yeah, just like Dad did.

Kathryn wiped another tear before taking a sip of wine and then pulled her cell phone from her backpack. Maybe Neil would take her call and give her some answers. Her fingers were shaking so hard she had to enter his number three times before getting it right.

After four rings a nasally woman's voice answered "We're sorry, you have reached a number that has been disconnected or is no longer in service. If you feel you have reached this recording in error, please check the number and try your call again."

Kathryn punched in his number and double checked to make sure she entered it correctly. She heard the same recording.

You've thought of everything, haven't you, Neil?

She suddenly remembered seeing Neil's sleek laptop on his office desk. Jumping up from the glass table, she corked the bottle, tucked it under her arm and picked up her full wineglass before carefully walking to his office. She flung the light switch on while opening the laptop. Waiting for the computer to power up, she found a tissue and wiped droplets of wine off the cool, smooth desk that had splashed from the glass.

"Maybe you can give me some answers," she whispered to the bright screen.

A password prompt appeared. Kathryn took a guess and typed in her own name.

Wrong, of course.

She tried a variety of birthdates, his social security number, driver's license number, but to no avail. She mused for a while, then finally typed "Miranda", the name of Neil's deceased little sister. He'd told her about his sister only once, but she could tell that even twenty-five years after her death, he still grieved for the girl who'd had the misfortune to be born with Rett Syndrome. When she had asked other questions about Miranda a few months later, he had snapped at her and told her to never bring her name up again.

Kathryn was rewarded with the desktop menu but then guiltily glanced at the door. She tried reassuring herself that Neil had forfeited his right to privacy when he packed his belongings and left.

Having no idea what she was looking for, she started with his calendar. She located the current date and noted that he had an appointment at ten o'clock that morning with a Ms.X.

Who's Ms. X? Is she a lover or co-worker, informant or client?

Kathryn flipped to the preceding date.

When nothing appeared she started scrolling back through the days until one week earlier she found another appointment with Ms. X at ten o'clock.

With her heart pounding and her palms starting to sweat, she went back another week. There she found another appointment with Ms. X at ten o'clock.

"Please let there be an innocent explanation for this," she whispered.

She continued searching the calendar, going back week by week, finding each appointment with Ms. X, until she had scrolled through six months, to the first logged appointment. By this time her pounding heart felt like it was going to rupture and her head felt as if it were gripped in a vise. In a daze she started hunting through his Word documents after taking a gulp of wine.

She found that most of the document titles were related to newspaper and magazine articles he had composed as a freelance writer over the course of several years, but one title caught her eye. She clicked on "mynovel", entered Miranda's name at the password prompt, and was astounded to find it contained over one hundred pages of writing. Quickly reading, she discovered he had been writing a novel based on a voyeur spying into an apartment across from his, when the mirrored windows became transparent during the time the morning sun passed over them. He vividly described graphic sex scenes involving a beautiful blonde prostitute and a violent older john. She blushed while reading what was only a step away from pornography and was nauseated by the violence inflicted on the woman, all the while continually worrying that Neil would come home and catch her on his computer.

The stress finally took a toll on Kathryn. She pushed herself away from the computer, stretched and tried to rub the knots out of her neck. She found her backpack in the kitchen, retrieved the USB flash drive and saved the novel and Neil's calendar to the device, to read at another time on her own computer. After carefully wiping her fingerprint smudges from the keyboard and desk, she made sure she logged off before shutting down the computer. She straightened the computer on the desk, noted everything else was in order, shut off the light and stumbled off to bed more than a little drunk.

The ringing telephone jarred Kathryn into consciousness.

"Dammit, Neil, answer the phone," she muttered under her breath, rubbing her throbbing head.

When the phone finally stopped ringing, she opened her dry, gritty eyes and grimaced at the intruding sunlight. Abruptly she was fully awake and she leapt out of bed and grabbed the phone to see if Neil had left a message. Disappointment swept over her when caller ID identified her office number. She rubbed her puffy eyes and ran fingers through her tangled hair.

After listening to Marianne's brief voicemail, Kathryn calmed herself and called her back.

"Landry Designs, how may I assist you?" Marianne said, sounding efficient.

"Hi Marianne, it's Kathryn," she replied, her words coming out with a croak. "I'm returning your call."

"Are you sick? Your voice sounds hoarse!"

"It's probably allergies from the Santa Ana winds. What did you need?"

"I didn't want to intrude but I was getting worried about you. You're always at the office by eight or at least call and there wasn't anything on your appointment calendar. I tried your cell phone but didn't get an answer, so I was, well, worried…" Marianne's voice trailed off.

Kathryn glanced at her crystal bedside clock while sniffling. "I can't believe it's nine-thirty already! I'm sorry to worry you, Marianne, but I overslept."

"Are you sure you're not coming down with something? I'm surprised Neil didn't call the office to let me know."

She paused a moment and her voice cracked. "I guess he's been kind of busy this morning."

She heard Marianne exhale. "Are you sure you're okay? I don't want to pry, but if you need anything…"

Kathryn choked back the sob wanting to escape and tried to enunciate her words. "Neil packed up and left yesterday. He didn't tell me he was going, and I think he's having an affair. On top of that, I drank an entire bottle of wine last night."

"Oh Kathryn, I'm so sorry about Neil."

"I know you never liked him but he's the only family I have," she said, trying to control her quaking voice. "I don't know what I'm going to do."

"You're not alone. You know Richard and I consider you the daughter we never had. Would you like me to come over? Bring a box of Godiva?"

"Thanks, Marianne, but I don't think I should have any more calories anytime soon," she said with a hiccup, trying to calm herself down. "I'll be okay, but I don't think I can make it to the office today."

"Don't worry about the office, I'm sure I can manage anything that comes up."

"The only pressing item is finding out when Customs will release John's art and schedule the delivery for Saturday morning." Kathryn paused to wipe her nose. "You'll find the phone number and invoice on my desk."

"I'll call Customs right away and let John know the status. Just take care of yourself, and please, let me know if there's anything else I can do."

"I'll check in with you later. And Marianne? Thanks."

Kathryn hung up the phone, changed into black yoga shorts and a royal blue tank top, then stood in front of her creamy marble-topped vanity. She muttered when she saw her reflection in the mirror. Red, puffy eyes. Dark circles and bags. Hair standing every which way.

I look like Johnny Depp in Alice in Wonderland.

Averting her eyes, she harshly brushed her hair and then clipped it into a ponytail. She pulled open her makeup drawer and grabbed her birth control pills. Neil usually had her pill sitting on the breakfast table. She briefly wondered if she even needed to take them now.

Putting the container back into the drawer, she saw Neil's thyroid medication. He was meticulous, bordering on paranoid, about taking it. After having surgery to remove a cancerous thyroid when he was a teenager, Neil's body was dependent upon the medication. She was certain he would not have missed packing his prescription nor would he have left his laptop. She shivered at the thoughts running through her head.

You're imagining things. Anyone who reads his calendar would know he was having an affair. Don't be so dramatic.

Kathryn remembered Neil's description about the transparent windows in his novel and wondered if there was some truth behind his story. She hurried to her living room and peered into the apartment opposite, mesmerized as the dark opaque glass slowly turned translucent when the brilliant morning sun passed over it. The apartment appeared to be empty. The two rooms that she could see into held no furniture and a beautiful blonde woman wasn't walking around or having sex.

Going to the kitchen, Kathryn pushed the power button on her coffee machine, anxious for her first cup of scalding hot Kona coffee. The toasty fragrance of the beans filled the air and she was reminded of touring coffee plantations in Hawaii with Neil on their honeymoon. Really a double-celebration trip since they'd both graduated from college the week before and had married a few days later before enjoying themselves in Hawaii. She closed her eyes trying to remember how he used to love her so many years ago.

Neil, why did you shut me out of your life? Why did you leave?

Knowing she didn't have the answers, she poured a cup of coffee and talked herself into calling the police. She couldn't ignore the fact that Neil had left two items behind that were of utmost importance to him.

She tried to keep her voice steady as she gave her name and address to the husky-voiced sergeant, who asked for a physical description of her husband, and when she last saw him. He said they would send a detective to her home as soon as they could, but she should call back if Neil returned or made contact. Kathryn hung up the receiver to wait by herself in the silent apartment.

She recalled with distaste, while vigorously cleaning her granite countertops and travertine kitchen floor, the ordeal her mother, Evelyn, had gone through when her father disappeared. The young detective who questioned them made it apparent from the beginning that he considered the case family abandonment and not worth his time. Her mother didn't try to dissuade him and it wasn't long before the case was closed. Each day after that, Evelyn became more withdrawn, more haggard, until she barely resembled the mother Katherine once knew.

Kathryn's eyes blurred as she remembered coming home from her first day of classes at the community college and finding her mother sleeping in the hot, stuffy bedroom. Only she really wasn't sleeping. A brand new bottle of prescription sleeping pills lay empty beside the still body, a half-empty bottle of vodka perched on the nightstand.

The police quickly labeled it suicide even when Kathryn asked them to look into the prescription. The label didn't seem genuine and she had never seen her mother take a drink of alcohol in her life. But authorities shook their heads and told her to forget about it.

The sudden chiming doorbell startled her and Kathryn hesitated, while drying her hands, before walking to the door. She didn't want to see anyone, but didn't want to take the chance of missing someone bringing a message from Neil. She quickened her step at the insistent chime and yanked open the heavy door.

"Good god, Kathryn, you look awful!" said John Selton.

Chapter Three

"Thanks, John," Kathryn replied sarcastically, trying not to notice how his crisp white buttoned-down shirt was cut to emphasize his broad shoulders and narrow waist. "You look great too."

"No, I take that back." His liquid brown eyes swept over her tight tank top and form-fitting yoga shorts. "You look terrific."

"I'm assuming you didn't come here to exchange compliments, so what can I do for you?"

"I dropped by the office to see you and pried the story of Neil's affair out of Marianne. I thought I might offer my services."

"I know Marianne. She wouldn't gossip about my personal business. What did you bribe her with?"

"Teuscher dark chocolate champagne truffles, flown in fresh from Switzerland. She made me go back to Fashion Island and buy another box for you."

"Fine, Mister Johnny on the Spot. Hand over the chocolate and you can come in. I think I could use your *professional* services."

She opened the door and John stepped in. As he handed her the box of truffles, he leaned down and brushed his warm full lips across her cheek. His freshly shaved face had a clean, woodsy scent.

Kathryn abruptly backed up. "John, I meant your private investigator services. I'm not sure about the affair, but Neil's disappeared. I've already called the police and reported him missing, for whatever good that will do. Maybe you can find him?"

"You can't blame a guy for trying." John ran his hand through wavy black hair and flashed a smile, his white teeth accentuated by his deeply tanned skin. "I wish you would have called me before the police though. They complicate everything. But, if you really want to find Neil, of course I'll help."

She quickly explained finding the prescription and the laptop that was left behind as she led John to Neil's office. The room was a contrast of black and white. White tiled marble floor topped with a woven black bamboo area mat. His black desk was immaculately organized with brushed stainless steel desk accessories and clutter free. The framed black-and- white oak tree landscape photos on his wall were meticulously straight. A black vase held snow-white Phalaenopsis orchids. Not a speck of dust in sight.

Kathryn turned on the computer. "I found his calendar. It looks like he was meeting a woman every week, but I can't believe it was an affair. He never would have left his prescription or laptop if he ran off with someone."

John scanned through the computer files, randomly opening some before focusing on the calendar.

"Would you like some coffee or something to drink?" she asked.

"No thanks, I'm fine. Have you looked at the rest of his files?"

"I scanned the titles. Most of them seem to be articles he's written for freelancing jobs, but there were too many to open and look at. There is one that is a, um, novel he was working on."

"Oh? An aspiring novelist? Is it any good?"

"I, um…" stammered Kathryn, turning beet red, "…really can't say."

John laughed. "Is it that bad? I thought he wrote for a living."

"No, I'd say it's well written. But it's about a subject I'm not comfortable with.

The only reason I mention it is that it could be connected to his disappearance. I know I'm grasping at straws but I don't want to overlook anything."

"What was Neil's reaction to your lack of enthusiasm for his novel? Was he crushed?"

She lowered her eyes and softly said, "I never knew about the novel until last night."

"Oh, so Neil has some secrets…" John's voice trailed off. "There are a lot of documents here so I think the best thing would be to take the laptop to my office and have my technicians start going through the files. Is that okay with you?"

"That would be fine, except I don't have the combination number for the security device."

"Oh? More secrets? Shouldn't be a problem. I'll send someone over to make a hard drive backup. Is there anything else you can think of that I should know?"

"No, I can't think of anything else right now. I feel like I'm in a fog." She shivered and wrapped her arms around her midriff. "This brings up so many bad memories from when I was a kid."

"Can I ask what happened?" John looked up from the laptop.

"My dad disappeared when I was fourteen. We came home and all his stuff was gone, just like Neil."

"Your dad disappeared too? Poor Kathryn, you've been through a lot, haven't you?" He reached up and took her hand into his. "Did you ever find out where he went or what happened to him?"

"No, nothing. He worked for the *Register* and they ran a series of articles on him but he never turned up."

"I seem to remember something like that. What was your father's name?"

"Jack Muir."

John studied her for a moment, then nodded. "How about your mother, can she stay with you, or some other relatives or friends?"

"My mother died when I started college. She had a brother but I only met him once, right after my father left. Neil didn't have any family either. Neil's the only one I have," Kathryn said, her voice quivering.

John stood up and drew her to his shoulder while putting a protective arm around her. Kathryn sniffled, but didn't give in to the desire to sob her heart out. Instead she surprised herself by noticing again how nice John smelled, wondering if it was cologne or the soap he used.

The ringing phone startled them both. Kathryn pulled away and answered. After listening to a brief message she replaced the receiver.

"The detective's on his way up. John, can you stay and help me get through this?"

"You're not alone, Kathryn. I'll be here as long as you want me to be. Why don't you freshen up and I'll meet him at the elevator. I know quite a few guys on the force and I can fill the detective in before he talks to you."

Kathryn quickly changed into slacks and a blouse, brushed her hair and applied some lipstick. She opened her front door and waited for them to arrive. She saw John walking towards her with a scowl on his face. The detective closely followed. He wasn't in uniform, but was dressed in dark blue jeans, a collared white shirt and a brown suede-looking sports coat. As the pair of men walked down the hallway from the elevator, Kathryn could see the detective was about six feet tall, salt-and-pepper-splashed hair, which was neatly trimmed, and pale blue eyes set in a rugged, tanned face.

John reached her door first and brusquely said, "Kathryn, this is Detective Williams. Detective, this is Kathryn Landry."

The detective put out his hand to shake Kathryn's, but she was frozen in time. Her mind whirled back to being fourteen years old and meeting another Detective Williams. She tried to remember what he looked like, but only remembered cold blue eyes.

John nudged Kathryn, bringing her back to the present.

"Oh, sorry Detective," she stammered as she shook his hand. "I met a Detective Williams about twenty years ago under very difficult circumstances, and I was wondering if you were the same person."

"It could have been. I've been on the force for twenty-five years now. Some people think being fifty years old makes me ancient and decrepit but I know that I'm making the baddies shake in their boots when they see me coming after them," Detective Williams said with a chuckle. "What was the case about? Maybe I'll remember that far back if my senile brain hasn't forgotten."

Kathryn liked his deep, gravelly self-deprecating voice, but then reminded herself that if this was the same detective, he had grievously wronged her and her mother.

"My father, Jack Muir, disappeared twenty years ago. Unfortunately, my husband, Neil, disappeared in almost the same way. All their personal belongings gone, no trace, no note, nothing," she broke off with a choke.

She saw Detective Williams suddenly pale at her father's name. John was intently studying the detective as well.

"Jack Muir. Mrs. Landry, I can't tell you how sorry I was that we couldn't find any leads on your father," Williams replied. "And your husband is now missing?"

"Oh," Kathryn said abruptly, "so you are the same detective. Do you think you can do any better finding my husband?"

"Mrs. Landry, we'll do everything humanly possible to solve Mr. Landry's disappearance. We have advanced technology at our disposal that wasn't available twenty years ago," Detective Williams answered, his eyes pleading with Kathryn. "Please believe me when I say I'm truly sorry about your father's case not being resolved."

"I hope you're right. Why don't you both come in and have a seat so we can talk about Neil," she said. "Can I offer anyone coffee or tea before we get started?"

"No, nothing," both John and Detective Williams replied at the same time. John glared at the detective, whose furrowed brows caused deep lines to appear in his forehead.

Kathryn led them to the living room, with the large picture window looking out to the neighboring apartment building and the Pacific Ocean glittering in the distance. Kathryn chose the overstuffed sofa and sank down into the cushions. John sat in the matching wingback chair next to her and patted her hand. Detective Williams shrugged his shoulders, sat on the opposite end of the couch, took a notebook out of his sports coat and started writing. Kathryn couldn't help but compare John and Detective Williams. John was dressed in a custom-made Hugo Boss shirt and Dolce & Gabbana black wool trousers. He had a Breitling watch and his John Lobb leather shoes were shined to perfection. Detective Williams, on the other hand, looked clean and neat, but not very successful. He wore a simple Timex watch and his cowboy boots were scuffed.

"Mrs. Landry, is your husband the Neil Landry who used to write the sports column for the *Register*?"

"Yes."

"I was a big fan of his. He has a great sense of humor and I was shocked when they discontinued his column."

Kathryn paused to wonder why everyone else thought Neil was so humorous. Why didn't she get to see that side of him?

"Thank you, Detective. He was disappointed they dropped the column as well. However, it allowed him to successfully expand his freelancing endeavors."

"First, do you want the media involved? Will you be contacting them?" Detective Williams asked, his mouth turned down at the corners.

"Oh, definitely not. I don't want a circus going on around here if we can avoid it," she answered, while looking at John to see if he had a different opinion.

"Then we'll do everything to keep it quiet for the time being," Williams answered.

"Thank you."

The detective started asking a question but, before he gave Kathryn a chance to answer, said, "Are you sure you want Mr. Selton here?"

"Mr. Selton is a private investigator who has agreed to help me out. If you recall, the police never figured out what happened to my father," Kathryn snapped.

She felt some satisfaction when she saw him grimace.

"Okay then," Detective Williams said, "let's get started."

He asked questions for about fifteen minutes, taking notes the entire time. Kathryn was embarrassed to answer some of them with John there, but kept telling herself that he was going to help and he needed to have the information as well. She couldn't help wondering why John wasn't taking notes. Once or twice he gave her shoulder a reassuring squeeze and a brief nod when the detective asked a particularly personal question.

"Well, that about wraps up all my questions," the detective said. "I'm sure I'll be asking more as the investigation continues. Is there anything else pertinent I should know?"

"No, nothing that I can think of." Kathryn's brows scrunched together. "I think it's important to re-emphasize, though, the only thing Neil left behind was his Synthroid prescription and his laptop. He would never do that voluntarily."

"I'll need the name and phone number of Mr. Landry's doctor and pharmacist," the detective said. "We'll check if he's gotten a refill. I'm also going to have our computer guy have a look at Neil's laptop and take it down to our lab. I'd do it, but I've never quite caught up with all this technology."

Kathryn almost snorted. "You mean all the advanced technology that is supposed to help you find my husband?"

John suppressed a snicker while the detective glared back.

Detective Williams grunted. "You've got a point. However, we have teams who do nothing but focus on the technology while we grunts do the legwork. It's more efficient that way."

"Just a moment, Detective," John interjected, "I don't think there's any reason you need to take Mr. Landry's computer. It's personal property of my client."

"Are you trying to help find Mrs. Landry's husband or interfere with my investigation?" Williams asked.

"Since you botched your last investigation involving Mrs. Landry, I'm helping, which is why the computer should stay here," John said. "Mrs. Landry and I will need access to the data."

"Then perhaps you should back the computer up and access the data that way," the detective replied. "One way or another, that laptop is going to the lab tomorrow afternoon. End of discussion. Now, if you don't mind, I'd like to take a look around your apartment, Mrs. Landry."

"That's fine. Do you want me to show you around?"

"No, I can find my way. I'll try not to be too intrusive."

When the detective left the room, John got up from his chair, sat beside her and held her hand. "You did great, Kathryn."

Lowering his voice to almost a whisper, he said, "Why didn't you tell the detective about the calendar and novel?"

"I'm afraid he'll jump to the conclusion that Neil was having an affair and left me. I don't want him dumping this investigation before he even starts. Maybe he'll find another explanation before they see the calendar."

"Excuse me." Detective Williams had returned, eyebrows raised. "I don't mean to interrupt but my office just paged me. I have some urgent business to take care of so I'd like to come back tomorrow and take another look around. I'll need to talk to some of your neighbors and the building manager then."

Kathryn immediately withdrew her hand from John and said too loudly, "He was trying to console me and wanted to make sure I didn't forget to tell you anything that might be significant. Unfortunately, I can't think of anything else I haven't told you already."

The detective let the silence linger before he handed her a card. "Here's my business card with my work number and cell phone in case you think of something. I'll call you tomorrow morning and let you know what time I'll come by."

Once the detective was out the door, John said, "What a jerk! I was hoping one of my buddies would be assigned your case."

"Do you know Detective Williams?" Kathryn asked. "There's a lot of tension between the two of you."

"Not really. I've just heard my buddies complaining about him all the time. You know those old-timers: they're always right and you're always in their way. Williams has quite a reputation down at the precinct."

"What's his reputation?"

"A loner; a real hard-ass. I suppose he's competent, but perhaps you should complain and see if they'll put someone else on it. Especially with the way your father's case turned out."

"I'll give it some thought and see what happens over the next couple of days. I don't think I can go through another interview like that with a new detective." Kathryn exhaled deeply before sinking into the wingback chair. "Thanks for everything you've done for me today, John. I don't know how I would have gotten through it without you."

"Glad to help out. Why don't you let me take you to lunch? I know the perfect, quiet little spot down by the beach."

"Thanks, but I'm really not up to going out. I'm exhausted."

"Okay, I can order in Chinese."

"I appreciate all you're doing for me but I feel like being by myself for a while."

"No problem, I get the hint," he answered while winking at her.

Kathryn started to get up, but John walked over and gave her a peck on the cheek. "No, stay where you are and I'll let myself out. I'll see you tomorrow."

After he left, Kathryn fixed herself herbal tea, opened the box of Teuscher chocolates and bit into the dark, creamy morsel, the sweet richness coating her tongue. The sharp bittersweet smell reminded her of Easter as a very young child. Her mom and dad playing hide-and-seek with chocolate eggs. Laughing. Tickling. Yelling "warmer" or "colder." Sharing candy together after the games. Childhood memories almost forgotten.

She stared out her large picture window towards the empty mirrored apartment. Her jumbled thoughts fought for answers and she became more agitated. Pacing back and forth in front of the window, she noticed her doorman talking to the other apartment building's doorman fifteen floors below her.

"Of course!" She grabbed her purse and sprinted out the door.

Chapter Four

The elevator doors opened with a chime and Kathryn stepped into the lobby. Her low-heeled slingback shoes clicked on the glossy white marble floor as she headed to the dark mahogany reception desk next to the front entrance. A short, stocky young man, dressed in a long-sleeved gray uniform, stood behind the counter. A captain's hat sat angled on his black, close-cropped hair, and his dark black eyes darted continuously around the lobby.

"Good morning, Mrs. Landry," Tommy said. "Shall I call a taxi for you or will you be driving today?"

"Hi Tommy," Kathryn replied. "I'd like to talk to you, if you have a few minutes."

"Sure. Is everything okay?" He leaned in closer to her. "What's up with the police?"

Kathryn berated herself for not thinking of talking to Tommy sooner. He knew everything that went on in the building.

"Tommy, I'd like to keep this confidential, okay?" Kathryn paused, looked around the lobby, then lowered her voice before continuing. "Neil disappeared yesterday. The detective who came to talk to me about it seems to have other things going on at the moment. Can you tell me when you last saw my husband?"

Tommy pursed his lips together and seemed to examine the ceiling for a moment before answering. "It would've been the day before yesterday. He went out for his usual run around three-thirty in the afternoon and came back about an hour later."

"You didn't see Mr. Landry at all yesterday?"

"No, but maybe he left while I was on a break? I wish I could be more helpful."

"Would you have any idea how Neil could have taken his clothing out without you noticing? Did you see anyone carrying out a lot of boxes or suitcases yesterday?"

"The Smiths moved out yesterday. They lived on the floor above you," Tommy said while rummaging through a file folder. "Here's a business card from Arcade Moving Company. They're the ones who did the loading. There were a lot of boxes and furniture going out but I never saw your husband."

"Is there a chance he could have gone out through the back service entrance?"

"It's not likely," the doorman replied. "About three years ago we were having problems with break-ins using that entrance, so the door has an alarm. It will go off even if it's opened from the inside, unless you have the pass code. The alarm never went off yesterday."

"Thanks, Tommy. I'm sure the police will eventually be asking you the same questions." On a sudden hunch, Kathryn asked, "Do you know the doorman across the street? Did anyone move out of that building yesterday from the fifteenth floor?"

"The answer to your question is 'yes' and 'yes.'" Tommy chuckled when he saw Kathryn's confused expression. "My cousin, Tomas, is the doorman, and their tenant shared the moving van with the Smiths. I thought it was strange since the Smiths are quite elderly and the tenant across the street is a young woman. But maybe they're related somehow, or got a good deal on the truck."

Kathryn laughed. "Your name is Tommy and your cousin is Tomas?"

"Yeah, I know. My grandfather's name was Tomas, and my mother and my aunt both wanted their firstborn named after him. My aunt gave birth to my cousin a few hours before I was born, so they got the official name. My mom settled for Tommy."

"Sounds like it could be confusing."

"Oh it is, especially since Tomas and I could pass for identical twins." He grinned. "You should have seen the stunts we pulled when we were in school. Those were the good old days. But enough about me. Is there anything else I can help you with?"

"Did you see the woman who moved out yesterday?" Kathryn asked, holding her breath. "What does she look like?"

"She's young, maybe early twenties, blonde, tall, well developed if you get my meaning. And drop-dead gorgeous with no disrespect to you, Mrs. Landry. I believe she lived on the fifteenth floor, directly across from your apartment. She only showed up at that apartment once a week for a short while. My cousin likes gossip, which is why I know so much."

"Do you remember seeing her yesterday?"

"I think she arrived a couple hours before the moving van showed up. She's hard not to notice. But with the bustle going on around here with the Smiths moving out, I didn't see her leave."

"Would your cousin mind if I asked him some questions too?"

"I'm sure he'll be happy to talk to you, Mrs. Landry. Tomas loves to talk, especially to pretty women. I'll call him right now and tell him you're on your way."

Kathryn walked across the cobblestoned drive, giving the splashing marble dolphin fountain a wide berth. She wrinkled her nose at the smell of faint smoke fumes blowing in on the winds and scanned the eastern sky for sooty plumes. Even though the intense sun radiated heat on her bare arms, she shivered when she saw a brown smudge creeping towards the city.

Entering the apartment's lobby, she found that it was an exact replica of her own building and, just as Tommy had said, a man who looked like his twin brother, wearing an identical uniform, was hanging up the phone. His coal black eyes quickly slid down her body then rested on her face, before he introduced himself.

"Hello, Tomas," Kathryn said, reaching out her hand to shake his. "Thanks for taking time to talk to me."

"Not a problem. Tommy mentioned you had a situation. I'm happy to help any way I can." Tomas frowned. "Even if it means talking to the police."

"I appreciate it." Kathryn pointed towards the flat-screen television mounted in the lobby. "Has there been any news about a fire today?"

"No, but I thought I caught a whiff of smoke when you came through the door. Do you think one started?"

"I'm afraid so. I saw brown haze moving towards here." Kathryn winced. "I hate these winds when it's been so dry. And then crazies start fires and so many people lose their homes."

"I know. My uncle came close to losing his in the Malibu fire a few years ago and they never caught those arsonists." Tomas scowled. "Maybe the winds will die down and they'll get this under control quickly."

"I hope so."

"So what can I do for you, Mrs. Landry?"

"Do you remember seeing a young, blonde woman leave yesterday after her belongings were moved out?" Kathryn pulled a small notebook out of her purse, prepared to take notes.

The front desk phone rang. "Excuse me, Mrs. Landry, I need to answer this. Here's the remote. You can change the channel and watch whatever you want."

She moved closer to the flat-screen television and, using the remote, searched for a local news channel while waiting for Tomas to end the phone call. She jumped when he cleared his throat, directly behind her.

"Sorry to startle you. Now what was it that you wanted to know about Helene?"

After repeating her question, Tomas scratched his head. "I recall seeing her come in but I didn't see her after that."

27

"But wouldn't she have left the apartment key? And what about a forwarding address for her mail?"

"One of the movers dropped the key off at my desk and said that Helene would be in touch later about forwarding mail."

"Didn't you find it odd not seeing her leave the building?"

"I just assumed she left while I was on break and, since she didn't see me, had the movers leave the key."

"Do you know what Helene's full name is? Was the apartment registered in her name?" Kathryn paused for air. "Could she have gone out another way without you noticing?"

"Whoa, you have a lot of questions!" Tomas chuckled. "Her name is Helene Monterrey. I'll have to check the records for her application. Her apartment was a rental, not owner-occupied. What was your other question again?"

"Sorry," Kathryn said while frantically writing in her notebook. "My mind is getting ahead of myself. Is there another way she could have left without you seeing her?"

"We have a service entry but it's alarmed, so she couldn't have used it."

"How do people get in to make deliveries?"

"If it's a company that comes on a regular basis, they have the key code to open the door and disarm the alarm. If it's a new company bringing deliveries, they ring my desk using a phone in the service entrance and I go open the doors for them."

"Wouldn't the moving company have used the service entrance?"

"Since Helene and the Smiths from your building were sharing the truck, management let them use the front entrance. Besides, she didn't have much to move out."

"Would you mind if I take a look at the apartment?" Kathryn gave him her sweetest smile. "I assume it's still empty."

"I don't see why that would be a problem. Just don't tell the manager on me," Tomas said, winking at her. "Let me get the key, and once we're done looking around up there, I'll check the lease records."

They took the elevator up to the fifteenth floor and Tomas unlocked the heavy oak door, then held it open for her. "Ladies first."

The apartment was bare. Kathryn walked into the living room, her feet sinking down into the plush cream-colored carpet. Glancing out the window, she noticed there were no draperies or blinds. Looking towards her apartment, she saw that the mirrored glass on her windows had dulled and was thin in several areas. She thought she might be able to make out the shape of a lamp in her living room, but wasn't sure if her eyes were playing tricks on her.

She left the window and began to walk through the empty rooms, hunting for anything that would give her an indication Neil had been there. Tomas noisily opened and closed cabinets in the kitchen, humming softly to himself. The apartment was completely empty and appeared to have been cleaned after the movers left. Kathryn checked the trash for any scraps of information under the bathroom sinks. Nothing. She joined Tomas in the kitchen and opened the huge built-in Sub-Zero refrigerator, which looked brand new, straight from the factory. Kathryn saw that all the appliances, countertops and flooring were high-end and sparkling clean.

"I wonder why the owners would sink so much money into an apartment and not live here," she muttered.

"Did you say something?" Tomas had his head wedged into the trash compactor that had been cleverly designed to blend into the cabinetry.

"Nothing important." She bent down to see what he was doing. "Did you find anything?"

"I see a piece of paper stuck behind the compactor." He pulled his head back out, reached in a long arm, then slowly pulled the sheet out. He glanced at it and handed it to Kathryn.

Smoothing the rumpled paper out, she found a charge card statement to Bloomingdales for Helene Monterrey with an address in Rancho Santa Margarita. Miss Monterrey had been a very busy shopper. Jewelry, make-up, handbags, perfume, shoes, lots of shoes, and designer jeans. Kathryn was curious about what Helene did for a living that allowed her to afford two different residences and shopping sprees at Bloomingdales.

"Thanks, Tomas. I think this is exactly what I need."

"Not a problem, Mrs. Landry. Shall we go look at her lease application?"

Waiting for the elevator to take them back down to the lobby, Kathryn asked, "Did Helene have any visitors when she came to the apartment?"

Tomas shook his head. "No. She always came in alone and left within a couple hours, alone."

"But did someone ever come in after she arrived, or leave right before she did?" Kathryn persisted.

"No, no one that didn't live here, that didn't belong."

"Would you recognize my husband, Neil, if I showed you a picture?" Pulling a photo out of her wallet, Kathryn's voice quivered. "Did you ever see him here?"

"No, I never saw him in this building. Once in a while I'd see him leave your building, but that's all."

Once they reached the lobby Tomas checked to make sure no residents were in sight, then quickly let her into the manager's office. He briskly walked to a dark wood filing cabinet, pulled open a drawer and retrieved a file.

He pointed to a desktop computer. "Lucky for you our manager is old school. Records are supposed to go on the computer but this guy likes to hang on to the paper copies."

She peered over his shoulder as he opened the file. "Can you tell who rented the apartment?"

"This is odd. Her file doesn't have much in it. Usually there's at least a ten-page application tenants have to fill out. Helene's name isn't anywhere on the lease either." Tomas pointed at a single sheet of paper. "FLZ Corporation is written in the reference part of the form, but no names, no phone numbers, no addresses. The only other information in the file is a receipt stating the apartment was paid in full for one year's lease, in cash, but doesn't state what the amount was."

"That is strange. Do you think Helene worked for FLZ Corporation?"

"I've never heard of that company. I don't understand why management wouldn't require a completed application for Helene. They're a stickler for dotting the i's and crossing the t's."

She jotted the company's name into her notebook. "Thanks, Tomas. You've been a big help."

"No problem, Mrs. Landry. I'd better get this back before the manager comes back from his doctor's appointment. I'm not supposed to get into these files but I want to help you out," he said, giving her another wink. "Tommy has nothing but nice things to say about you and your husband. I hope it works out for you."

"I wouldn't want you to get into trouble for this, so I'll be on my way."

She turned to leave when she heard Tomas clear his throat, "Hmpf, hmpf."

Looking back she saw him rubbing his thumb and forefinger together, intently studying the vaulted ceiling, whistling something that vaguely resembled "Zippity-Do-Da". Puzzled, Kathryn froze a moment before comprehending. She pulled her wallet out of her handbag and handed Tomas a fifty-dollar bill.

"It's been a pleasure helping you out, Mrs. Landry."

"Thanks, Tomas," she replied as she walked out the door, clutching Helene Monterrey's address firmly in her hand.

Chapter Five

Kathryn rushed back to her own apartment building, barely giving the darkening smoky sky a glance.

Tommy opened the glass door for her. "Mrs. Landry, your assistant has been trying to reach you. She would like you to come to the office as soon as possible."

"I guess I forgot to un-silence my cell phone." Kathryn grimaced. "Thanks for taking the message, Tommy."

"Not a problem. I hope Tomas was able to help you out?"

"He gave me a few things to think about. Unfortunately he didn't see Neil moving out either."

"I'll keep my ears open and let you know if I hear anything new," the doorman promised.

Kathryn quickly drove the short distance to her office keeping a close watch on the now-larger cloud of mushrooming smoke drifting towards the coast.

"Kathryn, are you all right?" Marianne jumped up from her desk and ran to give her a hug. "I was worried when I couldn't reach you at home or on your cell."

"I'm sorry. I forgot to turn the volume on my cell back on after talking to the detective." Kathryn studied the older woman's face. "What's so urgent?"

"I didn't want to bother you but John insisted I call. He's frantic right now!"

"I was just with him an hour and a half ago and everything was fine. What's the problem?"

"The carpenter finishing up the crown molding at John's house called and said there's a slab water pipe leak and part of the downstairs guest room and powder room are flooded. I called John and he says it's impossible for him to deal with it right now and he wants you to oversee the repairs. He said to add the expense to his contract." Marianne paused for breath. "I called a plumber and the restoration company after I made sure the carpenter had turned off the water main."

"It sounds like you've got it under control, Marianne."

"Richard and I have been through slab leaks a couple times already. It's an inconvenient nuisance but getting the right people on the job quickly speeds up the recovery." She handed Kathryn a large manila envelope. "He'd like you to bring this contract to the house for his signature."

"Contract for what?"

"John didn't tell you this morning?"

"No, we only talked about trying to find Neil." Kathryn opened the envelope and pulled out the documents.

Marianne pointed to the property address. "John closed escrow on a vacation home in Palm Springs and wants you to work with the general contractor on the remodel for the design and decorating."

"Okay, but why does he need it delivered to his house right now?"

"I hate to pass this message along, Kathryn, but John insisted. Apparently Trieste will be there after school and needs to be watched for an hour or so until he can get away from work." Marianne shook her head. "He really should be more considerate; we're not a babysitting service."

"It's not a problem. John's doing the best he can, considering he's a single dad." Kathryn smiled. "Besides, I need a break from what's going on with Neil, and Trieste will take my mind off him. I never thought I'd enjoy being around kids but she's changed my mind."

"She is a sweetheart and she certainly thinks the world of her dad. And you too." Marianne hesitated, and then cleared her throat. "I know you have so many other things on your mind right now and I hate to bother you about this, but can you deposit some money into the company's account today?"

Kathryn frowned. "I thought our invoices were current."

"They are, or were. I don't know what's going on but two of our vendors called and said that our checks were returned for insufficient funds."

"That's impossible! Neil told me he deposited five thousand dollars last Friday."

"I'm sure it's just a glitch at the bank but can you log into the account and see if there's an explanation?"

She glanced at her watch. "I should have time to stop by the bank before Trieste gets home from school and clear this up."

"It'll be quicker to look at your account online, Kathryn, then I'll know how to respond to those vendors."

"Um, Neil never gave me the password." She massaged her temples, trying to stave off a headache, wondering what else was going to go wrong.

Marianne's mouth dropped open, then she quickly closed it. "Okay. When you figure it out, let me know so I can resend the checks."

***

Easing into traffic, Kathryn headed her pearly white Lexus towards her bank, located adjacent to the Fashion Island shopping center. The palm trees in the parking lot were whipping frantically in the increasing wind and she could see whitecaps crashing on the glittering ocean.

She signed in and took a seat in the bank's waiting area, the plush cushions of the low chair cradling her body. There were no other clients waiting but she could see that two of the bank's representatives were talking on the phone. Impatiently glancing at her watch, she was ready to give up and leave when a young, twenty-something woman called her name.

She introduced herself as Doris and then proceeded to type on her computer with bright red nails that matched her silk blouse, ignoring Kathryn.

"Excuse me, are you the person I should talk to about my business account?" Kathryn kept her voice quiet.

Doris barely looked up. "Account number and identification please."

She passed the most recent checking statement along with her driver's license to the woman. "There seems to be a mistake. My assistant says checks have been returned for non-sufficient funds."

After tapping on the keyboard and clicking the mouse several times, Doris brushed her pixie-cut brown hair away from her forehead and pursed her ruby-red lips. "No mistake. Your balance was only ninety dollars and that was before we charged you twenty dollars for each NSF item. As of this moment your balance is fifty dollars."

Kathryn's heart stuttered in her chest while a dull roar filled her ears. "But my husband deposited five thousand dollars on Friday. That was only four days ago!"

Once again Doris tapped away on her computer keys, frowned, then clicked some more before handing the statement and license back. "Nope. No deposit was received. You'd better discuss this with him."

"Can you check my personal account?" Kathryn whispered.

Doris sighed and rolled her eyes. "I'm a business account specialist, not personal accounts."

"Please?" Kathryn begged. "I'm going to need to transfer money to my business account, so you'll need to handle that transaction anyway."

"Fine." She practically spat the word out. "What's the account number?"

Handing the surly woman a blank check from her personal account, Kathryn held her breath while the red nails flew over the keyboard.

Another sigh filled the air as Doris handed Kathryn the blank check. "Do you have another account with us?"

"Why? There should be enough to cover my business account, isn't there?"

"No, ma'am. There isn't." Doris finally looked Kathryn in the eye. "You only have fifty dollars in this account too."

Kathryn's face flamed red and she leaned forward to grip the edge of the desk. "How, how did that happen?"

More clicking, then silence, as Doris studied the screen in front of her. "Looks like Neil Landry made a withdrawal last Friday afternoon for twelve thousand, seven hundred and fifty dollars."

***

Driving south on the Pacific Coast Highway, Kathryn meandered along the street lined with quaint little restaurants, boat yards, upscale shops, tourist joints and quick glimpses of the Newport Harbor in between buildings. But she didn't see any of it. All she saw was Neil's signature on a withdrawal slip wiping out their account.

Neil, what have you done to me? What did I do to make you hate me so much? How am I going to survive?

Ever since she and Neil had become a couple their first year in college, he had taken control of her finances. When she started her interior design business, Neil had been the one to deal with the banks and manage her money. She wasn't sure she was capable of understanding what needed to be done since he'd never allowed her to learn how the financial side of her business was set up. All she knew was that when Marianne said they needed to pay invoices, Neil would deposit the money and Marianne would forward all payments from clients directly to Neil to administer.

After she turned inland and drove past Pelican Hill Golf Club, the guard at the private community recognized her and waved her through the gate. John's Spanish style home sat against the emerald green golf course and the blue Pacific Ocean could be seen from the terraces.

Kathryn shoved thoughts of Neil and bankruptcy from her mind and concentrated on the work at hand. If she was going to survive this, she was going to have to keep her business successful. She parked behind the plumber's van, hurried into John's home and, once she had determined that

Trieste wasn't there yet, went to see what damage had been done.

"Mrs. Landry, I'm so glad you're here," Timothy said. "I was working on the crown molding in the library when one of my guys found a flood coming out of the guest room down the hall. I turned off the water main as fast as I could but there was still a lot of water gushing. It's a good thing someone was here when it happened or the entire floor would have been ruined."

"Thanks for acting so quickly. I guess I'd better talk to the plumber and see how long it's going to take to fix."

"I don't think Mr. Selton's going to like the answer," he said, shaking his head.

Kathryn walked down the wide hallway and gingerly stepped on dark wood flooring still damp with water. Reaching the guest room she stopped at the door and her mouth fell open. All the heavy, dark Spanish-style furniture had been shoved to the middle of the room. Holes had been knocked into two walls. Newly installed custom-made base boards had been ripped from the walls while plaster and wallboard littered the floor. Several huge fans were pointed at the holes in the walls. The plumber stood poised over a jackhammer, ready to blast through the imported French Oak flooring.

"Stop," Kathryn yelped. "Do you really have to ruin it?"

The plumber carefully laid the jackhammer down and wiped dripping sweat from his bald head with a red bandana. "Sorry, miss. It's the only way to reach the pipe that's leaking."

"Then what happens?"

"I'll repair the damaged pipe, pour new concrete over the hole, and then you'll have to get your contractor to replace the flooring and patch the walls," he explained. "The fans and dehumidifier need to run for at least a couple days to dry out the walls. Looks like the leak's been here for a while."

"How long is it going to take to fix all this?"

"Hum, my experience is if you wait on the insurance company, it can take five or six weeks for all the work to be done. If you pay for it yourself, a couple weeks."

"Timothy's right, John isn't going to like either answer," Kathryn muttered to herself.

"So, miss, can I get on with the job?"

"If you're sure it's the only way."

Kathryn walked back to the dining room shaking her head, wondering how she was going to break the news to John.

She was startled out of her thoughts by a young girl shrieking her name. "Kathryn, what's going on?"

"Your dad has a bad plumbing leak," Kathryn told the seven-year-old girl who shared John's chocolate brown eyes.

Trieste shook her waist-length curly black hair and gestured dramatically. "Mom has to fly to Chicago for an emergency meeting so I'm staying with Dad for a few days. He says he's busy this afternoon but I can stay with you until he gets home tonight."

"Mrs. Landry, I hope you don't mind the imposition," a sultry, feminine voice floated from the hallway, borne on the waves of a heavy floral scent.

The former Mrs. Selton gracefully glided into the dining room on stiletto heels and gave Trieste a kiss on the cheek, leaving behind a dark coral smudge. "John said it would be okay. Our nanny is on vacation this week and I can't possibly put this trip off."

"Uh, no, it's fine, Mrs. Selton," Kathryn stuttered. "I'm just afraid that it's not going to be much fun for Trieste. There's no water because of the leak and the plumber is going to start his jackhammer any moment."

"You can call me Amanda." She fluffed her platinum blond hair and swept her appraising sapphire blue eyes over Kathryn. "John's house is large enough that Trieste can stay upstairs away from all the workers, and there should be plenty of bottled water. My daughter has a lot of nice things to say about you so I'm sure she'll be in capable hands."

"Thank you. Is there anything I should know about staying with Trieste until her dad gets home? Does she have homework?"

"She's self-sufficient and knows what needs to be done so you don't need to worry." Amanda fluffed her hair again before turning towards her daughter. "Trieste, be good for Mrs. Landry and tell your dad I'll call in a couple days to let him know when I'll pick you up."

As Kathryn watched the tall, graceful woman sweep out of the room and up the walkway to the waiting town car, Trieste moved closer to her and took her hand. "Come show me the surprise! Dad said you have my room ready for me."

Laughing, Kathryn gave the slight girl a quick hug. "I think your dad wanted both of us to show you your new bedroom, but since he's not here I guess we'd better take a look now."

Just then the jackhammer started up with a deafening, throbbing noise. Trieste screeched, covered her ears and took off with a bound up the stairs to her bedroom. Once Kathryn stepped in behind her, the small girl swung the oversized door shut.

"I hate loud noises!"

Kathryn quickly gave her a hug, then turned her towards the room and stepped into a fantasy land. Pale ballet-slipper peach, gold and sparkles graced the room. One side of the room had a dance stage, the wall mirrored and a ballet barre in position. Painted curtain backdrops ready for performances, and a spotlight overhead for the star, framed the stage. Trieste chose the princess castle backdrop and pulled it to cover the mirror. Donning her ballet shoes, she whirled and twirled herself across the wooden dance floor.

"I love it," she gushed, while hugging Kathryn. "Now I can practice my dancing whenever I want to. I'm going to be a ballerina when I grow up and it takes lots and lots of practice."

Kathryn spent awhile showing Trieste all the special, thoughtful things her father had included in the room before asking, "Do you have homework?"

"Yeah, but do I really have to do it today? I want to play in my new room," she pleaded.

"Yes, you have to, but I'll get you a snack to eat while you're working on it. Okay?"

"All right." She opened her backpack and piled school books on the spacious built-in desk, outfitted with a laptop and color printer.

Once Trieste was settled in with snacks and homework, Kathryn made several phone calls lining up contractors to repair the damage to John's house and had just finished when John walked through his front door.

"Kathryn, thank you for rescuing me!" John said, taking her hand. "I was helping my Uncle Gerald out with some negotiations for a new land development and couldn't leave."

Kathryn tried to push her financial troubles from her mind and focus on what John was saying. "Wait a minute. Did you just say Uncle Gerald? As in former State Senator Gerald Selton?"

"Yes. I thought you knew he was my uncle."

"Honestly, I never made the connection. He's so well known for his involvement in the community but I never heard about his family."

"Well, he's my uncle and he provides most of the work I do."

"It must be rewarding to work for such an impressive man." Kathryn studied John's face, looking for similarities to his uncle. "It's amazing how successful he is at raising money for so many charities on top of everything else he's involved with."

"Yes, he is an impressive man." John placed his briefcase in an alcove. "So, how was your afternoon? I appreciate you looking after Trieste. She adores spending time with you."

"Trieste is an angel and it was a treat getting to show her the new bedroom." Kathryn smiled, then shook her head. "Unfortunately the repairs for the slab leak are going to take quite a while to finish, but I have all the contractors lined up to expedite as quickly as possible."

"Daddy!" Trieste squealed, throwing herself into his arms. "I love my new bedroom! Thank you, thank you, and thank you!"

"You're welcome. Kathryn and I had a blast designing it for you," John said, lifting her up and giving her a tight hug. "Maybe you can put on a ballet performance for us after dinner?"

"Oh yes! I know just the dance I want to do with the princess castle backdrop," Trieste said while bounding up the stairs. "I'll go practice it now so I'll be ready."

John laughed. "Okay, I'll call you when dinner is on the table."

"I really should be going," Kathryn said, looking at her watch. "I've left the contract for your Palm Springs home on your kitchen counter and I'll give you a report and an estimate of the repairs for the plumbing leak by tomorrow afternoon."

John took her hand again. "The report and estimate can wait. I think you need to stay for dinner and a very special ballet performance, otherwise Trieste will be heartbroken."

"How can I say no to that?"

Besides, all I have to go home to is a house that's as empty as my bank account.

"I don't think you can, which is why I suggested it." He grinned. "Since you're staying, how does barbecued salmon with grilled asparagus sound?"

After dinner and an adorable "Sleeping Beauty" ballet performance, she made her way to the front door.

"Thank you for a lovely evening," she said, giving the young girl a hug. "Dinner was delicious, John. And Trieste, I can tell you're going to be a famous ballerina one of these days."

Trieste said goodbye and went back to her room to finish homework while John walked Kathryn to her car.

"You made the evening special for Trieste," he said softly. "Thank you for staying."

"I'm glad I did. I had a nice time."

He took her hand and gave it a squeeze. "Kathryn, this is hard for me to tell you, but we're uncovering some things about Neil that aren't going to be pleasant for you."

"What? Have you found him?"

"No, but we're pretty certain he was having an affair and we're close to locating the woman."

"Who is she?"

"I can't say until we have absolute proof. I just thought you should know so that you can prepare yourself."

Kathryn rubbed her face with both hands and took a long, deep breath.

John leaned towards her, wrapped an arm around her shoulder. "Kathryn, listen to me. You have to believe that there's life after Neil. This isn't the end for you and I want to be the one to help you find a new beginning."

"I can't think about endings or beginnings right now." She took another deep breath. "I'm going to have to get through this in my own way and in my own time. But thank you for caring and thank you for trying to find Neil for me."

He gave her another hug, then helped her into her car. "I just want you to know that you're not alone and if you need anything, no matter what time of day or night, just call me."

Kathryn looked up into John's face and was blinded by the sudden glare of bright headlights as a vehicle pulled up directly behind her car.

"What the hell is he doing here?" John hissed.

The deep, gravelly voice of Detective Williams bellowed out, "Good evening, Mrs. Landry! I've had a heck of a time tracking you down. Don't you believe in answering your cell phone?"

Chapter Six

The detective strode to Kathryn's car. John held his ground.

"What can we help you with Detective?" John asked, placing his hand protectively on Kathryn's arm.

"My business is with Mrs. Landry so if you'll excuse us, I'd like to have a chat with her."

Kathryn looked up at John. "It's okay, I can handle this. I'll call you tomorrow afternoon with the estimates."

"Are you sure? I'll stay if you want me to."

"The lady said she was okay. You can leave now," Detective Williams snapped.

John gave Kathryn's hand a squeeze, then slowly made his way back to his house. The detective waited until John was inside the house with the door closed before turning to Kathryn.

"Do you always ignore your phone calls?"

Kathryn felt her face heat up. "No, but I've been having problems with my cell battery holding charges. That must be why I didn't get your call."

Kathryn's face turned a deeper red when her cell phone rang. She fumbled through her handbag, retrieved the phone, glanced at the caller ID and answered it.

"Hi Marianne."

"Kathryn, I was so worried about you. Detective Williams has been trying to call you but couldn't reach you. I hope you don't mind that I told him you were working at Mr. Selton's house?"

"It's okay, Marianne. I don't understand why I didn't get the calls, but Detective Williams is here right now so I'd better go unless you need something else."

"No, that's all. I just wanted to make sure he connected with you. I'll talk to you tomorrow."

Kathryn replaced her phone and noticed the detective trying to hide a smile.

She took a deep breath to regain her composure. "So, what's going on that you needed to track me down?"

"One of your neighbors saw your door wide open and your apartment ransacked. They called the police and I responded."

"How could that happen?" her voice quivered. "How did they get in?"

"We're looking into that. From what I could tell the only thing missing was your husband's computer. I'll need you to take a look and see if anything else was taken. I'll follow you home."

Kathryn's hands shook as she started her car and the drive home was a blur. When she pulled into her parking space the detective parked behind her car, boxing her in.

"There's a guest parking spot over by the exit." Kathryn pointed towards the opening.

"I'm fine here," he said, locking his white, government-issued Ford Explorer.

Kathryn led them to her apartment and stopped at the front door. Her eyes stung as she surveyed the damage. Chairs were knocked over, cushions strewn about. Lamps were lopsided and end tables were toppled.

She made her way through the living room mess and stepped into Neil's office. A snapped anti-theft cable dangled from the desk and there was an empty space where the laptop had once sat. Filing cabinets had been pried open; papers littered the floor.

"Why would someone do this?" she whispered, massaging her temples.

"The damage is limited to Mr. Landry's office and the living room," Detective Williams said. "Can you tell if anything else is missing?"

"I really don't know about Neil's office. He keeps everything locked and I don't have the key. But I'll check the rest of the apartment."

Kathryn walked back to the living room. She started picking up chairs and cushions and straightening up the mess. She turned to see the detective leaning against the doorway watching her.

"Detective Williams, what's the black powdery stuff on everything?"

"I had a team come through and lift fingerprints. Sorry about the mess, they're not exactly housekeepers," he said with a chuckle. "This reminds me, I need to take your fingerprints and anyone else's who has been in here."

"We have a maid service come in once a week. I'll get the company's phone number for you. The only other person would be Neil." She paused for a moment. "Oh, and John."

His eyebrows raised and his mouth puckered into an "O."

"It's not what you think," she stammered.

"Thinking can be dangerous. I normally avoid danger. So tell me, what should I be thinking?"

"You're jumping to conclusions about my relationship with John. It's strictly business."

"You'll have to admit, Mrs. Landry, it does appear to be a very cozy business relationship. A person has to wonder if it has something to do with your missing husband."

"I knew you'd try to blame me just like you blamed my mother when my father disappeared," Kathryn replied hotly. "And you wonder why I enlisted John's help? At least I know he'll try to find the truth without taking the easy way out."

"If I was a sensitive type of guy, your words might wound me." The detective's ice-blue eyes narrowed. "But since I'm not, I'll warn you that Selton had better not interfere with my investigation. I think it's more than coincidence that Neil's laptop was stolen the night before my computer team was supposed to take possession of it."

"Are you insinuating that John took the computer?" Kathryn almost snorted. "I was with him and his daughter all evening, so it's impossible."

"Like I said, a cozy situation, Mrs. Landry."

"Unbelievable! I don't think this conversation is going anywhere, so I'll check the rest of my home to see if anything is missing."

She went to her vanity and checked on her jewelry. It was still there. The plasma-screen television was in its place, mounted to the wall. Opening her nightstand, she found her iPad. She opened her bureau drawers and gasped when she saw all her lace panties were missing.

She stumbled back to the living room.

"What's wrong, Mrs. Landry? You're white as a sheet!"

"They stole all my… all my… underwear," she stammered.

"Anything else missing?"

"Nothing else that I could see."

"Sit down, you still look like you're going to pass out." Detective Williams guided her to the sofa. "I'll get you a glass of water."

Kathryn greedily drank the cold water, then rested her head on the back of the soft sofa and closed her eyes. "I feel so violated, knowing they took my, um, things."

"I understand. It's a normal feeling to have," he said in a gentle voice. "Is there family you can go stay with for a few days? The lock on the front door is broken so you shouldn't stay here until it's repaired. I also want to make sure your building corrects their security issues before you come back."

"No, I don't have any family."

"How about Neil's family?"

"No, he didn't have family either. It was just the two of us."

"Then how about close friends you can stay with?"

"Hm, not really. I work long hours and Neil was always doing his business thing, so we don't socialize much."

Kathryn's eyes met the detective's icy blue eyes and thought they seemed to melt a little. "What?"

"That's a sad place to be in life. No family and no friends."

"It is what it is. I suppose I can impose on my assistant and her husband. I really don't feel like being alone in a hotel right now."

Besides, I don't have any money to pay for a room.

"That's a great idea. She seems genuinely concerned about you."

"Yeah, she's a caregiver when given the chance."

"Why don't you go pack some things, Mrs. Landry, and I'll follow you to her house."

"I'll do that, but please call me Kathryn. Mrs. Landry sounds so formal."

"All right, if that's what you want, Kathryn," he answered with a small smile on his lips.

She walked towards her bedroom, then turned back to the detective. "Thanks for being nice to me right now. I know it seems like we've been at odds every time we talk but I feel like you put me on the defensive."

He cleared his throat and hesitated before answering, "I think Selton brings out the worst in me. Then I have to question why you spend so much time with him."

"What do you have against John? You don't even know him!"

"What gave you that idea? Of course I know him. He was a rookie on the force when your father disappeared and Selton made quite a reputation for himself. Not a good reputation."

"Oh, I didn't know. I thought I heard John say he'd never met you."

The detective arched his eyebrows.

"You're doing it again." She pointed at his face.

"What?"

"I can tell you're skeptical by the look on your face. Besides, that was a long time ago and I'm sure John is a much better man than you remember."

"Guess we'll see about that, but I reserve the right to remain skeptical," he answered with a grin.

Kathryn went to her bedroom, switched on the light and quickly made a call to Marianne, who enthusiastically agreed to the stay. She pulled her largest suitcase out of the walk-in closet and started stuffing it with sleepwear, casual pants and shirts, and then carefully folded tissue paper around a few silk blouses and wool slacks and skirts to keep them from wrinkling. She made a mental note to shop for new underwear the next morning. Laying out ten pairs of shoes, she looked at her almost-full suitcase and decided she'd better eliminate half the shoes. She collected her toiletries from her vanity area and stuffed them into the suitcase. Her shoes were wedged around the edges of the bag. She added a new hardback novel, the iPad, then put her favorite feather pillow on top. Kathryn closed the top of the suitcase, straddled it and started fighting with the zipper.

"Need a hand?" Detective Williams said, standing in the doorway. "I've never seen anyone take that position with a suitcase before."

"Ha, ha. You should try packing for an indeterminate amount of time and see if you can get it to all fit in one suitcase."

"I said you might need to stay with Marianne for a few days but I never said you couldn't come back here."

"I guess I didn't think about that." Kathryn stood up and as she released her weight from the suitcase, her feather pillow popped the lid open.

"A pillow? Doesn't Marianne have pillows?"

She smiled sheepishly. "I sleep so much better with my own pillow. I never travel without it."

"All right, go ahead and hold down the lid and I'll try to zip it for you."

They struggled, but in the end the suitcase zipped tight. He picked it up to carry to the door.

"Did you pack bricks? This must weigh as much as you do!"

"Are you always a complainer?" she retorted. "Or maybe I should carry it so you can save your strength."

"Naw, I'm fine. I've never understood how a woman can pack a suitcase so heavy. I think you're all in league to give us poor guys hernias or back problems."

"I'll let you in on a little secret. It's called shoes. Every woman owns numerous pairs of shoes and we can't leave home without our favorites. I did you a favor and only packed five pairs instead of the ten pairs I think I need."

"Ten pairs of shoes? Two pairs should work just fine: sneakers and black shoes to wear to the office."

"Women can't survive with one pair of black shoes for office wear! What if I wore blue or brown slacks? Black wouldn't work. Then the hem length determines which size heel to wear, so you need at least three pairs of shoes in each color. You also have open toe, closed toe and sling back. The possibilities are endless and we need all of them."

"Truce, I give up." The detective shook his head. "Is this all you need? Are you ready to go?"

"I just need one thing from the kitchen but I won't pack it in the suitcase."

"Good. I'd hate to add any more weight to this thing. I'll carry this ton of bricks to the door while you get whatever it is you need."

Kathryn walked through the dining room on her way to the kitchen and pulled one of the dining room chairs with her. She climbed up on the chair and started a frantic search in the upper cabinets.

"Are you looking for something I shouldn't know about?"

"No, it's nothing illegal. I'm just looking for chocolate. I know there's a box of Godiva truffles in here somewhere and I want to take them to Marianne."

"Wouldn't you remember where you put them?"

"It's complicated."

"I think I'm intelligent enough, unless it's something like women and their shoes."

"Okay, but you can start looking in the cabinets over by the oven while I tell you."

"What exactly am I looking for?"

"You don't know what a box of Godiva chocolates looks like? It will be a gold box. You do know what gold looks like, don't you?"

"Very funny. So, tell me why we're conducting this very thorough search."

"Neil's a fitness buff and thinks I shouldn't eat chocolate. I liked to keep a box on hand, just in case, but he hides it when I bring it home."

"Just in case what?" The detective turned from the open cabinet to look at her.

"Just in case I needed it, like tonight. I can't show up at Marianne's without a hostess gift. Aha!" Kathryn exclaimed. "That tricky little devil. He put a cookbook dust cover over the Godiva box and hid it with my mother's cookbooks. I knew it had to be in here. I could smell it."

They collected her suitcase and headed to the lobby. As they were stepping off the elevator, Tommy grabbed an envelope off his desk and trotted up to Kathryn.

"Mrs. Landry, this was delivered for you about ten minutes ago," Tommy said, slightly out of breath. "I'm sorry I didn't call you but the phones have been going crazy and I haven't had a spare moment. There they go ringing again."

He shoved the envelope into Kathryn's hand and trotted back to his desk. She looked down at the plain white envelope with her name written in blue ink on the front. Her hands started shaking and her lips trembled.

"What's wrong, Kathryn?" Detective Williams asked, trying to balance her suitcase.

"It's from Neil. This is his writing."

Chapter Seven

Kathryn's shaking hands started tearing the envelope open when the detective's warm fingers stopped her.

"Please don't open it yet. I want to protect any fingerprints that might be there," he whispered.

"Oh, of course. I didn't think of that."

He grabbed the heavy suitcase in one hand and with the other guided her to Tommy's desk. As soon as Tommy hung up the phone, it started ringing again.

"Don't pick that up," the detective snapped. "I have a couple questions you need to answer."

Kathryn rolled her eyes at the detective. "What Detective Williams meant to say is, we'd like to ask a couple questions, if you can spare a moment, Tommy."

"Of course, Mrs. Landry. How can I be of assistance?" he answered smoothly, taking his hand off the ringing phone.

"I'm assuming the detective was wondering if you knew who dropped off this envelope."

"No, I didn't see it delivered. Like I mentioned, it's been a zoo in here this evening and about ten minutes ago I noticed it sitting on the counter."

"Detective, is there anything else you'd like to ask Tommy?"

"Would you be able to kindly provide me with this building's management phone number this evening?" he asked politely, suppressing a grin. "I would like them to secure Mrs. Landry's apartment as soon as possible."

Tommy quickly wrote down a name and phone number on embossed notepaper and then handed it to Kathryn. "Is there anything else I can help you with, Mrs. Landry?"

"I think that's it for now," Detective Williams answered, taking the notepaper from Kathryn's hand. "Thanks for taking the time to help us out."

As they walked to their vehicles, he asked, "So all these years my method in obtaining information has been wrong?"

"Maybe being harsh with the bad guys works but for us innocent civilians a little politeness goes a long way."

"Hmmm, I'll try to remember that next time I have to talk to innocent civilians," he said with a laugh.

"How long are you going to make me wait to open Neil's note?" She gripped the envelope tightly.

"I have some disposable gloves in my truck so as soon as we can get those on you can open it."

After stowing her luggage in the back of his SUV and donning the gloves, Kathryn carefully ripped open the envelope and slid out a folded letter-sized sheet of white paper.

Unfolding the letter with shaking hands, Kathryn read, "Stop trying to find me. I'm in love with someone else. Get over it and let me go. Neil."

The detective took the page from Kathryn's hand, then handed her a tissue to wipe the tears threatening to spill from her eyes.

"That's pretty heartless of Neil, don't you think?" he asked while studying the note with his flashlight.

She hiccupped. "He wasn't the most considerate person, but I can't believe he'd be this cruel."

"I find it strange that he wrote your name with pen on the envelope yet the note is a computer-generated print, including his name. I would think he'd at least sign his name."

She wiped her eyes. "Why do you think that?"

"I'm no psychologist, but I think signing one's own name would indicate that he's in charge, he's making the statement in a stronger manner."

"Or he's making a statement that he's disconnected from me on all personal levels, including signing his name."

"Could be. Like I said, I'm no psychologist." He patted her arm. "If you don't mind, I'd like to come back to your apartment after dropping you off at Marianne's and get a sample of Neil's writing. I'll take both of them to the lab tonight."

"It's fine with me, if you think it's necessary." She sighed and looked at the envelope. "This is definitely Neil's writing. More scribble scrabble than writing and almost illegible."

***

After parking in Marianne's driveway, Kathryn shook her head as she watched Detective Williams park his Explorer next to a fire hydrant and noisily grunt while lugging Kathryn's bag to the front door. Trying to ignore the comically heavily breathing man standing next to her, she rang the doorbell and admired Marianne's snug little Corona del Mar house with its cheerful rose garden illuminated by Malibu lights.

Marianne opened the door and immediately gave Kathryn a hug, fussing over her before pulling her into the house. The detective followed behind with the suitcase and placed it in the hallway.

"Marianne, this is Detective Williams," she said once they were inside the house. "Detective, Marianne Patton."

"Nice to meet you, Detective. Thanks for bringing Kathryn over. Let me introduce you to my husband, Richard."

Richard came walking down a long terra-cotta-tiled hallway from what looked like the kitchen area, where the warm, sweet scent of fresh baked cookies wafted. He was tall, well over six feet, thick gray hair, and had the look of a lean runner with deep creases lining his tan face. He was wearing a frilly pink polka-dotted apron and carrying a hot pink oven mitt.

"Excuse my costume. Marianne has me on cookie duty." Richard shook the detective's hand. "Nice to meet you. We'll make Kathryn as comfortable as possible during her stay with us. We're sure sorry about the trouble that she's found herself in!"

"I appreciate you letting me stay."

"Nonsense, we're happy to have you," Marianne gushed.

Detective Williams pulled out a pen and a business card. After quickly writing a number, he handed it to Kathryn. "Here's my cell phone in case you need to reach me. I'll call you in the morning and let you know if I have any new information."

"You're not leaving already, are you?" Marianne asked. "We were just sitting down for dessert. Please join us."

"I'd love to, ma'am, but I really need to get to the office and follow up on some leads."

"Well, at least let me pack some oatmeal chocolate chip cookies for you to take. Richard just pulled them from the oven."

"Really, that's not necessary," he said, embarrassed. "I don't want to impose,"

"It's no trouble at all. I always cook enough for twelve people so there's plenty to send..." Marianne's voice trailed off as she headed towards the kitchen.

Richard smothered a laugh. "She's always been like this, cooking too much food, then wanting to find someone to pass it on to. I've gained thirty-five pounds since we married thirty years ago and finally had to take up running to keep in shape."

"I've been a recipient of her food as well," Kathryn added. "You're in for a treat. She's a great cook."

Marianne scurried in carrying a paper bag bulging with Ziploc baggies of cookies. "I put a couple extra cookies in there in case you get hungry later."

"Thank you, Marianne, you're very generous." He sniffed the fragrant bag. "These smell delicious! I haven't had homemade cookies since my grandmother passed away several years ago."

They walked out to the front yard with the detective, the wind buffeting their bodies.

"I think I'm going to have to close up the windows tonight," Marianne said, sniffing the air. "The smoke seems to be getting stronger."

"Yes, ma'am, it is." Detective Williams ran his fingers through his short hair. "The firefighters haven't been able to control the blaze that started out in the Cleveland National Forest last night. The brush up on those mountains is dry as a tinderbox and I'm afraid it's going to keep burning until these winds to die down."

"I don't think that's going to happen anytime soon," Richard said, shaking his head. "At least not according to the weather reports."

"I hope it isn't another arsonist this time." Marianne looked towards the east, squinting. "A few years ago you could see the glow from the fire all the way down here."

"Unfortunately, they suspect it was an arsonist who started this blaze. Something about these winds makes the crazies go even crazier." The detective stuck his hand out to Marianne and then to Richard. "Thanks again for the cookies. I'd better get back to the office."

After he left, Marianne took Kathryn by the arm and led her down to the kitchen, telling Richard to place the suitcase in the guest room. She poured each of them a glass of Duckhorn Cabernet and placed a platter of cookies on the table.

Kathryn raised her eyebrows. "Wine and cookies?"

"Just wait until you taste them together. You'll never go back to milk and cookies again." Marianne raised her glass of deep red wine. "Cheers!"

Just then Richard walked into the kitchen, picked up his glass of wine with one hand and started rubbing his shoulder with the other. "What did you pack? Bricks? Wait, let me guess. Shoes? I thought Marianne packed heavy but I don't think I'll ever complain about her suitcase again."

Marianne flicked Richard with her dish towel. "Be nice to our guest or no cuddling for you tonight."

"Promises, promises," Richard retorted.

Kathryn laughed at their good-natured ribbing and apologized for the weight of her suitcase. "I wasn't sure how long I'd need to stay so I wanted to be prepared."

"Honey, you know you can stay as long as you need," Richard assured her. "Now sit down and tell us everything that's happened."

It was nearly two o'clock in the morning before Kathryn tumbled into bed and fell into an exhausted sleep. She'd made Marianne promise to sleep in and not rush to the office early the next morning, since she'd kept her up so late.

The jarring sounds of her cell phone ding-a-linging dragged her from a deep, dreamless sleep.

"Hello," she answered with a croaking voice.

"Kathryn?" John Selton asked.

She glanced at the bedside clock. "John, it's six in the morning. Is everything okay?"

"Yeah, everything's fine. I was calling to find out how you are since I didn't hear from you after Mister Dirty Harry hauled you away."

"He didn't haul me away. My apartment was broken into and Neil's computer stolen. He needed me to check if anything else was missing."

"Oh my god! Are you okay? You should have called me. You know I would have been there for you."

"Thanks, I do know that. But you have Trieste and I didn't want to call and wake her up."

"You shouldn't worry about that." John covered his cell with his hand and Kathryn could hear him talking to someone else, their voices muffled. "Sorry for the interruption. Can we meet for coffee around nine o'clock this morning and review the Palm Springs contract? You can tell me what happened last night then."

"Yes, that should work. How about meeting at my office?"

"I was thinking Starbucks in Fashion Island."

"Okay, I'll see you then."

After ending the call, Kathryn unpacked the remaining items in her suitcase, took a long, hot shower, dressed in khaki slacks and a white ruffled blouse, and pulled her hair up and secured it with a barrette. She applied as much foundation as she could to diminish the black half-moon circles under her eyes, put some mascara and lipstick on and decided it was good enough to get her through the day.

Kathryn made her way to the kitchen where she smelled coffee brewing.

"Good morning, Kathryn," Richard said cheerfully. "I hope you slept well. Can I get you some coffee?"

She breathed the dark, sharp fragrance in deeply. "I'd love some; it smells heavenly. And yes, I slept incredibly well."

Kathryn sat and sipped the hot beverage, hoping the caffeine would give her a boost.

"Marianne's in the shower right now, but she said to offer you some of her Banana Chocolate Chip Muffins for breakfast. Are you hungry?"

"Yes, I'd love a muffin. Marianne's brought some to the office before so I know how delicious they are."

"Nutritious too, according to Marianne." Richard chortled. "But I think she overstates the nutrition a bit since she adds so many chocolate chips to the batter."

"Hey, who said chocolate wasn't nutritious? I've read it's very good for you."

He shook his head. "I give up. Chocolate for breakfast should be on everyone's menu."

Kathryn was just finishing her muffin and a second cup of coffee when the doorbell rang.

Richard answered the door and Kathryn could hear Detective Williams apologizing for dropping by so early without calling. Richard invited him in for muffins and coffee, which he declined.

Once Richard poured a cup of coffee and excused himself, the detective glowered at her. "As usual, a certain someone doesn't answer or check their messages on their cell phone."

Kathryn groaned. "I must have been in the shower."

"No dead battery this time?"

Feeling her face on fire, Kathryn sputtered, "Nope, I don't think that's the problem this time."

"Besides checking on you, I wanted to let you know I had a very interesting conversation with the lab technician this morning."

"About Neil's note?"

"Yes, and other things."

"Well, what did the technician say?" Kathryn asked nervously.

"There were absolutely no fingerprints on the note and your name on the envelope was a forgery of Neil's writing."

Chapter Eight

"How can it be a forgery?" Kathryn stammered. "I'm positive that is Neil's writing!"

"That's not all, Mrs. Landry. I also find it very interesting that John Selton's fingerprints are all over your house, including your bedroom."

"What?"

"I have to wonder, Mrs. Landry, if your husband left because of your involvement with Selton or if you decided he was a nuisance and needed to be gotten rid of."

Kathryn gritted her teeth together. "You're joking, right? I don't find your humor very funny, Detective Williams."

"You're good, Mrs. Landry. You pulled me in last night with your damsel-in-distress act and I fell for it. 'Please call me Kathryn.'" He mimicked her high-pitched voice.

"You are so wrong about me." Kathryn balled her hands into a fist. "I have no idea what happened to Neil but I do know that you're trying to take the easy way out and blame me."

"I'm just looking at the facts, ma'am. And they add up." He stood. "Please give my regards to the Pattons."

"That's it? What am I supposed to do now?"

"If I were you, I would start looking for a good attorney," the detective answered, his lips curved into a sneer. "Don't bother getting up. I'll let myself out."

As soon as the front door slammed shut, Marianne came bustling into the kitchen. She took one look at Kathryn's angry face. "Did the detective have bad news for you? Is it Neil?"

"Oh Marianne, I'm so confused and afraid," she whispered. "Neil's note is apparently a forgery and they found John's fingerprints all over my apartment, including the bedroom. So now they think that I had an affair and either Neil ran off or I did him in."

"I know you had nothing to do with Neil's disappearance. It makes me so darn mad Detective Williams would insinuate otherwise!" Marianne sputtered. "The truth will come out, honey, so don't let it get to you."

"I'm sure you're right, but I feel so helpless." Kathryn suddenly stood up and snapped her fingers. "I almost forgot. Marianne, I don't think I'll come to the office today unless there's something urgent. There's someone I need to talk to that might have an idea where I can find Neil."

"Of course that's okay. But shouldn't you let the detective talk to them?"

"No, definitely not until I've had a chance to talk to her. He would only put his spin on it and I might never know the real story."

"All right, if you think that's best." Marianne turned to the kitchen sink and started washing dishes, her shoulders hunched over. "Kathryn, did you talk to the bank yet? I hate to bother you about this, but two more vendors called after I talked to you yesterday afternoon. I didn't want to bring it up last night after all that had happened."

Kathryn massaged the back of her neck and appeared to study the flat metal geometric sculpture hanging on the wall above the table. "I… I don't know exactly how to answer that question."

Marianne turned to face Kathryn. "What's going on? Either you talked to the bank or you didn't."

"I talked to them. They just didn't have the right answer for me." Kathryn covered her face with both hands and rubbed her temples, avoiding eye contact. "Apparently Neil cleaned out all our bank accounts and I have nothing."

"Oh my god, Kathryn, that's awful!" Marianne rushed to give the younger woman a hug. "Richard and I can loan you some money until you figure out what you need to do."

"No, I can't accept that from you. I think we can stall the vendors and the bank for another week or two and hopefully I'll be able to track Neil down and get my money back. I'm going to try to sell his precious little car too, which should give us some cash in the meantime."

"What about asking John for an advance on the Palm Springs job?" Marianne suggested.

"I don't see how I can ask for a big enough advance to make a difference without telling him why. I really don't want John to find out about this." Her eyebrows drew together and her shoulders slumped. "He's already acting like my knight in shining armor and the last thing I need is for Detective Williams to find out that John's financially supporting my company now. I think I'm just going to have to figure this out on my own, Marianne."

"Well, if you change your mind, Richard and I would be happy to loan you some money."

She hugged Marianne. "That means a lot to me, but I've got to work this out."

***

Kathryn found John sitting at a small round table at the back of the crowded coffee shop, two iced lattes sitting in front of him, along with two croissants.

"Hope you don't mind, but I went ahead and ordered for us." John handed her one of the cold drinks. "Iced skinny pumpkin spice latte?"

"Thanks." She took a sip before opening the manila envelope sitting on the table. "Do you have any questions about the contract?"

"Looks fine to me. My contractor's business card is in there. He's expecting your call and can talk about the scope of work." John placed his company's check on top of the papers. "Here's a five-thousand-dollar advance for your work. We can talk about the schedule of payments once you start."

"This isn't necessary." She handed the check back. "You know that's not my standard operating procedure."

"I know, but I figured with Neil gone you might be kind of strapped for cash. Hopefully this will give you some breathing room." He tossed the check back to her and grinned. "I think I've got a couple referrals to send your way too, as long as you don't let them interfere with my project."

"That's very thoughtful of you, but I don't feel comfortable accepting the advance."

"C'mon, Kathryn, I trust you and know you'll get the work done."

She tucked the check into her purse. "Thank you."

He leaned back in his chair and crossed his arms. "So, I tried calling your apartment this morning before I called your cell phone. Where were you?"

"I'm staying at Marianne's for a few days until the lock on my door can be replaced."

"You should have called me last night. You know you're more than welcome to stay at my house."

"John, that's not appropriate. Questions are being asked about whether you're the reason Neil left and I'm uncomfortable with that."

"I've told you that I'm collecting evidence that Neil is the one having the affair."

"An affair is one thing, but why did he disappear? I need to tell you that a note was delivered to me last night at my apartment building that looked like it was supposed to have come from Neil."

"What did it say?"

"Basically that he's found a new love and that I should stop trying to find him," Kathryn whispered quietly, sniffing back a tear.

"See, I've been trying to tell you that. Do you have the note with you?"

"Detective Williams has it. He was with me when the note was delivered."

She furrowed her brows. "I'm positive that it was Neil's writing, but the lab said it was a forgery, so now they think I had something to do with his disappearance."

John swore softly. "I wish you wouldn't have gotten the police involved in this and trusted me instead. They make everything so much more difficult, especially Williams."

"I wish I hadn't called them either, but it's too late now." Reaching out to grasp John's hand, she said. "I need your evidence that Neil was having an affair and you need to find him soon so we can prove I'm innocent."

"I'm doing everything I possibly can. Your husband seems to be very adept at covering his tracks." John sneered. "And I'm sure Williams isn't doing anything but blaming you?"

"That's how it's looking right now." She sighed. "Speaking of Detective Williams, I heard that you were a rookie police officer and worked at the same precinct at the same time?"

"Yeah, a long, long time ago. He was just as cocky then as he is now."

"Oh, I didn't think you knew him."

John scowled. "What's it matter whether I knew him or not? Has the dee-teck-tive been telling stories about me?"

"No, and there's no reason to get upset. I was merely curious. I never knew you were a police officer. Why did you get into the P.I. business?"

"My uncle suggested it and set me up. It's turned out to be a huge asset for both of us, especially with the security aspect. Better hours and pay too." John chuckled, then looked at his watch. "I hate to cut our conversation short, but I've got a meeting to get to. Can I take you to lunch today?"

"Thanks, but I don't think that's a good idea. I need to catch up on a lot of things at the office."

"Okay, then how about dinner? Trieste says she has another ballet dance she'd like to perform for you."

"Thanks, John, but I really need to pass. Give me some time to figure things out, please?"

"All right, if you insist. But I'm going to call you often to let you know my progress and I want you to promise to call me if anything new comes up, okay?"

"Okay, that's a deal."

***

Kathryn drove to the same bank branch, tried to summon up courage and signed in.

Neil, you bastard, you're not going to steal this money from me.

Once again Doris called her name and loudly exhaled when she saw her customer.

"Account number, please," she said once Kathryn sat down across the desk from her.

"I'm here to open a new business account," Kathryn replied, slapping the check onto the desk. "And I want to close both my old accounts and transfer those funds to the new account."

"What type of checking product do you want?" Doris asked, tapping on her keyboard.

"I don't know," Kathryn grimaced, embarrassed because she didn't know what Doris was talking about. "What would you recommend?"

After scrolling through several screens, Doris finally answered. "You'll probably want our basic free checking with a minimum of one hundred dollar balance required and up to fifty checks allowed on the account per month. All I need is your tax identification number and social security number."

Kathryn dug through her wallet and produced her social security card. "I'll have to call my office for the tax number."

Doris almost smiled. "You can use my phone if you want."

Marianne quickly gave her the information she needed, which she passed on to Doris. After signing several documents and discussing what to do with any further checks returned for non-sufficient funds, Kathryn left the bank and programmed her car's navigation system for Helene's address.

She chose her favorite playlist on her iPhone, a variety of Harry Connick

Jr. songs, and pulled into traffic on the 405 Freeway. Heading south, she made her way to the 241 toll road to Rancho Santa Margarita. The brown, arid hills rimmed the shimmering blacktop road while puffs of ash and dust drifted across the lanes, borne on the wild Santa Ana winds. Irvine's Great Park Orange Balloon was barely visible against the smoky valley floor, and somewhere on the western horizon she knew Catalina Island danced in a glittering ocean.

Kathryn drove through cookie-cutter-tracts. Neutral-colored stuccoed houses with tiled Spanish terra-cotta roofs. Neat, trim lawns, palm fronds thrashing in the wind and gardens bursting with colorful flowers. Some of the houses had Halloween decorations up, and while there were kids' toys in a few yards, the neighborhood appeared deserted. Helene's home had pink and white impatiens blooming in flowerbeds and window-box planters. A plastic hot pink jack-o-lantern sat on her steps.

She parked at the curb in front of the house, climbed out of the car and winced at the scorching hot wind. Wrinkling her nose, she tried to not breathe in the sooty air. Making her way slowly to the front door, she tried to figure out what to say to Helene.

Kathryn rang the doorbell, waited a couple of minutes, then rang the bell again. This time she faintly heard a woman's voice and the door finally opened. A tall, young woman stood dripping wet, with a tiny hot pink towel covering part of her curvaceous bosom and barely reaching to the top of her slender thighs. She looked expectantly at Kathryn.

"I'm sorry to disturb you. Are you Helene Monterrey?"

"No, I'm her roommate, Roxie. Or I should say I was her roommate," the young woman answered, swinging her dripping blonde tresses, splashing Kathryn with a few drops of water.

"Would you happen to know how I could reach Helene?"

"No, sorry. I really don't know where she went." Roxie tugged her thin towel up a little higher on her full breasts, each displaying twin butterfly tattoos.

"I know this is an inconvenient time for you, but would you mind if I came in and asked you a few questions about Helene? I just drove from Newport

Beach and would like some information before driving back."

"Oh, is that your car? Awesome! I've always wanted one like that," the wet woman enthusiastically said. "Sure, come on in. I'll go put something on so make yourself comfortable."

Kathryn stepped into the house and was greeted by pink everywhere, with splashes of white. She sat on the pink floral sofa and wondered where a person could find so many pink items to furnish a house. Roxie walked back into the living room wearing a cotton-candy pink robe that wasn't much larger than the towel she had been wearing earlier.

"Are you a friend of Helene's?" Roxie asked.

"No. I suppose I should have introduced myself. My name is Kathryn Landry. I just happened to stumble across Helene's name and address after my husband disappeared two days ago."

"Oh, that is sooo weird. That's when Helene left. Two days ago I think." The very young woman examined her Frosty Strawberry nail polish. "I came home from work around four a.m. after working the evening shift. Helene had the day shift and all her stuff was gone. She didn't even bother telling me she was leaving. At least her part of the rent was paid up until the end of the month but now I gotta find a new roommate."

Kathryn suddenly chilled and tried to compose herself. She hoped her voice wouldn't crack. "So what company did Helene work for?"

Roxie looked confused for a moment, then giggled. "We don't work for a company. I guess you could say we are in the entertainment business, self-employed. Yeah, that's what it is."

"But you said you had the night shift and Helene worked the day shift. So what kind of…" Kathryn's voice trailed off when she guessed what work Roxie and Helene did.

"You're not with the police, are you?"

"No, definitely not. I'm trying to track down my husband since the police are blaming me for his disappearance."

"Well, just don't get me in trouble, okay, Kat? Is that what people call you? Kat?"

"My parents used to."

"It fits you. Anyway, Helene and I had an agreement. She found clients who wanted to see her during the day so I had the house to myself. I had clients at night so she had the house then. It was a pretty good arrangement. Sometimes we had a client together and then we'd take a few days to vacation and soak up the sun down in Cabo San Lucas."

"Do you know any of her clients' names?"

"I think their names were John Smith." Roxie's laugh ended in a snort.

"I'm not here to pry into your clients' lives, Roxie, I'm just trying to figure out if my husband was connected to Helene."

"What was his name? Helene would sometimes talk about her clients, but not this last one. He demanded confidentiality and paid well enough for it. Although I can't understand why she put up with the abuse for so long."

"My husband's name is Neil Landry. Was Helene seeing her last client for a while?"

"Your husband's name doesn't ring a bell. I guess Helene was seeing this last guy for about six months? I lose track of time. He only wanted to see her once a week and paid her enough money so that she wouldn't take any other clients the rest of the week either."

"Is that strange for your business?"

"You bet it is! It's kind of like a Cinderella story. Except this guy was a pervert. Helene had to put up with a lot even for the money she was making."

"What do you mean a pervert?"

"Some guys like to hit you or knock you around some to get off. This guy came easy enough for being an old guy; it was afterward that he beat on Helene. She said his ice-cold blue eyes positively burned when he abused her. He never touched her face though, or hurt her bad enough that she needed to see a doctor. She tried hiding the bruises and cuts from me but since there's no lock on the bathroom door, she couldn't hide them for long. The worst part was the way he cut her using his pirate ring. He actually scratched symbols onto her skin. Ick!"

Ice-cold blue eyes. Sounds like a hard-ass detective I know.

"Pirate ring?" Kathryn squinted her eyes, thinking she'd misheard.

"You know, like from *Pirates of the Caribbean*?"

"Oh, you mean skull and crossbones?"

"Yeah, that's what I meant. He had one of those in some kind of silver metal sitting on a black stone. He wore it on his pinky."

"Why would Helene stay with a client who treated her like that?"

"The money, honey. In this business you know you have a limited number of years, looking great, to make the most money. We know we're eventually going to have to do something else unless we find a Prince Charming to rescue us. Look at the movie *Pretty Woman*. Now there's a movie to dream about. Helene was getting tired of the business and she thought if she could put up with her rich pervert another six months, she'd have enough money to put herself through college and still live well."

"Do you think she decided she had enough money now and decided to leave and start over somewhere else?"

"I guess that's what she did. Maybe her Prince Pervert offered her something she couldn't pass up. You'd think she'd say good-bye though, huh?"

"Out of curiosity, how do you hook up with your clients? Do you have a, um, pimp?"

Roxie snorted again. "In our league, we don't call them pimps. That's so, oh, what's the word? Cliché? We have a manager who refers us and takes a small percentage. We can refuse a client and if we find our own client we don't have to pay the fee."

"Was Helene's last client referred to her?"

"Yep, through the usual channel. Helene told me that after the arrangements had been set up, a really handsome guy approached her on behalf of the pervert and made sure she knew and understood the terms of her employment. She even had to sign a contract. She was disappointed that he wasn't the client. You know, tall, dark and handsome? Wore an expensive suit and jewelry too. He had one of those watches that pilots like to wear." Roxie paused for a breath. "One of my clients owned a jet and initiated me in the mile-high club. He wore one of those watches. Starts with a B.

"Do you mean Breitling?"

"Yep, that's it. Those watches are too complicated for me."

Kathryn immediately thought of John Selton but then dismissed the idea as absurd. Helene's go-between was probably some flunky. She was now positive that Neil couldn't have been the client involved with Helene. He certainly didn't have that kind of money, even after stealing hers. Still, there was a nagging doubt that he might have fallen in love and run away with Helene to start a new life together.

"How about her family? Does she have any?"

"Her mom and dad live in a podunk town somewhere in Kansas. They thought she was a model. About once a year she'd go home to visit but never stayed more than a week."

"You wouldn't happen to know their phone number or address, would you?"

"Nope. Sorry."

"Thank you for talking to me, Roxie. I really appreciate it." Kathryn handed her a business card. "Here's my work phone number and cell number. Please call me if you hear from Helene."

"No problem, Kat."

Kathryn walked back to her car and got in. Directly across the street she saw a middle-aged blond man sitting in a beat-up, older model, black Cadillac. When she caught his eye, he immediately looked away. Shrugging, she figured he must have been one of Roxie's friends. Making her way back to the freeway, she decided to continue south on the toll road for a late lunch in Dana Point. Maybe sitting at a serene waterfront restaurant in a town where no one knew her would help her think more clearly. Her mind kept going over everything Roxie had told her, trying to figure out if there was anything that would lead her to Neil.

The miles flew by on the lightly travelled toll road, empty arid hills seemingly untouched by humans. Busy with her thoughts, Kathryn didn't notice the vehicle behind her until a loud crunch and the jolt of her car startled her. Her car swerved into the shoulder, throwing up gravel and dust as she fought to regain control.

Back on the asphalt pavement, she glanced in her rearview mirror and yelled, "Watch where you're going, idiot!"

Stunned, she recognized the blond man who had been sitting in his black Cadillac across from Roxie's house. She watched in disbelief as he slowly gained on her, edging his car up to her left rear fender. Fearing that he would ram her again, Kathryn punched the gas pedal down and her Lexus responded immediately with a surge forward. She was grateful that she was on an open road with little traffic. The powerful engine rapidly accelerated the car and she was confident that she could outrun the older sedan.

She was horrified, though, when the black car kept pace with her. Her palms started sweating and she had a hard time gripping the steering wheel as her car went faster and faster, the foothills becoming nothing more than a brown blur. She still couldn't break away from the menacing car. Seeing a curve in the road ahead, Kathryn gritted her chattering teeth and started slowing down, praying the black car would do the same. Instead, the blond man maneuvered his car to the left of her fender again and gently tapped her bumper.

Her Lexus spun into an open area between two dusty hillocks, hit a shallow ditch, rolled several times and landed top-side-down on a steep incline. The airbag deployed, knocking the air from her lungs. Kathryn was shocked by the rapidness of the spin and felt dazed from hitting her head. She struggled to reach the emergency call button located on the ceiling of her car and pushed it before her world went black.

Chapter Nine

Kathryn slowly regained consciousness and groaned when her head began throbbing. She heard several sirens shrieking in the distance, getting closer with each second. Her car windows were spidery webs of cracks and she could make out dark, dusty dirt sitting at the top of her window. Confused for a moment, she finally realized she was still strapped in, upside down. Her breathing quickened and her heart rate escalated as she struggled to release the seatbelt. Tiny beads of sweat dripped up her back and onto her neck. The sirens got louder and finally a pair of black-booted feet stood next to her side window.

"Miss, can you hear me?" a deep, masculine voice called.

"Yes, I can hear you. Can you open the door, please?" Kathryn yelled as loud as her headache would permit. "I really need out, now! Like right this second!"

"We'll have you out soon. Your door is jammed so we have to cut it open with the Jaws of Life. Try to remain calm, miss. It won't be much longer."

She closed her eyes and tried to breathe in slower, hold a breath and then slowly exhale. The heat made it difficult to inhale the heavy air and she struggled harder to undo her seatbelt.

"Miss, please stay still," the rescuer pleaded. "We need to check for injuries before we move you."

Finally, she was pulled from the totaled car. Despite the heat she started shivering, shaking from head to foot. A fireman found her a place to sit, away from her car, and wrapped a blanket around her while a paramedic took her vital signs. The ambulance and tow truck all arrived at the same time, blocking the right lane.

A California Highway Patrol officer circled around her car, then strode over to her.

"How are you feeling?" the officer asked.

"Except for a splitting headache, sore ribs and a totaled car, I'm great." Kathryn tried to smile but found it hurt her head too much.

"Looks like you're going to have a hell of a shiner," he said, bending his head close to her face. "Have you been drinking this afternoon?"

"No, sir." Kathryn peered up at his name badge. "Officer Callahan."

"Did you fall asleep at the wheel?"

"No. A guy in a Cadillac pushed me off the road and I rolled."

"Do you think it was road rage?"

"I have no idea why he did this to me and no idea who he is." Kathryn winced, rubbing her neck with shaking hands. "I was visiting a friend in Rancho Santa Margarita and noticed him sitting in his car across the street. I didn't realize he was following me until he hit me the first time. I was able to keep control of my car so I sped up trying to get away from him. That's when he hit me again and you know how it ended."

"You're very lucky to be alive. If you had rolled another hundred feet up the road, you could have crashed down a steep cliff."

He finished taking down her information, along with a description of the black Cadillac and the blond man, then left to measure skid marks and take photos of her car. The paramedic came back and insisted she let the ambulance take her to the hospital for a thorough exam. They loaded her in and made their way to the hospital. Kathryn was thankful they drove without their sirens.

**

While waiting for her turn with the emergency room doctor, she called John. "Hey, it's Kathryn."

"Hi, what's up?" He sounded brisk. All business.

"Did I catch you at a bad time?"

"I'm just wrapping up a meeting with my uncle, but I can spare a moment for you."

"I don't want to bother you. I'll call Marianne."

"No, really, it's okay, Kathryn. What's up?"

"I was in a car accident and I'm at St. Joseph's waiting to see the doctor."

"Are you okay? I can be there in less than a half hour."

"I'm fine. Just a headache and some bruising. I'll call Marianne and have her pick me up."

"No, I insist. I'll come down right now."

Kathryn looked at her watch. "I'm sorry, I forgot you have Trieste. Isn't she getting out of school soon?"

"She's going to a friend's house after school and I don't have to pick her up until eight o'clock tonight."

"If you're sure you can leave the meeting it would mean a lot to me," Kathryn whispered. "I'm having a really bad day."

"I'm on my way right now. Is it St. Joe's in Mission Viejo or Orange?"

"Mission Viejo."

"Okay, I'll see you soon."

Just then the silver-haired emergency room doctor entered her tiny curtained cubicle. "Well, young lady, I'd say you have yourself quite a shiner going on."

"So I've heard. I haven't seen it myself."

"Can you tell me if anything hurts?"

73

"Everything hurts, but my head is the worst." She massaged her neck. "I think I have a few bruises on my left arm and leg but they don't seem to be too bad. I can walk and use my hand just fine."

He took a look at her eyes, checked her vitals and had her walk in a straight line. He asked about her accident and how long she estimated she had been unconscious.

"I pressed my emergency call button, then passed out," Kathryn answered. "When I woke up, I heard sirens in the distance. I guess it was less than five minutes."

"You have a mild concussion, but it shouldn't be anything serious," the doctor declared. "I'll give you some Motrin before you leave and write a prescription for it as well. It will help with the headache. Get plenty of rest, but you need to have someone wake you every two hours overnight, to make sure you're okay. Try to take it easy tomorrow as well. If you think your symptoms are worsening, call your doctor immediately."

Kathryn signed all the release forms, took the prescription form to the in-hospital pharmacy, then waited for John.

John finally rushed into the emergency waiting room. "You look awful, Kathryn. That's a hell of a shiner!"

"I seem to be hearing that a lot lately. I think I'm starting to get a complex."

"How are you feeling? Are you really all right?"

"My head is better but still aches some. And yes, I'm really all right."

"Let's get you out of here and you can tell me what happened on the way home." He wrapped his arm around her waist and guided her towards the exit.

Just as they walked through the automatic double doors, a young woman entering the hospital reached out and tapped Kathryn's arm.

"Kathryn, what happened to you?"

"Angela, what are you doing here?" Kathryn leaned over, gave the slight woman a hug, then looked into her haggard face. "Is everything okay?"

"It's Kris." Stepping to the side of the entrance to let people pass, Angela swiped her curly red hair away from her teary hazel-colored eyes. "She started having seizures last night. I thought we'd be lucky and not have to go through this."

"Oh no!" Kathryn reached out to hold the woman's trembling hand. "Is there anything I can do? Can she have visitors?"

Kathryn jumped when John nudged her. "Oh sorry. Angela, this is John Selton. John, meet Angela Casey, my running buddy and Kris's mother."

"Nice to meet you, Angela. I'm sorry to hear about your daughter." John reached out and shook her hand. "How old is she?"

"Kris turned seven last month." Angela looked towards the hospital doors. "I'd better get back to her. I ran out to grab a bite to eat and I hate to leave her alone for long."

"John, do you mind if I say hi to Kris for moment? I promise I won't be long."

"I'll come up with you, if it's all right," he replied. "I have a seven-year-old daughter and I can't imagine seeing her in a hospital bed. Do you think she'd like a balloon?"

Angela smiled. "I know she'd love a balloon. Thank you."

While Kathryn told Angela about her accident and waited for the elevator, John hurried into the gift shop and purchased a pink-and-purple mylar balloon, whose words read, "Get Well Soon."

As they rode the elevator up Angela said, "I should warn you, Kris is going to look a little freaky. They're running a forty-eight-hour EEG on her and her head looks like a science experiment gone wrong. Wires coming every which way out of her head."

"Do they suspect epilepsy?" John asked, holding the elevator doors open for the two women when they reached the fifth floor. "I'm sure with the correct medication she'll be okay."

"Unfortunately, Kris's situation is much worse than epilepsy," Angela answered, her shoulders sagging. "She has Rett Syndrome. That's why Kathryn and I have been training for the charity half marathon. We want to raise funds to find a cure for my daughter and all the other girls like her."

"Rett Syndrome? I've never heard of it."

"Most people haven't," Kathryn piped in, "even though it affects about one in every ten thousand girls born each year."

They followed the young mother into the sterile white hospital room that smelled of pine tree disinfectant. Lying in a small bed was a very thin girl watching a Disney movie on a pink iPad. A small wheelchair, decorated with pink ribbons and pink pillows, was parked next to the bed. Angela leaned over and kissed her daughter's forehead, then clasped her hand. Wires protruded from every surface of the gauze that wrapped the girl's head, leading to a solid mass of cables hooked up to a machine showing green bouncing lines running across the surface of the screen. A steady flow of quiet beeps came from the machine.

Kathryn leaned over the opposite side of the bed. "Hey Kris. I see you've got *The Little Mermaid* on."

The little girl turned towards Kathryn. Her brilliant green eyes widened and a small yelp escaped her lips as she smiled.

"I'm happy to see you too." Kathryn pointed to John. "I've brought a friend with me. His name is John."

"It's nice to meet you, Kris." John walked over, placed the balloon in the child's hand and noticed the plastic braces wrapped tightly around her arms. "Did you hurt your arms, sweetheart?"

Angela shook her head. "No, that's part of Rett Syndrome. Uncontrollable and repetitive hand movements. If she doesn't wear the braces her hands are always in her mouth causing sores and dental complications."

Kathryn laughed. "Are you flirting with John, Kris? Look at her bat her eyelashes at him."

Kris gave John a huge smile, waved her balloon at him and started cooing.

"She loves handsome guys, always giving them her goo-goo eyes" Angela explained. "And when she has a handsome therapist, she's willing to work harder and longer without complaining."

John patted the young girl's hand before turning to her mother. "I gather she can't talk?"

"No, she lost her few words when she was eighteen months old. She's never walked either."

"It must be heartbreaking," John said, shaking his head. "I'd like to make a donation towards your charity run. Where should I send the check?"

Angela grabbed a tissue and dabbed at her eyes before digging in her handbag, grabbing a card and handing it to John. "That's very kind of you. We all truly appreciate it. Here's the website with the donation information."

"We'd better be going." Kathryn gave Kris a kiss and hugged Angela. "Please let me know if you need anything."

As they rode the elevator back to the lobby, Kathryn explained that Angela was a single mother with no family living in the area to help her out. "I honestly don't know how she manages it all on her own. Between Kris, work and then training for a half marathon, she's got to be stressed out."

"I'll look into some of my uncle's charitable foundations and see if there's anything they can do to help," John promised.

As the elevator doors opened, Kathryn saw Detective Williams striding purposefully through the front entrance door.

"He's like a bad penny," John muttered under his breath.

The detective caught sight of them. "Mrs. Landry. Wow, you have a…"

"I know, I know. A hell of a shiner. I'm getting kind of tired of compliments like that." She looked at John before stepping away from him.

"I suppose you've got a point," Detective Williams replied, his eyebrows furrowed together. "I heard about your accident and thought I'd drive you home so that you can tell me about it."

"I'm driving Kathryn home." John scowled at the detective. "We were just leaving."

"That's mighty nice of you, Mr. Selton, but I think Mrs. Landry should come with me since I have reason to believe this accident may be connected to her husband's disappearance," the detective said with authority. "I also have other questions I need to ask her that pertain to, ah, my unfortunate remarks this morning. Shall we go, Mrs. Landry?"

"It was just an accident. Why would you think it had anything to do with Neil?" John sneered.

"Guess you're not in the loop, are you, Selton?"

"John, someone intentionally ran me off the road. I think I'd better go with Detective Williams." Kathryn saw John's scowl deepen. "I'll call you later and explain. And thank you for all you did for Kris."

Kathryn followed the detective out the door. He led her to his Ford Explorer, which was parked in the red zone, with one tire up on the curb.

"Oh look, someone stuck a red curb under your tire," Kathryn said, tossing her hair back.

"P-P."

"Excuse me? What does that mean?"

"P-P. Police privilege."

She rolled her eyes as he opened the passenger door and helped her in.

"I'm not an invalid, you know."

"It's just my childhood training, ma'am. Open the door for ladies."

"Oh? Well, thank you," she replied sullenly.

"I thought we'd take a look at the scene of your accident." The detective started the Explorer and pulled out of the parking lot, heading east toward the 241 toll road. "You might remember something by being in the actual spot."

She didn't say anything and the silence hung between them for several miles.

Clearing his throat, he asked, "This Kris person. Is it someone I should know about?"

"No. Just a little girl of someone I know, who's in St. Joseph's for some tests."

"Oh." He cleared his throat again. "I hope it's nothing serious."

"Just a life sentence imposed by Rett Syndrome." She hugged her arms in closer to her midriff and looked out the passenger window.

"Rett Syndrome? I've never heard of that." He quickly glanced over to Kathryn before giving the road his attention. "What is it?"

She told him about it, her voice turning gentle and warm when she talked about Kris.

"Sounds devastating. That poor mother." He paused for a moment, then asked, "How are you feeling? Are you hurting?"

"I have a mild concussion but the Motrin kicked in so I'm feeling better."

They returned to silence until he pulled over to the side of the road, turned off the engine and opened his door.

"Let's take a look. I would like to hear the entire story of why you were down here and why someone ran you off the road."

Kathryn climbed out of the Explorer and shivered when she saw the steep cliff not far from where her car had come to rest.

"Are you cold?"

"No, just thankful to be alive."

"So what's the story?"

"I was visiting a friend in Rancho Santa Margarita. When I left, I noticed a guy sitting in a beat-up black Cadillac. Next thing I know, he's ramming into me. I have no idea why he did it or who he is. I lost control of the car and rolled. End of story."

"This isn't exactly the direction home from Rancho."

"I wanted to go to Dana Point for some lunch," she answered, holding her grumbling stomach. "I haven't eaten anything and I think the Motrin is making me nauseated."

"Some gourmet food will help with that. I know the perfect place just up the road."

Once they were belted in, he gunned the engine and drove across the steep grassy center divider and headed north.

"Isn't this kind of dangerous?" she said, clutching the seat with both hands, hoping the SUV wouldn't roll before it reached pavement.

"I'm a trained professional."

The detective took an exit Kathryn had passed earlier in the day and went through McDonald's drive thru. He ordered two Big Mac meals with Diet Cokes. Once he had the food, he found a corner in the parking lot and backed in.

"Bon appétit, Mrs. Landry."

Finishing his burger, Detective Williams turned to her. "Kathryn, I think there are a lot of things you're not telling me."

"What do you mean?"

"A friend in Rancho Santa Margarita? Just yesterday you said you didn't have any friends."

"Okay, so this is more an acquaintance. So what? Am I not supposed to be doing something?"

"I guess I should apologize for what I said to you this morning." The detective sighed. "I was angry because I thought you were playing me. I still need to know why Selton's fingerprints are all over your apartment and why there were none on the note."

"John must have taken a look around my apartment when I first asked him to look into Neil's disappearance. It's the only logical explanation," Kathryn whispered, brushing a strand of hair from her face. "I have no idea about the note. I feel like someone's playing with my emotions, yanking me around."

"I think you know more about what's going on than you're letting on. Or you have information that you don't think is important." He looked her in the eyes. "Is that it?"

She looked away and clamped her lips together.

"Look, we need to clear the air. Your anger could hinder my investigation."

"I have every reason in the world to be angry with you. I can't believe they would put you in charge of this investigation and leave you in charge once you found out the connection to my father!" Kathryn yelled, all her pent up emotions spilling out. "Then you have the audacity to accuse me of an affair without any evidence to back up your accusations just so you can conveniently 'solve' another case and go your merry way."

He waited for her to calm down.

"You have every right to be angry with me and I owe you an apology that can never make up for what you lost. As I've said before, I am truly sorry for what happened with your father."

"Your apology doesn't make it any better," Kathryn said bitterly.

"Okay, if you're not going to believe that I'm sorry, then let me tell you my side of the story. You have the time, right?"

"I suppose."

"Your father's case was my first big investigation. I was young and wanted to make my mark on the department and pave the way for future promotions. My wife and I had been married for two years and she was expecting our first child so I was motivated to try even harder to provide for them. A week into your father's investigation, I discovered some information that led me to believe there was corruption within our precinct and that there was a cover-up involving your father's disappearance. I also believed he had already been murdered. I tore into it like a bulldog, determined to solve the case and bring the perpetrators to justice." Detective Williams took a deep breath. He sat silently with his eyes closed for several long seconds.

"That's when my wife started receiving threatening letters at the school where she was teaching, telling us that if I didn't drop the investigation something terrible would happen to her and our unborn child. It shook me up but I still kept at the investigation. Then she received an actual photo of an aborted baby with a note saying that's what our child would end up like if I didn't drop the case. My wife was so shocked she miscarried. I closed the case. I left you and your mother with nothing but the fear of never knowing what happened to your father, and for that I am truly sorry."

"How awful for your poor wife!" Kathryn gasped. "But did you just say you thought my father was murdered? And they got away with it?"

"Yes, I never found out how, why or by whom, but that was what my informant heard on the street."

"I suppose I always knew he was dead, but without knowing for sure, I hoped that he was alive somewhere and would come back." She brushed tears from her cheek.

"Kathryn, I screwed up with your father's investigation. I don't want you to think I'm going to do the same with Neil's disappearance. Whatever you know or suspect, you need to tell me."

She hesitated. "Detective Williams, there might be a few things, but it all seems to point to Neil having an affair."

"Since we're going to be working together on this, please call me Mike." He gave her a tentative smile. "I think we can do away with the formality, now that we're on the same side. Aren't we?"

She told him about the novel, finding Helene's address and her conversation with Roxie.

Mike absently stroked his lightly whiskered cheek. "I'm going to need a copy of the novel and whatever else you copied from Neil's laptop. Do you believe there's a connection between his novel and Helene?"

"It seems a likely possibility. Especially after Roxie described some of the injuries Helene sustained during her, ah, encounters." Kathryn shuddered. "It's somewhat consistent with Neil's novel. I can't imagine allowing myself being systematically scratched and cut with a pinky ring. What was that girl thinking?"

"She was probably thinking of the money. Describe the skull and crossbones ring for me."

"There's not much to tell. Roxie said it had some sort of silver skull and crossbones on black onyx stone. Do you think it's significant?"

"Hard to say. Somehow it all points to Helene right now. Do you feel up to talking to Roxie again today?"

"If you think it's important, I guess we can stop by. I feel bad about involving her with the police when I told her I wouldn't get her into trouble." Kathryn massaged her neck, which was stiffening up. "Roxie seems like such a nice girl, sort of."

"I promise I won't arrest her."

Just then the detective's cell phone rang. He had a short, clipped conversation, then started up the vehicle.

"Change of plans. Someone just reported a beat-up black Cadillac with a blond guy sitting in it. He seems to have a hole in his head."

Chapter Ten

Detective Williams rolled down his window, attached a flashing red light to the roof of his vehicle and floored the Ford Explorer's gas pedal. Kathryn flinched when he reached over and flipped a switch, causing the siren to screech.

"You okay?" he asked, glancing at her from the corner of his eye.

"I'm okay. The siren startled me."

"I'm going to have to take you to the scene with me but I'll have one of the uniforms drive you to Marianne's as soon as possible."

"Can't I go to my apartment? I'd want to pick up Neil's car and a few things."

"I'd rather you wait until I can go with you."

"I'm sure I'll be fine," she answered, crossing her arms.

He gave her a quick look before returning his attention to the asphalt racing beneath them.

The SUV swerved around a slow-moving car and Kathryn gripped the seat. "Really, don't worry about me. I can take care of myself."

"Your accident is clearly more than a coincidence now that there's been a murder. You're very lucky to be alive with no major injuries." He paused, waiting to clear the string of cars he was passing. "We can only guess that the questions you've been asking hit close to home and whoever is behind this has decided you might be a liability. Or maybe they're only hoping to scare you off."

"You were frightened off a case before. What's going to happen when they, whoever they are, start threatening your wife again?"

He slowed the vehicle a fraction before answering. "Melanie passed away a few years ago. Breast cancer. I have no other family that they can threaten this time."

"I'm so sorry. I know how painful it is to lose a loved one." Kathryn let the silence linger a moment. "Even after years go by, the loss still hurts."

Once they reached the 405 heading north, traffic slowed them down even with the red light and siren. The detective skillfully wove in and out of the impeding vehicles.

"Where did they find the car?"

"Huntington Beach. Deserted frontage road along the Santa Ana riverbed."

They pulled up to a barricade manned by a police officer blocking the cul-de-sac. Numerous civilians stood on the curbs, craning their necks to see what was happening. Detective Williams flashed his badge and drove into the cul-de-sac once the barrier was pulled aside. He parked in the middle of the street, behind several black-and-white police vehicles, all with flashing red lights.

"No curbs available for you to run over?" Kathryn asked.

"Nope, looks like they're all taken."

An ambulance was parked to the side, the paramedics casually leaning against the hood talking to one of the officers. Wide yellow crime scene tape hung between two gray concrete block walls guarding the entrance to the frontage road. Several officers were standing on the other side of tape, talking and laughing.

A motorcycle officer pulled up alongside them and motioned for the detective to roll down the window. "Hey Williams, what are you doing in our neck of the woods? Don't you have enough crime down your way to keep you busy?"

"Naw, I was bored so thought I'd be a looky-loo."

"You gonna introduce me to the lady?"

"Sorry, crime scenes make me so excited I forget my manners. Mrs. Landry, this is Officer Peña, one of Huntington Beach's finest."

Kathryn leaned across the detective to shake the motorcyclist's hand through the open window.

"Nice to meet you Mrs. Landry," Officer Peña said. "That's a…"

"I know, I know," Kathryn interjected. "I've heard it too many times to count today."

The officer turned back to Detective Williams. "So what's the story?"

"Short version is the deceased may have been the perp who ran Mrs. Landry off the road today, almost killing her. We're here to make an I.D."

"Identification? Like we're going to look at the dead body?" Kathryn choked. "I don't want to look at a dead body!"

"We have to be certain this is the same guy. Do you think you can start by taking a look at the car?"

"If I really have to."

Officer Peña escorted them through the crime scene tape and walked them towards the black Cadillac. Kathryn began to hobble, her muscles tensing and tightening from the accident. She searched her handbag and found her prescription Motrin to relieve the symptoms. She was sorry she didn't have any Valium to prepare herself for seeing a dead body.

The frontage road ran parallel to the riverbed, heading to the Pacific Ocean. A long, gray concrete block wall provided the homes and businesses backing the dry riverbed with privacy, while scraggly grayish-brown trees and bushes grew erratically along the narrow, dusty road. There were two investigators combing through the car.

"Can you tell if that's the vehicle?" Peña asked, stopping thirty yards from the car.

"It certainly looks like it," Kathryn answered. "If there are dents with white paint, the color of my car, can't we assume it's the same? I don't want to look at the body!"

Williams sighed. "I'll go take a look and then decide."

He strode to the car, spoke with the investigators for a few minutes and donned the plastic gloves handed to him. He circled the car, paying special attention to the front right bumper. He looked at the dead man and then walked back to Kathryn.

"There are dents on the Caddy, and the paint is consistent with your car. The investigators will compare the dents with those on your car and call me."

"So I don't have to look, do I?"

"I'd like to give you a pass but I'm afraid you're going to have to do this."

"Do they know who it is?" Kathryn asked, nervously looking around for an escape.

"Nope. No ID on him, which is another reason I'd like you to take a look." Mike grimaced. "No car registration either. Probably a stolen vehicle, if I had to guess."

Crows cawing overhead made her shiver. "Can't I wait until tomorrow to look at him? I'm going to have nightmares as it is, just thinking about it."

Taking her arm he pulled her gently towards the dusty, dented car. "It's not going to be as bad as you think."

Against her better judgment, Kathryn allowed herself to be pulled closer to the car. She looked into the riverbed, at the clouds, at the darting gray lizards running into the scraggly brush. Anywhere but up ahead at the dead man waiting for her. She tripped over a small stick and yelped. Mike gave her a quizzical look, then gripped her arm tighter.

When they reached the door of the Cadillac, he whispered into her ear, "You're going to have to open your eyes. It's pretty hard to see anything if you keep them shut."

"I'm fine just like this." She squeezed her eyes shut even tighter. "Can we go now?"

"Not until you take a quick look."

She opened her eyes and concentrated on the dented door of the car, then ever so slowly raised them until she was staring into the face of the body. Blood had dried into rusty red rivulets down the man's cheek, while flies buzzed around the dime-sized hole in the middle of his forehead. His hazel eyes were wide open, staring at her, accusing her.

Her hand flew to her mouth to stifle a scream, her breathing became labored and her world went dark.

"Kathryn, Kathryn! Can you hear me?" Mike's face was close to hers, his arms cradling her. "Wake up, Kathryn."

"What? What happened?"

"You passed out." He shook his head. "Are you feeling better?"

She struggled to a sitting position and noticed they were back by the yellow crime scene tape, hanging between the two block walls. The officers standing there were politely ignoring her. "How did I get here? The last thing I remember is his eyes. Staring at me."

"I, ah, carried you. I didn't want you to have to see him again." He ran a hand through his short cropped peppery hair. "I'm really sorry, but I'm going to have to ask you if you can ID the guy."

"It's the same man I saw at Roxie's house and then when he rammed me, but I have no idea who he is," she whispered, almost choking on the words.

"All right. I'll get a ride home for you." He patted her arm, then stood and waved to Officer Peña. "Would you mind asking one of the black-and-whites to drive Mrs. Landry to Corona del Mar? I'd like to stay around here awhile longer and I know she's already had a long day."

"But I want to go to my apartment."

The detective clenched his jaw. "No buts, Mrs. Landry. You're going to Marianne's."

"Okay, whatever you say," she conceded, hobbling after Officer Peña, grateful to be away from the crime scene.

"I'll call you later this evening!" Mike yelled after her.

She lifted her hand in a half wave, without looking back.

Officer Peña quickly found an idle policeman who volunteered to drive Kathryn. After introductions were made, she sat in the front seat of the patrol car while the officer, looking barely out of high school, drove towards the beach.

"Would you mind taking me to Newport Beach instead of Corona del Mar?" She sweetly asked. "I need to pick up my husband's car so I can drive to work tomorrow."

"Sure, if that's what you want, Mrs. Landry," he answered.

They drove in silence except when she needed to give directions. When he pulled into the circular drive in front of her apartment building, skillfully missing the curb, Kathryn thanked him and stiffly walked into the lobby.

"Mrs. Landry!" Tommy exclaimed. "What happened to you?"

"Too much has happened to me today, Tommy. But a car accident is what gave me this beautiful shiner," she answered, trying not to grimace. "Did the lock on my apartment get repaired yet?"

"Your detective must know what strings to pull because they fixed it late last night. Let me get the new keys for you," he answered, bounding towards his desk.

She walked through her door, eager to be in her own home but sighed when she saw the papers still strewn around Neil's office and the black powdery residue on all the hard surfaces. After a long, hot shower to soothe her sore muscles, she changed into a t-shirt and sweatpants and went to work straightening Neil's office while hunting for his car keys.

Curiosity got the better of her and she spent time browsing through Neil's papers and documents before she placed them neatly into the banker's boxes she had pulled from his closet. Most were articles he had written or interviews he'd participated in while looking for the next big story. Not all were sports related. There were also political and community leaders profiled. Nearly done reading through his papers, she laid down on the floor to stretch her aching back and saw a manila envelope wedged beneath Neil's small white sofa. She pulled it out and found it contained her birth certificate, their passports and a single sheet of white paper with Neil's scrawled handwriting. It appeared to be columns of lists.

Not having the patience to decipher the list, she put it aside and studied her birth certificate. She traced her mother's name with her finger and saw her mother's young age. Only twenty when Kathryn was born. Her father had been thirty. Seeing her mother's maiden name, Stone, suddenly made her remember an uncle who had come briefly to their house right after her father disappeared. She wondered if any of her mother's family were still alive and if she should try to contact them now that she had no family left. She wasn't sure if they had even been notified of her mother's death sixteen years before.

She tucked her birth certificate and Neil's paper back into the unlabeled file folder, and opened Neil's passport. She studied his photo closely. The handsome, chiseled face remained stonily impassive, as it so often had when he was displeased with her.

Where did you go, Neil?

She placed his passport in the file folder and, as she picked hers up, a folded sheet of paper fell out. Opening it, she found a copy of a bank statement for Neil and Kathryn Landry from a bank that she had never used. Checks had been written on the account for several thousand dollars each, the last one clearing ten days before. The balance was close to a quarter of a million dollars.

Kathryn exhaled, not realizing she had been holding her breath.

So this is where you've been stashing our money. How long have you been squirreling it away? I think I'll be visiting this bank tomorrow and making a very large withdrawal. Let's see how you like being left penniless.

She opened her passport and saw colorful stamps, collected during their third wedding anniversary celebration, island-hopping in the Caribbean. She thumbed through the pages, whispering the names of the different islands.

Barbados... Neil had surprised her with champagne and crystal glasses on the deserted beach in front of their bungalow at midnight, followed by a moonlit swim.

Turks and Caicos... a rented catamaran for two, a secluded bay at sunset, more champagne, coconut massage oil...

What happened to you, Neil? Why did you stop loving me? Why have you given me nothing but a peck on the lips for the last five years?

She turned to the photo page, wishing she could go back to being as naïve and carefree as she had been all those years ago. But instead of looking at a younger version of herself, the photograph of a raven-haired, dark-skinned beauty stared back at her.

Chapter Eleven

Kathryn shook her head to quiet the buzzing in her ears. There had to be a mistake. She checked the signature. It was her handwriting. The name was still Kathryn Evelyn Landry. But the face wasn't hers.

Neil, you son of a bitch. How long has this been going on?

With trembling hands she closed the passport and put it into the unmarked file folder. She threw her wedding ring, with its two-carat solitaire diamond, into the folder, but then put it back on after deciding she'd rather not have Detective Williams ask too many questions. She wrapped her arms around her stomach, rocking back and forth, wishing tears would come. But they wouldn't. Not yet. After what seemed like hours, but was probably mere minutes, she struggled to her feet. She pulled the bottom drawer out from the filing cabinet and taped the file, containing the passports, to the back wall after shoving the bank statement and Neil's unintelligible list into her purse. She carefully inserted the drawer back into the cabinet and slammed it shut. Neil's betrayal was going to remain her secret.

She went to her bedroom and stared. Had she and Neil always been strangers? Had she ever really known him?

Shaking her thoughts aside, she found her jewelry box still sitting on the vanity and opened a tattered velvet ring box. A small sapphire sat mounted between twisted vines of white gold. Her mother's wedding ring. Her father had remained faithful to his wedding vows, of that she was certain. She slipped it onto the fourth finger of her right hand. It fit perfectly. She remembered her mother carefully placing it into the velvet box each night before rubbing lotion into her gentle hands. Sometimes she'd massage young Kathryn's hands and arms with the lavender-scented cream before tucking her into bed.

Her ringing cell phone jarred her back to the present. "Hello."

"Hi Kathryn, it's Marianne. I haven't heard from you today so I was wondering if you were going to have dinner with us."

She glanced at her watch. "Is it seven o'clock already? I can't believe it's that late."

"I hope I didn't disturb anything, but I was getting worried about you."

"No, that's okay. I apologize. I should have called earlier," Kathryn answered. "I can be at your house in about an hour, but please don't hold dinner for me."

"Nonsense, we'll wait for you. We usually don't eat until late anyway."

"Thanks, Marianne. I'll be there as soon as I can."

Hastily putting the remaining files and papers into boxes and shoving them into the closet she then grabbed paper towels and Windex and quickly cleaned up the black powder. Next she began opening up Neil's desk drawers, hunting for his car keys. They were nowhere in sight. She searched his closet, which had been converted to hold office supplies. Nothing. She sat on the couch wondering where to look next when she saw a few stray papers beneath his desk. She crawled over to retrieve them and saw a small metal box affixed to the bottom of his desk. She pulled it open and was rewarded by the sound of jingling keys falling to the floor.

***

Seated in Neil's sporty BMW M5, Kathryn carefully pulled into traffic.

Making her way to Corona del Mar she looked in the rearview mirror frequently, checking to make sure she wasn't being followed. She tried to convince herself that the accident and then the murder had been a coincidence, but by the time she pulled up to Marianne's house her heart was pounding and she had to wipe her sweaty palms on her pants before ringing the doorbell.

Richard opened the door. "Oh my, Kathryn. You look like you've had a hell of a day!"

"It's been an unbelievably bad day."

"What happened to you? Was it that detective? Marianne said he was being a jerk this morning."

"Richard, don't make Kathryn stand around in the hallway!" Marianne hollered from the kitchen. "Let her come in and relax."

As soon as Marianne saw Kathryn's face and limping steps she bustled around getting a bag of frozen peas for her eye and poured her a glass of Grgich Hills Chardonnay. Kathryn breathed in the warm, comforting smells of bread baking and saw colorful red bell peppers, orange carrots, yellow squash and green baby spinach lined up next to the white sink, prepped for dinner. Pungent Parmesan and glossy black olives sat in red porcelain bowls next to a pot of water waiting to boil.

Once Kathryn was settled, Marianne asked, "Are you sure you're okay? What happened?"

She quickly explained her accident, avoiding the fact that she could have been killed. "I meant to drop by home and get the keys to Neil's car then come straight here. But I got distracted by the mess and ended up staying a long time going through his files. I'm sorry I worried you, Marianne."

"You know you could have called us from the hospital," Richard said, patting her free hand. "Honey, you're not alone in this. We're here whenever you need anything."

"Thanks, it means a lot to me, especially now. But you've done so much for me already I hate to be a bother."

"You're not a bother at all." Marianne paused to toss the pasta, vegetables, cheese and olives together. "We love having you here."

Over a comforting dinner of pasta and lemon poppy seed cake for dessert, Kathryn gave the Pattons more details about her accident but tried to downplay the murder of the hit-and-run driver, insisting it had nothing to do with her. After helping clear the dinner dishes, she gave Marianne the new business account checks before borrowing their laptop and settling in the guestroom with her iPhone playing calming classical music into tiny ear buds. She retrieved the flash stick from her handbag and pulled up Neil's novel. She browsed through sections until she found what she was looking for: the physical description of the "john." She pulled Neil's scribbled handwritten list from her purse and tried to decipher his writing. Certain phrases popped out from one column that coincided with his novel's description: salt-and-pepper hair; icy blue eyes, cruel sneer; rugged, tan face.

Why does this keep reminding me of a certain detective I know?

She soon figured out that the next column listed a woman's physical attributes, which seemed to match Helene's description. The third column listed sex acts. Kathryn didn't try to decipher that column.

Exhausted, she turned off the laptop, returned the flash stick to her handbag and took another Motrin. Before climbing back into bed she groaned, remembering that someone was supposed to wake her up every two hours. She crept out of the room determined to go it alone if Marianne was already in bed. However, she was still up, sitting in her kitchen chatting with Richard and John Selton.

John was running his fingers through his wavy black hair when Kathryn walked into the kitchen. He was dressed in blue jean shorts and a white t-shirt, which she noticed accentuated his well-developed biceps.

"Kathryn, I'm so sorry if I woke you," he said.

"I wasn't asleep yet." She yawned while collapsing into a chair. "What are you doing here so late?"

"I was worried sick about you since I haven't heard from you after that pompous ass pulled you out of the hospital." He scowled, frown lines furrowing his brow. "I tried calling you several times this evening but you didn't answer your cell phone."

"I'm sorry, John, I think my battery must have died. I forgot to recharge it." She shrugged. "How'd you find Marianne's house anyway?"

"I'm an investigator, remember? It's my job."

"Actually, John called a while ago so I invited him over so we could tell him in person about that murdered man." Marianne and Richard both stood up. "I think we'll say goodnight, and let the two of you talk. We'll see you in the morning, Kathryn."

Before John could say anything, Kathryn jumped up. "Marianne, can I talk to you in private for just a second?"

"Sure."

When they were out of hearing distance from the kitchen, she whispered, "I have a huge, huge favor to ask. The doctor said I had to be awakened every two hours tonight to make sure my concussion didn't get worse, otherwise they wanted to keep me in the hospital overnight for observation."

"Of course I'll do it. But why did you have to ask me in private?"

"John will want to stay and look after me. I feel awkward and it doesn't make it easier after listening to Detective William's accusations, even though he's completely wrong."

"Well, it's obvious that John cares about you beyond your client relationship. It doesn't hurt to have as many friends as you can right now, Kathryn."

"Friendship is one thing, but I think John wants more and I'm not ready for that. He doesn't want to hear that either."

"Don't worry, it will work itself out once Neil's disappearance is solved."

"Yeah, as long as it doesn't turn out like my father's case." Kathryn sighed.

Marianne gave her a gentle hug and they walked back to the kitchen.

John asked, "So what was that all about?"

"Just some girl talk. John, you should know better than to pry," Marianne scolded. "Come on, Richard, let's say goodnight."

After the couple left, Kathryn quickly asked, "Don't you have Trieste tonight? You really didn't have to drive all the way here to check on me."

"Trieste spent the night with her friend." John leaned back in his chair and studied her behind his long fringed eyelashes. "If I didn't know better, I'd think you were avoiding me."

"It's not that, I promise. It's just been a long and exhausting day."

John scowled. "I know and I want to help but you're not letting me."

"What do you mean?"

"First, I can't believe you didn't tell me that someone purposely ran you off the road, causing your accident. Instead, I had to hear it from Williams. That aggravates me. And then I really can't believe you didn't call and tell me the same man was murdered a short time later."

"John, it's complicated."

"I think it's that pompous ass making it complicated. I wish you would stop letting him interfere with us," he hissed.

"I'm sorry this is turning out to be difficult and I'm making you unhappy. But do you mind if we continue this conversation tomorrow?" Kathryn rubbed her eyes. "I really don't feel that well."

John's face softened and he took her hand. "I'm being an insensitive bastard, aren't I?"

"Just intense, which is more than I can handle right now."

"Okay, sleep well tonight, but I'm going to pick you up at nine tomorrow morning and take you out to breakfast. Someplace where Williams can't follow and kidnap you again."

"Whatever you say." She yawned.

I guess Neil's bank will have to wait until after breakfast.

"Dress casual, but no jeans," he directed.

After locking the door when he left, Kathryn plugged her cell phone in to charge, then tumbled into bed and slept soundly. Marianne was true to her word and woke her up every two hours, bringing water and Motrin halfway through the night. At eight the next morning, Marianne knocked on Kathryn's door and stuck her head in.

"I'm leaving for the office in a few minutes. How do you feel this morning?"

"Not as bad as I thought I would." Kathryn stretched. "You're an angel, Marianne! I think the extra Motrin last night really helped."

"Richard is leaving for an appointment too, so there's a spare key on the kitchen table with the alarm security code. Would you mind setting it when you leave?"

"No problem." Kathryn glanced at the bedside clock. "Oh no, is it really that late already?"

"There's no rush for you to do anything this morning. Sleep some more or at least have a lazy morning. There's coffee ready to brew and help yourself to whatever else you'd like."

"John's coming at nine to take me to breakfast since I didn't have the energy to do much talking last night. I'll drop by the office after breakfast."

"Good. I mean 'good' you're going to have breakfast with John. There's no need for you to rush to the office. You should take it easy today."

She hurried through her shower, dressed in a flirty floral skirt with a white silk blouse and topaz-looking bejeweled sandals. She was finishing trying to conceal her black eye when John arrived. He looked well rested and ready for business wearing a light gray Prada dress shirt, which complemented Tiffany silver cufflinks. Italian wool black slacks accented with a Hermes belt at his waist, and Bally shoes shined to perfection, completed his ensemble.

"You look beautiful this morning, Kathryn," he said as he brushed his lips against her cheek. "Here, I brought you a little gift."

She took the Chanel shopping bag, plucked out the tissue paper and found a bronze quilted leather handbag, with Chanel's logo stitched on the front.

"It's beautiful, John, but why a handbag?"

"Actually what's inside the purse is the real purpose of the gift."

Kathryn slowly zipped open the top, admiring the supple leather. Inside she found a case containing oversized Chanel sunglasses, bronze to match the handbag and complement her hair color.

"I thought you might want something fashionable to help cover your black eye. Plus, I need to apologize for being so insensitive last night. Apology accepted?"

"This is perfect! Thank you so much, and yes, apology accepted," Kathryn bubbled, giving him a quick hug. "Can you wait a couple minutes while I transfer my purse contents to the Chanel?"

"Sure, take your time."

Kathryn quickly organized her new handbag and put the sunglasses on before joining John.

"I'm curious about one thing. How did you manage to buy these when South Coast Plaza doesn't open until ten? I know they had to have already been closed by the time you left here last night."

He winked and lowered his voice. "Oh, I have connections."

"Wow! Connections a girl would kill for!" She admired herself in the mirror. "Well, thank your connection for me. These sunglasses are just what I needed."

She turned from the mirror and John pulled her into his arms and pressed his lips against hers. She wanted to pull away but instead found her lips and body responding to his sensual kiss. His tongue began to tentatively explore hers and he pulled her tighter against his muscular body, showing her how aroused he was.

An insistent ringing cell phone caused him to pull away and, swearing softly, he answered it while his eyes roamed over Kathryn's body.

"Uncle Gerald, good morning," he said, rolling his eyes.

She could hear a man's deep voice but couldn't make out the words.

"I'm meeting Mrs. Landry for breakfast this morning to discuss her case. Can I drop by later? How about eleven-thirty or noon?"

After Gerald belted out a few commands, John disconnected the call.

"Now, where were we?" His voice was husky.

Kathryn blushed. "I think we were heading out the door for breakfast."

"Are you sure? I don't have to be anywhere until noon," he pleaded, grabbing her hand.

"John, there are so many reasons why this isn't a good idea right now."

"No one has to know."

"But I'll know. And I know it's not right for me at this point in my life. Please be patient with me."

John reached up and stroked Kathryn's cheek. "I'll be on my best behavior and wait until you're ready."

"Thanks for being understanding."

"No problem. Do you think I can try again next week?" he asked with an impish grin.

She swatted his hand away. "Come on, let's go have some breakfast and talk about murder."

***

John gunned his 911 Turbo Porsche down the 73 toll road and took the Bonita Canyon Drive exit. The Santa Ana winds were frantically whipping the trees lining the street, pushing dark dingy clouds from eastern foothills towards the city. The ruby-red machine glittered in the smoky sunlight and when he stomped on the accelerator, Kathryn could feel the aggressive horsepower as the car hugged the curvy road.

"How fast have you gotten your car to go?"

"About one hundred and sixty."

"And you didn't get arrested?" she asked, shocked.

"I was on a racetrack. I wouldn't endanger other people's lives by driving recklessly on a public road. If you're interested, I'll set it up so you can drive my car that fast," he said with a huge grin.

"I think I'll pass, but thanks for the offer." She leaned back into the form-fitting seat and watched the brown hills race by. "So where are we going?"

"Shady Canyon Golf Club. They make killer Eggs Benedict."

"You're a member?"

"My uncle. He owns a house there."

"One of those connections, huh?"

"Yep, handy to have when you need them."

"So why did you pick Shady Canyon for breakfast?"

"First reason is that Williams can't track you down here. Second, we have to turn off our cell phones, so we'll have uninterrupted time to talk."

"You've thought of everything, haven't you?"

"That's my job."

Kathryn relaxed and enjoyed the scenery racing by. Feeling the car jump as John pushed the accelerator down even more, she looked over and saw him intently watching his rearview mirror. She turned around and saw a black car following close behind.

"What is it?" her voice trembled.

"Nothing to worry about. Just some bozos from a job I've been working on for my uncle."

She watched him masterfully handle his powerful car and when she looked back again the black car had fallen back, but then just as quickly caught up and rode the Porsche's bumper.

John grimaced and began slowing down, the black car keeping pace. Before pulling over to the shoulder of the road he reached across Kathryn's lap, opened the glove box and extracted a nine-millimeter Glock pistol.

Chapter Twelve

"What's that?"

"It's a gun. What do you think it is?"

"I know it's a gun, but why?"

When his car hit the graveled shoulder, John slammed on the brakes and released his seatbelt. "My motto is better safe than sorry."

He bolted out the door and made a beeline for the black car, which was still rolling towards the Porsche.

Kathryn pulled her cell phone from her handbag, wondering if she should call 9-1-1. She twisted around in her seat trying to see what was happening. Her hands started quivering and she could hardly hold on to her phone. She could see that the car following them was a new Cadillac CTS-V, and she was glad that the two men had not gotten out. John was waving his arms around, the gun still in one hand. She could hear him and one of the men shouting at each other but couldn't make out the words.

When John finally strode back to his car, she quickly turned around to face front and imperceptibly dropped her phone back into her handbag. The

Cadillac roared past them throwing gravel onto the hood of the ruby-red car.

He gave them the middle-finger wave, jammed the Porsche into first gear and almost spun out trying to catch them. Out of the corner of his eye he could see Kathryn looking pale and shaking.

"Too much excitement?" he asked.

"I think I've had enough excitement this week to last me a lifetime!" She shivered.

He slowed down and held her hand. "I'm sorry. Those goons were only trying to intimidate me. They couldn't hurt a fly if they wanted to. I would never do anything that would put your life in jeopardy."

She didn't reply, and instead tried to slow her breathing and shaking by thinking calm thoughts.

***

They were shown to a table in the corner of the elegant dining room, overlooking the golf course. The tawny hills surrounding the green course looked like sentinels. After the friendly server took their orders and John provided his uncle's club number, Kathryn looked around admiring the beautiful furnishings.

"We're the only ones here."

"That's my third reason for choosing this place. We can talk without people overhearing." He covered her hand with his and gave it a gentle squeeze. "Are you okay now?"

"I'm okay." Smoothly retrieving her hand, she picked up her orange juice and took a sip. "This is fresh squeezed. It's delicious."

John compressed his lips and lowered his eyebrows.

"What?"

"We didn't come here to talk about the merits of fresh-squeezed orange juice. I'm trying to patiently wait for you to tell me what the hell's been going on."

"Oh. You mean besides being chased a second time in two days by a black

Cadillac?"

"I'm sorry about that. I guess I was mistaken about no one being able to track us here."

"Your car isn't exactly inconspicuous."

"You have a point. But this meeting is about you and not my problems."

"So much has happened in the last few days, I don't know where to start."

"Then start at the beginning. We have as much time as you need." He took a notebook and pen from his hip pocket. "Maybe I'll hear something that you forgot to tell me before or I'll see it in a new context."

Kathryn quickly told him about how she discovered Neil missing, since he had already heard the story. She went into great detail about how she discovered and tracked down Helene and Roxie, pausing only when the young server came with their food and coffee refills. Sometimes it was difficult to remember all that had happened and John asked pertinent questions to get her back on track. She was gratified to see him taking detailed notes. When she started talking about her accident, Kathryn shivered.

"Why would someone try to hurt or kill me?"

John waved the approaching server away. "Maybe he was looking for a thrill and you were in the wrong place at the wrong time."

"I don't know. Especially since he was murdered a short time after."

"Maybe when the police ID him, his name will help you figure out if there is any connection to you or Neil."

She shivered again. "Don't remind me about the identifying. I'll never get that haunted look on his dead face out of my mind."

"I'll never forgive Williams for putting you through that ordeal," John quietly said while running his fingers across her forearm.

Kathryn pulled her arm away and clasped her hands in her lap, appearing to examine her nails. Clearing her throat, she said, "There's one more thing I haven't brought up yet."

When she hesitated, John quietly asked, "What is it?"

"When Neil's note was analyzed for fingerprints, they didn't find any. Absolutely none. But when they got the fingerprint results from my apartment, after the break-in, they found several prints. Mine and Neil's obviously. Our housekeeper's. And your prints. Your prints were all over the place, including my bedroom." Kathryn's voice quivered. "Can you explain that to me?"

John remained silent but his face turned dark red and his eyes narrowed as he crossed his arms.

"Well, can you answer my question?"

"Let me guess, that Williams guy you've been hanging around has dropped this bombshell."

"Yes, he was doing his job. I think it's normal for them to take fingerprints when there's a crime scene."

"Kathryn, he's trying to drive a wedge between us and you're letting him," John hissed.

"You're deflecting and not answering my question. I think I have a right to know the truth."

"You want the truth? Then stop listening to what that detective tells you. He puts a spin on everything to discredit me."

"Your fingerprints in my bedroom? Did he make that up?" Her voice went up an octave.

"No, he didn't make that up. But he's trying to insinuate something that hasn't happened." John sighed and leaned in. "Is that why you've been avoiding me?"

"I haven't intentionally been avoiding you. Just a lot has been going on," she answered, massaging her temples. "But don't sidetrack me. I want to know why you were in my room."

"It's not what you think. You asked me to investigate Neil's disappearance and I needed to see his surroundings and look through any belongings he may have left behind. I wanted to do it without being distracted by you." Taking her hand into his, he smiled. "And you do distract me."

She pulled her hand back. "Why didn't you ask me, or at least tell me you were going to do that? I was completely blindsided by Detective Williams."

"I'm sorry, I should have."

"How did you get into my apartment?"

"Trade secret."

"Okay then, when did you go through my things?"

"The day I had the water leak and you were at my house with Trieste."

"Oh… So you were at my apartment right before it was broken into?"

"I swear I didn't take Neil's computer and I made sure the door was locked when I left."

She avoided making eye contact. "Did you know my underwear was stolen?"

"I swear I didn't take anything. I opened some drawers and closets, and, um, maybe unlocked some of Neil's filing cabinets, but that's it." He stroked her forearm with the tips of his fingers and softly said, "Please, you have to believe me. I wouldn't lie to you."

"I believe you." She sighed and shook her head. "I'm so tired of not knowing what's going on and being kept in the dark. I wish you would have told me."

"I won't keep things from you again, Kathryn."

"Does that mean you'll tell me how you got into my apartment?"

John laughed. "Tommy and Tomas do some odd jobs for my uncle on occasion. Tommy let me in, or maybe it was Tomas. I can't tell them apart, but whichever one it was, he would never mention my visit to anyone."

"Ah, more connections."

"Can't ever have too many."

Once they were back in John's car, he checked his voicemails. "Would you mind if we stop by my uncle's office before I drop you off at home? I have to pick up some documents before he leaves for a meeting."

"That's fine."

"He wants to meet you anyway."

"I thought I would stay in the car. I'd feel awkward meeting Senator Selton looking like this." She touched her bruised face.

"You're still beautiful. Besides, he knows about the car accident so don't worry about it."

***

Stepping into the former senator's office, Kathryn admired the paintings of several local artists arranged tastefully to complement the sleek white and chrome furniture being cradled by plush steel-blue carpet. White orchids sitting on pristine glass tabletops graced the room. John asked her to wait in the reception area for a few minutes while he discussed business with his uncle.

The young, blonde receptionist, dressed in a very short leopard-print skirt and low-cut black silk blouse, brought her chilled Perrier in a Waterford goblet along with some magazines. Kathryn stood at the floor-to-ceiling window, admiring the view of Newport Beach from eighteen stories up, sipping her water before lazily flipping through *Architectural Digest*. She was startled to hear yelling coming from behind the closed doors of the senator's office.

The receptionist giggled when she saw Kathryn's expression. "Don't pay attention to them. They're just hotheaded Italians. They yell at each other and then afterwards act like nothing ever happened."

True to her word, John and his uncle walked out several minutes later. His uncle was laughing, but Kathryn thought John's smile seemed forced, his laugh brittle. The resemblance between John and Gerald Selton was almost nonexistent. The senator had salt-and-pepper hair, lines in his deeply tanned face, and aquamarine blue eyes, a sharp contrast to John's chocolate-brown eyes. Gerald wore a light gray Hugo Boss suit which accentuated a tall, angular figure.

"Uncle Gerald, let me introduce you to Kathryn Landry. She's the designer who has done wonders with my office and is now working on my home."

"I am so delighted to meet you, my dear. I am very impressed with your work and wish I'd met you before I had this office redecorated two years ago," he said, shaking her hand.

"Thank you, Senator Selton. It's a pleasure to meet you." She wondered if all the Selton men held on to women's hands much longer than necessary. "Your office is beautiful and I wouldn't advise changing a thing."

"Please call me Gerald." The senator laughed and let go of her hand. "John, now I see why you're so enchanted with Kathryn. She's beautiful, talented and a diplomat."

She blushed at the compliment.

"I'm hosting a small cocktail reception aboard my yacht Sunday evening. I would like for you to join us," Gerald said. "It starts at four-thirty so we can cruise for a while before the sun sets."

"That's very kind of you to invite me, but I wouldn't want to impose."

"Nonsense, I insist you come," he commanded. "John will pick you up so you won't have to worry about directions or parking."

"Thank you. I'm looking forward to it."

"I hate to have to rush out after just meeting you, Kathryn, but duty calls." Gerald took her hand and gallantly kissed it. "I'll see you in a few days."

The senator dashed out of the office, the receptionist tottering behind him on four-inch high heels, trying to hand him messages and documents before he reached the elevator.

"He's an interesting man."

"Yes, he is," John agreed.

"I really don't know about attending the cocktail reception. I don't have any idea what to wear and I won't know anyone."

"I'll be there and will introduce you to everyone. I promise I won't leave you alone with anyone boring." John grinned. "I think your Donna Karan little black dress will be just fine."

"What did you do? Memorize my wardrobe while you were looking through my apartment?"

"Ouch, I guess I deserve that remark." He pretended to duck away from her. "No, I did not spend time looking through your clothing. You wore it when you came to my office to get the contract for my house design signed."

"I don't remember that."

"Oh, but I do," he answered, giving her a mischievous grin.

***

107

John pulled his car into Marianne's driveway and was climbing out of his car when he groaned. "This guy is like a bad penny. When's he going to give up?"

Kathryn turned just in time to see the front wheel of Detective William's Explorer jump the curb in front of the house and come to a screeching halt.

"John, go ahead and leave," she pleaded. "I think it would be better if I take care of this alone."

"I hate to throw you to the lions but I have an appointment I can't miss." He looked at his watch. "Are you sure you'll be okay?"

"Yes, I'll be fine."

"I'll call you this evening," he said, starting up the car.

Kathryn watched the ruby-red car back out of the driveway and jumped at the sound of the detective's voice in her ear.

"Having cell phone problems again?"

"What? No, I don't think so," she answered, turning towards the house.

"I've been trying to reach you for the last three hours." He scowled. "This is the third time I've driven by Marianne's house and I've been to your apartment just as many times. Your assistant is probably a nervous wreck right now wondering if you're okay."

"I was at a breakfast meeting with John and cell phones were prohibited," she answered defensively while searching her new Chanel handbag for the house key. "I guess I forgot to turn it back on and check for messages. I'm sorry if I worried you and Marianne."

"How convenient for Selton. No cell phones allowed." He brought his face closer to hers. "Don't you understand that you're involved in a missing person's case, possible attempted murder, and murder? I need you accessible twenty-four hours a day until this is resolved."

"You don't have to be so harsh. I said I was sorry." She opened the front door and rushed to punch in the code to deactivate the alarm. "What is so important that it couldn't wait a couple of hours?"

Detective Williams caught her arm and turned her to face him. "Someone tried to kill you. I think it's possible that they might try again."

Kathryn shuddered. "I think you're overreacting, Mike. I was in the wrong place at the wrong time."

"Maybe, but maybe not. I don't want to take any chances of you getting hurt. If I had my way, I'd have an armed guard escorting you around."

"Now you are going overboard." She pulled away. "So what's going on that has you so frantic?"

"The ID came back on the dead guy. Does the name Ernest Miller ring a bell?"

"No, not at all."

"He doesn't have a criminal record but he served in the Marines in 'Nam. What is really interesting is that his current employer is FLZ Corp."

"You mean the same company that leased Helene's apartment?" Kathryn gasped.

"Yep, one and the same. My computer guys are telling me it's a dummy company but they're working on trying to find out who or what it's sheltering."

"Maybe this guy thought I was connected to Helene? Have you talked to Roxie yet?"

"Not yet." The detective bit his lip and cleared his throat. "I was waiting for you to show up since you neglected to give me her address yesterday."

"Oh. I really am sorry about turning off my cell phone."

"There's one more thing. We searched Mr. Miller's apartment and found a black onyx ring etched with a skull and crossbones. My men are telling me that it was designed for a team of elite Marines at the end of the Vietnam War commemorating their 'brotherhood.'"

"Well, that proves he couldn't have been after me. Like I said, I was at the wrong place at the wrong time."

"That remains to be seen." His forehead creased into a frown. "Do you think you can spare the time right now to go see Roxie with me?"

"Let me check in with Marianne and then I can go."

Kathryn went to the kitchen and called the office. She reassured her assistant that everything was fine and that she was going to Rancho Santa Margarita with Mike.

"Um, Kathyrn?" Marianne chimed in before she could hang up. "I know you deposited John's check into the new account, but every check that I wrote last week is now being routed through the new account and we're already overdrawn on it. Two of our vendors are threatening to pull their employees off the job if we don't pay them within three days."

"Don't worry about it, Marianne. I found out where Neil has been putting my money and as soon as I get back from Rancho Santa Margarita I'll drop by the bank and make a deposit into the company's account."

"That's a relief," Marianne sighed. "My loan offer is still open though, if you need it."

"Thanks, but I should be okay. I'll call you when the money has been deposited." Kathryn rubbed her neck. "Would you mind bringing my laptop to your house? I feel bad dominating yours and I want to keep a closer watch on my account."

"Sure, no problem. I'll see you this evening."

They climbed into the detective's Explorer and he asked her for Roxie's address so that he could program the navigation system.

"I think the address got left in my totaled car and I can't remember it offhand. But I think I can find the way back to her house."

"Are you sure you can remember how to get there?"

"Of course," she replied confidently.

Once again they drove south and onto the 241 tollroad. This time there was a sharp smell of smoke permeating the air and a heavy sprinkling of dusty gray ash swirled around the vehicle.

As they drove through the cookie-cutter neighborhoods, Kathryn said, "Turn right here."

Mike turned the vehicle down the street.

"No, I meant turn left right here. Didn't you see the way I was pointing?"

"Um, no, I was busy paying attention to the other vehicles on the street. It's called safe driving." He shook his head.

She pointed back the way they had come. "If you turn around, Roxie's house is on the other side of the cross street."

They parked in front of Roxie's house, the front wheel of the Explorer perched precariously on the concrete curb.

Kathryn opened the door and eyed the errant wheel. "Didn't they teach you how to park at the police academy?"

"Nope." He let the silence linger for a moment while he looked up and down the street. "It's a nice neighborhood, especially for a hooker."

He jotted down the address and cross streets in his notebook before they walked up to the front door and rang the doorbell. They waited a couple of minutes before he used his knuckles to rap on the door. Roxie still didn't answer the door.

"Maybe she ran some errands," Kathryn said.

"I'll take a look through the garage window and see if her car's there. Keep ringing the doorbell."

Mike walked down the steps to the side of the house where the garage was offset to the home.

He came back very quickly. "No car in there. Come with me. I want to check the back and see if I can find a way in."

"You mean you want to break and enter?" Kathryn asked incredulously.

"No. No break, just enter."

She tried the front door handle, found it unlocked and pushed open the door. "Can't we just use the front door?"

"I was hoping her neighbors wouldn't see us sneaking in."

"Oh? It's better for them to see us sneaking in through the back door?"

Kathryn gasped and came to a sudden halt as she stepped into the doorway. The house was completely bare. No pink sofas and rugs. Not a stick of furniture in sight. And no Roxie.

Chapter Thirteen

She followed the detective blindly through the house, not believing that it could be so empty. She didn't even notice that he had removed his gun from his holster.

"Hello?" A man's shaky voice came echoing through the house. "Did the rental agency send you over?"

Kathryn and Mike quickly walked back to the living room and found an elderly man, dressed in a brown tweed sport coat, leaning on his ivory-handled cane. His unruly white hair and thick mustache reminded her of Albert Einstein.

He hobbled over to Mike and shook his hand. "I'm Carl Bellini, the neighbor next door."

"Nice to meet you. I'm Mike and this is Kathryn."

"Oh, I think I saw you here yesterday, Kathryn," he said, shaking her hand. "So are you here to rent the house? That agency sure works fast."

"Actually we were hoping to talk to the previous tenant. Roxie? Do you know how I can reach her?" Kathryn asked.

"No, I'm afraid I don't. She didn't tell me that she was moving out. I'm very sorry she left." Carl Bellini sighed. "She's such a sweet young lady, so full of life, always bouncing around."

Kathryn quickly coughed to cover up her laugh as she envisioned the elderly man watching Roxie's buxom bosom bouncing around the neighborhood. The detective raised his eyebrows at her but she ignored him. She had neglected to give him a physical description of Roxie and would have to remember to do so once Carl left.

"Did Roxie move out this morning?" Mike began questioning.

"Do you mind if I ask what this is about and why you're interested in Roxie?"

Mike pulled out his badge and showed it to Carl. "I'm investigating the disappearance of Kathryn's husband. Roxie might have some information on his whereabouts."

"I'm sorry about your troubles, my dear. I'm happy to tell you everything I know but I'm afraid it's not much." Carl shifted his cane to his other hand. "Roxie moved out yesterday, late afternoon. I think it was several hours after you left, Kathryn. I'm not a snoop but kind of the neighborhood watch dog. I enjoy being outdoors and with my gimp leg all I can do is slowly walk around the neighborhood, which I do several times a day."

"Did you speak with Roxie while the movers were here?" Detective Williams asked, taking out his notebook.

"No, funny I never saw her. She must have left before they got here. Once the moving truck showed up with a bunch of men, they boxed everything up, threw it in the truck and took off. I watched for a while. It's fascinating to observe that kind of efficient operation."

"Did you ask the movers where Roxie was or where they were delivering her things?"

"Yes, but they told me it wasn't any of my business." He huffed. "I'm very disappointed Roxie left without saying goodbye but at least she had her rent paid up until the end of next month."

"Do you remember the name of the moving company?"

"It was one of those national chain rental trucks." He scratched his white head. "I think it was Nationwide. You know the green-and-white trucks? It struck me a little strange since the movers looked like professionals."

Kathryn broke in with her own question. "Carl, did you know Roxie's roommate, Helene?"

"Not really. She wasn't as friendly as Roxie so I only saw her coming and going. Once in a while she'd wave as she drove off."

"Did you happen to see her move out?" Mike asked.

"No, I didn't see her either, but I watched the movers load up her things a few evenings ago. I believe it was Arcade Moving Company that came. Roxie was very upset since Helene didn't bother telling her she was moving out." He shook his head. "And then she did the same thing to me!"

"Do you know how I can get in touch with the owners of this house?" The detective handed a business card to Carl. "I'd like to have a look around and see if they left anything behind."

He stole a glance at the business card. "I'm the owner. I'd be happy to let you look around if you think it will help your investigation."

The detective quickly thanked him. "Would you happen to have Roxie's or Helene's rental application? That might provide some useful information."

"I'll call up the management agency and have the application faxed to me. If I recall, it only has Roxie's information since she was the initial renter. She was such a good tenant, I left it up to her to screen her roommate. I'll leave you to your search but I'll come back as soon as I get the fax."

Once Carl was out of hearing distance, Mike turned towards Kathryn. "What was so funny? I didn't see anything laughable."

"I forgot to describe what Roxie looked like when I met her yesterday." She giggled. "I know this is a serious situation but trust me, this is humorous."

After hearing the description of Roxie's attire and physical attributes, he chuckled. "I can't believe I missed seeing that. Talk about bad luck!"

"You men are all the same," Kathryn snapped back. "Only one thing on your mind."

"I hope you know I was only trying to joke." He became serious. "I'm not chauvinistic no matter what Roxie's profession was."

"I know. I was trying to joke too, but it came out wrong."

Together they walked through the house again before Mike asked Kathryn if she minded looking through the kitchen and bathroom while he took the bedrooms and living room. She agreed and started with the kitchen. He remained standing in the living room frantically writing in his notebook.

Kathryn began opening the white wooden drawers and cupboards, amazed that everything was immaculate. The white tiled floor looked like it had been polished as well. Either the movers had been professional cleaners or else Roxie was a cleaning fanatic. She couldn't find a speck of dust anywhere even in the back of the deepest shelves. The refrigerator was bare and the freezer was free of frost.

She moved to the bathroom and decided after having had two cups of coffee, it was time to use the facilities. Closing the door, she automatically reached for the lock, then remembered Roxie saying it didn't have one. She turned on the light and the overhead fan to alert Mike that she was in there, in case he decided to enter. The fan made a clicking noise, sounding like it was striking something. After finishing with the toilet Kathryn opened the door and started her search of the bathroom. The vanity and medicine chest were empty and pristinely clean. Remembering scenes from various movies, she checked the toilet tank hoping to find a hidden clue, but once again found nothing.

Kathryn switched off the light and fan and was relieved by the silence. Carl would need to have the fan fixed before the house was rented. A thought flashed through Kathryn's mind and she switched the fan back on again. She could envision the fan hitting a thick piece of paper on each rotation to cause the noise.

She called the detective into the bathroom and switched the fan on and off, each listening intently to the noise. He agreed that it was worth checking into and retrieved a small tool set and a flashlight from his vehicle. Climbing onto the vanity and using a Philip's head screwdriver, he took the cover off the vent housing the fan and handed it to Kathryn. He used the flashlight to shine more light into the dark hole to get a better look.

"Don't turn on the fan, okay? I'm going to reach my hand up there and I don't want to lose any fingers today."

"Do you see anything?" Kathryn asked impatiently.

He didn't answer and instead slowly reached in with his right hand and tugged on something. Kathryn could hear a ripping sound and held her breath. He slowly extracted a small book, which was covered with dust and had mutilated edges where the fan had been hitting it. A few pages were hanging haphazardly out and she could see what appeared to be a woman's handwriting.

Mike climbed down from the vanity, switched off the flashlight and opened the cover of the small burgundy leather book, which fit in the palm of his hand. Kathryn excitedly leaned into his arm trying to get a better view, conscious of his lean body.

The inscription on the inside cover said "Helen Montgomery" with an address in Wallace, Kansas.

"I have to assume that Helene Monterrey was really Helen Montgomery. She must have changed her name to something she thought was more glamorous," Kathryn said. "Roxie told me Helene's parents still live in Kansas so we should be able to track them down with this and see if they've heard from her."

Mike grunted beside her and turned the page. Several modeling agencies with addresses and phone numbers were listed with contact names. The next few pages listed several men's names with dates starting back five years previously. Some of the names had phone numbers.

"Looks like I've got a lot of phone calls to make," he groaned. "And for the record, there is no 'we'. I don't want you getting involved. You've already put yourself in enough danger."

Kathryn scowled at him but bit her tongue and remained quiet instead of arguing.

He continued leafing through a few more pages until he got to the last one written on, which contained only one entry dated just over six months previous. Instead of a name there was a series of numbers and what appeared to be a phone number written underneath it. The remaining pages were blank. The back inside cover had a pocket sewn into it where they found two thousand dollars in cash.

"Looks like she was saving up for a rainy day," Kathryn mused.

"Or a quick getaway."

Mike handed the book to her while he climbed back onto the vanity and replaced the vent cover. She found some paper towels and dusted off the book while he returned the tools and flashlight to the Explorer. She joined him at the vehicle where they could see the elderly man slowly making his way up the street, white sheets of paper in hand.

"Are you going to tell Carl about the book we found?"

"Yes, I think we have to, although not in detail. If any of this information proves useful in apprehending and prosecuting someone I want to make sure that the court acknowledges it was legally obtained. I'll have Carl sign a receipt for the book and cash before we take it."

They followed Carl Bellini as he slowly climbed the steps into the house. "Here you go, Detective. Hope this gives you something to work from." He produced the fax with a flourish. "Did you find anything of interest during your search?"

"Actually, we found Helene's address book with two thousand dollars in cash. She had it hidden in the fan vent in the bathroom. With your permission I'd like to take it with me for evidence. Would you mind signing a receipt?"

"What a strange place to keep an address book!" Carl frowned. "Of course if you think it's important you're more than welcomed to take it."

Detective Williams tore two blank pages from his notebook and wrote duplicate receipts. Once Carl signed and dated each original, Mike gave one to Carl and returned the second one to his notebook.

"Thank you for your help, Carl. Mrs. Landry and I will be on our way. If you can think of anything else, please let me know."

"Good luck to you," Carl said, before they started to drive away.

Just as the Explorer entered the northbound 241 toll road, the detective's cell phone rang. Kathryn could hear an excited male voice on the other end and Mike's face drained of color. He ended the call and, for the second time in two days, attached his flashing red light to the roof of the SUV and started the siren, while flooring the gas pedal.

Chapter Fourteen

"What's happened?" Kathryn shrieked, clinging to the seat with both hands.

"The fire jumped the firebreak and is out of control. The Santa Ana winds are pushing it straight for my house," he answered through clenched teeth. "I hope they catch the bastard who started this."

"Surely you're not going there, are you? The firefighters will be able to protect your property, won't they?"

"I have six horses, including a thoroughbred who's expecting her first foal, and two dogs I need to evacuate immediately." Mike hunched his shoulders over the steering wheel as he swerved around a car. "I can let you off at a gas station and you can call someone to pick you up, if you prefer. But honestly, I could really use your help right now."

"Of course I'll help. But I don't know the first thing about animals."

He took the off ramp too fast, making the vehicle's rear-end slide towards the guardrail. He fought for control, then punched the gas pedal down when they reached the straight section in the road. The smell of smoke infiltrated the vehicle and heavy dark ash fell all around them as they climbed higher into the foothills.

Mike leaned over and started fiddling with the knobs on the radio. The vehicle drifted to the shoulder of the road and he fought with the steering wheel to bring it back to the pavement.

"What are you trying to do?" Kathryn yelped.

"I want an all-news station so we can get updates on the fire and evacuations."

She finally found a station but, instead of fire related news, a reporter was giving a traffic report with the promise of more fire coverage in five minutes. Mike cursed.

"My neighbor is starting to load the horses so I only need you to drive this back to Marianne's house. I don't think the city will be very happy with me if I leave their property to burn."

"I can help you pack up things from your house if you want."

What are you saying? You shouldn't be here!

"Thanks, that would help a lot. I have everything I want to take by the front door so all you have to do is throw it into the back of the Explorer. You can be out of here within a few minutes."

"You were expecting to have to evacuate?"

"I never expected to but I like being prepared. I always pack my valuables the second I hear there's a fire within fifty miles of my property."

"Where are you going to take the horses?"

Mike remained silent while he negotiated a sharp bend in the road. Coming to a straight stretch, he visibly relaxed his hands on the steering wheel. "There's a stable in San Juan Capistrano that will board them."

"What about you? Where will you and your dogs stay? Please don't go back to the house and try to save it yourself."

"I won't go back. I'll leave it in the hands of the professionals and in the hands of the power above," he answered. "There's a hotel close to the stables that allows dogs. I have a friend who can dog-sit for me while I'm at work."

Kathryn felt a twinge as she wondered if the friend was a female. Shaking it off, she watched the bone-dry brown rolling hills covered with sage scrub and chaparral rush by, a tinderbox waiting for a single spark to start the conflagration. In some places the road narrowed and tall, ancient oak trees made a leafy canopy over them. She occasionally saw a house tucked between rocky cliffs while others were bordered with pastureland and oak trees. No livestock could be seen.

"I had no idea there was this much open land out here. I always think of concrete cities and asphalt freeways when I think about Southern California."

"This area borders the Cleveland National Forest along with Limestone Canyon and Whiting Ranch Wilderness Parks," Mike answered, slowing the vehicle down as they approached a roadblock. "I spend most of my free time out here. It's hard to believe someone would deliberately try to destroy this."

He came to a stop and rolled down his window when they reached the barrier. They were greeted by a blast of hot, sooty air. Kathryn thought the officer manning the barricade looked like a bandit. His cowboy-style hat was pulled low, mirrored sunglasses hid his eyes and a dark blue bandana covered his nose and mouth. His khaki-colored uniform had turned a dusty gray with matching combat boots.

"Hey Mike, glad you made it," the sheriff's deputy said after pulling down the bandana. "Captain says we can give you about twenty minutes to get in and evacuate your horses."

"Thanks, Rudy, I owe you one."

"Not a problem," the deputy answered, pulling the roadblock aside. "Just do me a favor and get out of here as quickly as you can. This fire has a mind of its own, jumping roads and firebreaks like I've never seen. I'd hate for you and your friend to get caught in the middle of it."

"Don't worry. We'll be out of here before you know it."

Kathryn started choking on the thick smoke that had swirled into the Explorer. Her breathing became more rapid and her palms started sweating.

What are you getting yourself into? Is it too late to back out?

Mike quickly rolled the window up and turned the air conditioning on high before finally turning off onto a single-lane blacktop road blocked by an elegant, wrought-iron electric gate. He pushed the remote button attached to the sun visor and the gate slowly opened. The road wound between pastures enclosed by once-pristine white fences, now grimy with soot. Drab olive-green eucalyptus trees lined the drive. The murky air caused the SUV's headlights to come on. They crossed a stone bridge under which a dry river bed ran, then turned a bend in the road and his house came into view. But they didn't notice. Instead, their eyes were riveted on the fifty-foot roaring flames shooting up from the hill behind Mike's house, less than a mile away.

Mike groaned as he maneuvered the SUV towards his house, his knuckles turning white as they gripped the steering wheel. "I always knew there was a chance fire could destroy my home when I built here but I never really thought it would happen to me."

"I'm sure the firefighters will do everything they can to save it," Kathryn said, trying to keep her teeth from chattering, unable to tear her eyes away from the shooting flames.

He came to a stop in front of his house, opened his door and popped open the SUV's back hatch. Furnace-like heat waves assaulted them and their eyes started tearing up from the smoke and dust swirling around them, made worse by the gusting winds.

"The front door should be unlocked, so start loading up the boxes and get out of here as soon as you can. I've programmed the navigation to get you back to Marianne's." He jumped out of the vehicle while donning a cowboy hat. "I'll call you after I drop my horses off."

As if in slow motion, she watched him run across the paddock area which separated the quintessential red barn from his sprawling ranch house, painted dove gray and trimmed with white accents. Next to the barn a large silver horse trailer was hooked up to a sooty, red, heavy-duty Dodge Ram pickup. Two Australian sheepdogs were running circles around Mike and she could hear their sharp barks along with the shrill sound of neighing horses. A man wearing jeans, a blue plaid shirt and a bandana over his nose and mouth walked out of the barn leading a blindfolded, and very pregnant, horse towards the open door at the rear of the trailer, and then walked her gently up the ramp. Mike gave the nervous animal a tender pat then turned and saw her watching him.

"Kathryn, get moving! You need to get out of here!" he shouted before disappearing into the barn.

Choking on the smoky dust, she made her way to the house and opened the front door with shaking hands. She quickly picked up one of two suitcases, lugged it out to the Explorer and flung it into the back cargo hold. Ash falling like snowflakes made her sneeze; her nose rebelled against the hot, acrid smoke forcing itself into her lungs. Her stinging eyes watered so much she could barely keep them open and she felt rivulets of liquid run down her cheeks. She trotted back towards the house and retrieved the second suitcase. Grunting from the heaviness, she struggled to carry it across the cobblestone walkway to the vehicle. Her foot caught on the edge of a stone and she stumbled and fell when her sandal strap broke. Wincing from pain, she picked herself up and saw red blood mingled with black soot oozing from scrapes on her shin and knee, but immediately forgot about the cuts when she saw the fire crest the hill.

She kicked off her sandals, fumbled to pick up the suitcase and carried it as fast as she could to the vehicle. Overhead she heard the loud drone of a bomber and looked up just as they dropped their load of bright red fire retardant on the blazing flames.

She saw Mike lead another blindfolded horse from the barn. Before he could pull the jet-black animal up the gangway to the trailer, the horse reared and lashed out with his front hooves, knocking Mike to the ground. He struggled to keep hold of the reins as he jumped to his feet and tried to calm his horse, which continued bucking. Kathryn could hear the shrill neighing cutting through the thick air and Mike yelling at his neighbor to bring water. The man scooped up a tin bucket full of water from the horses' trough and emptied it on the animal's hindquarters. Mike started frantically patting his shirt, where Kathryn could see an ember had ignited the cotton sleeve, before being doused by another bucketful of water wielded by his neighbor.

Once he had the black horse loaded in the trailer and closed the door, Mike grabbed a long hose, cranked on the water and started spraying down the roof of his barn. He turned and saw her standing there. "Kathryn, get out of here!"

"I only have to get two more boxes then I'll leave!" she yelled back, trying to make herself heard over the roar of another bomber preparing to drop its load.

Her leaden legs carried her back to the house where Mike had stacked two heavily loaded banker's boxes. She groaned but started carrying them out, one at a time, limping the entire way as her tender feet complained from the abuse they were taking on the rocky cobblestones. Before she toted out the last item, a twenty-five-pound bag of dog food, she took a quick glance around the detective's great room surprised at how inviting it looked. A huge gray river-stone fireplace was the central focus with dark leather love seats dotting the room. She wondered how he could afford his ranch and expensive home furnishings on a policeman's salary and wanted to see more of his house but the fire propelled her into a flight mode. She grabbed the bag of dog food, closed the front door and trudged down towards the Explorer.

Suddenly she felt herself lifted and thrown down to the ground, the air knocked from her lungs as the detective landed on top of her. His piercing blue eyes glittered from smoke-induced tears and Kathryn was mesmerized as he looked deep into her own eyes. His hard, lean body pressed into hers and time was suspended.

"Sorry about that. I hope I didn't hurt you." Mike rolled off her and helped her to her feet with dripping wet hands. "An ember landed on your shirt and caught fire."

"I can feel it stinging."

"I don't think it had a chance to seriously burn you but I'll take a look once we're out of the fire zone. Come on, we need to get out of here now!"

He looked at her bloody and scraped-up feet and knees as she limped to pick up the dropped dog food.

"Leave it. I'll buy more later," he barked as he scooped her up in his strong arms and carried her to the SUV.

He quickly put her into the passenger seat and slammed the door. Climbing into the driver's seat, he gunned the engine and headed towards the road. She saw that the horse trailer had already left.

"Didn't you need to drive your trailer?" her voice squeaked while her teeth clacked together.

"My neighbor said he'd meet us at the bottom of the hill and decide what to do then," he answered with clenched teeth. "I should never have put you in danger."

"You wouldn't have gotten your things out if I wasn't here to help." Kathryn wasn't sure how she sounded so brave when all she wanted to do was get away from the smoke and ash.

She looked back towards the house and the violent wildfire. She could see red and orange flames making their way down the hill, ferocious tongues licking at tinder dry grass and ancient gnarled oaks. Black smoke roiling skyward obscured the sun while floating ash mixed with red-hot embers rained down. Large yellow bulldozers were slashing wide brown dirt furrows into the pasture closest to the hill. Wheezing and coughing from the smoke, she shivered as she heard the mournful wail of sirens. She turned to face the road and saw boxy red fire trucks racing towards them.

"They'll do everything they can to save your house, Mike."

"I know. It's hard not knowing how it's going to turn out."

They rode in silence, away from the inferno, until they parked next to the horse trailer.

"I have a first aid kit in the back. Let me take a look at your burn."

"Really, it's okay. I can take care of it when I get to Marianne's."

"Kathryn, I insist. I saw you squirming in the seat trying not to put any pressure on it. I want to make sure you don't need professional medical attention."

"Okay." She turned her back to him. "You're right."

She felt him gently lift her blouse. "It's not too bad. It's only a small blister, but I'll put some ointment on it to stop the stinging. Sorry, your blouse is toast though."

He quickly retrieved his kit and donned plastic gloves.

"I don't have cooties."

"I know, only boys do." He chuckled. "My hands are so dirty I don't want to risk infecting your burn. Now turn around and be a good patient."

She did as he asked and only winced once when the cold salve touched the burn. By the time the bandage was on, the stinging had stopped.

"Do you feel capable of driving yourself to Marianne's?"

"Definitely. I'll be fine."

"I can't thank you enough for all you did today," he said as she climbed into the Explorer and started the engine.

"It's okay, I'm glad I was there to help. Now go take care of your horses and dogs."

Before leaving, he leaned through the window and kissed her cheek before whispering, "You were incredibly brave."

***

Arriving at Marianne's house, Kathryn tried to carefully parallel-park the government-issued SUV, but scraped the curb instead.

After locking the door, she stumbled to the front of the vehicle, looked at the offending wheel and sighed. "Just great. How do I explain curb rash after giving Mike a hard time about his parking?"

Deciding it could wait until later, she limped to the front door and rang the bell. Within moments Richard pulled the door open.

"Kathryn, what happened? Good god, you look..."

"Terrible?" Kathryn pushed her hair away from her face and saw ashes float towards the brick walk.

"More like barbecued!"

"I was with Mike, uh, I mean Detective Williams, and the winds pushed the fire towards his house," she said with a raspy voice, gasping for air.

"Richard, don't leave the poor girl standing out there!" Marianne yelled from the kitchen. "Let her get comfortable before quizzing her."

Richard shrugged, then grinned as he held the door open for her. "Sorry, it was a shock seeing you like that."

Kathryn walked down the hallway and glanced at herself in a mirror. Black sooty smudges covered her face amid rivers where her smoke-induced tears had trailed. Gray dots speckled her hair. The whites of her eyes were bloodshot, while the bruise was turning deeper shades of purple and green. She ran her hand over her hair and came away with charcoal grit.

"Ugh, no wonder you were shocked. I'm shocked too."

Marianne bustled down the hall and gently pulled Kathryn towards the kitchen. "Sit down, dear, and I'll pour you a glass of wine and let you relax before Richard starts quizzing you again."

"I think I'll take a shower and change clothes first. I don't want to get this stuff all over your house. Besides that, I feel really disgusting."

She took a shower and washed her hair, astonished at how much soot ran out even after a second shampoo. She dressed in comfy yoga crop pants and a beach t-shirt before rejoining them in the kitchen, where a glass of Far Niente Chardonnay awaited her along with antibacterial ointment and bandages.

She sipped her wine while detailing her afternoon looking for Roxie and the horrifying fire. Shuddering, she said, "I feel so sorry for Detective Williams losing everything. I felt incredibly helpless. And on top of that, I never made it to the bank, Marianne."

"Now, now, the bank will be there tomorrow. He was lucky to have you with him and you did everything you possibly could to help. At least his animals are safe and there's a good chance the firefighters will be able to save his home," Marianne murmured in a soothing tone. "Why don't you call him and invite him to dinner tonight? I'm sure he'd like to get his mind off the fire instead of sitting in a hotel room alone, waiting for news. He's more than welcome to bring his dogs."

"That's a sweet idea, Marianne. I'll go call him right now."

Just as she retrieved her cell phone from her room, it rang.

"Hi Mike, I was just getting ready to call you. Have you heard any news about your home?"

"No, nothing yet. The waiting is agonizing." He exhaled. "The reason I called was to let you know I'll pick up the Explorer tomorrow. If you're not going to be home, you can lock the keys inside since I have a spare with me."

"No problem. You can pick it up whenever you wish. The reason I was going to call is because Marianne would like to invite you to dinner tonight."

"I'd love to come but I'd better not. I can't leave my dogs alone in the hotel."

"Marianne specifically included the dogs in the invitation so you're all welcome to come."

He hesitated. "Really, I don't want to impose."

"Trust me, it's not an imposition. Marianne loves to have guests and she loves dogs."

"Okay, if you're sure."

"Great! Would you like for me to pick you up since I have the Explorer?"

"No, I'll drive my truck and worry about the Explorer tomorrow."

"Okay. We'll see you in about an hour?"

"Sure, that works for me. I'll see you soon."

Kathryn tucked her cell phone into her pocket and went back to the kitchen.

"He said he'd join us for dinner," Kathryn announced. "What can I do to help?"

"Not a thing. Just sit there and keep me company," Marianne replied. "I was planning on barbecued salmon but I think I'll bake it instead with a maple syrup and brown sugar glaze. I think you and Mike have had enough smoke for the day."

Kathryn told them about her harrowing ordeal, and just as Marianne pulled the cork from a new bottle of Far Niente Chardonnay, the doorbell rang.

"I'll get it," Kathryn volunteered, hurrying down the hallway while smoothing her hair and wishing she had taken time to put on mascara and lipstick.

Opening the door, she was face to face with two scowling men and two dogs baring their teeth.

"Uh, Mike, John, what a, um, pleasant surprise."

Chapter Fifteen

"Kathryn," Mike and John said in unison before glaring at each other, their scowls illuminated from the carriage lights framing the front door.

The dogs looked from one man to another, hackles raised. Kathryn felt her face heating up, not sure what to say.

"Tatum, Sandy, down," Mike commanded.

The Australian Shepherd dogs instantly obeyed, all signs of aggression replaced by placidity.

"Mike, how nice of you to join us. I've got a single malt scotch with your name on it!" Richard bellowed, walking down the hallway towards to the front door. "Oh, John. Nice to see you too. Would you like to join us for a cocktail?"

"No, thank you," John politely said. "I was hoping to have a quick word with Kathryn before I meet my uncle for dinner."

"Then Mike, why don't you and I go in and crack open that bottle?" Richard directed, opening the door wider. "Have a nice evening, John."

Before Mike could follow Richard through the door, John leaned over and whispered, "Just so you know, Detective, that chocolate is so passé."

Kathryn hadn't noticed until then that Mike had been clutching a white box with black lettering and accents of dark chocolates. Her mouth watered and she noisily swallowed. "John, don't be rude. Mike's had an exceptionally distressing day."

She turned and looked Mike in the eyes. "Thanks for bringing the chocolates for Marianne. I know she'll love them."

"No problem, Kathryn. Oh, and Selton? I don't need your advice," Mike said, walking into the house. The dogs obediently followed their master without another look at John.

"Mike?" John mimicked in a falsetto voice. "Since when are you on a first-name basis with the detective?"

"John, do you have to be so… Oh what's the word I'm looking for?" Kathryn scrunched her eyes shut and shrugged her shoulders. "So antagonistic?"

"What I want to know is why that guy is here and why you're getting so chummy with him. He's trying to jeopardize our investigation and you're helping him."

"It's not what you think and if you'd listen to me instead of making accusations you'd understand."

"Fine, try me. I'm listening."

"Detective Williams has a house in Santiago Canyon. The wildfires are close to destroying it and he had to evacuate his animals and belongings." She paused a moment to collect her thoughts, wondering how much to tell him. "Marianne, being the kind-hearted person she is, invited him to dinner since he doesn't have a home to go to at this point."

"And how did you find out all this? Did he just waltz in and spill his pitiful story?"

"Can't you show a little more compassion, instead of being sarcastic?" She stomped her foot. "I'm sure you didn't come over here to get into an argument. What is it you need?"

"I'm sorry." John lowered his eyes and ran a hand through his thick hair. "I think I'm finding out that I have a small jealous streak."

"Get over it. There's nothing going on between you and me for you to behave so rudely."

"But I thought after this morning..." John's sensual eyes bored into her, causing butterflies to dance in her stomach.

"How many times do I have to explain that I'm not ready? I have too many loose ends to figure out and it may take a long, long time until I feel like I can take that plunge again."

"I know. But I want you to know I'm here for you."

"Yes, you've made yourself abundantly clear." She sighed. "But really, you didn't come all this way to tell me that. What's going on?"

"Nothing. I just wanted to see you." He looked sheepish. "Trieste's mother picked her up this afternoon and I wanted to take you out to dinner. I know a quiet little place right on the beach."

She saw his casual Diesel jeans, which fit him just right, a trendy Tommy Bahama silk shirt straining against his muscular arms and brown Kenneth Cole loafers on his feet. "Not a good idea. I'm sorry."

"How about tomorrow?" His head hung low, scuffing his foot on the walkway like a small schoolboy.

"I'm exhausted. I don't want to think about tomorrow," she answered while an idea formed in her mind. "In fact, I think I'm going to check myself into a spa where no one can find me for a day."

I might as well spend some of Neil's money on myself.

"I think that's an excellent idea." He pulled his Crocodile leather billfold out from his hip pocket. "In fact, here's my membership card to The Spa at Pelican Hill. I'll have them charge it to my account. My treat."

"Thanks, but no thanks." She pushed the card back to him. "I'm going to locate a spa where no one can find me."

"If you change your mind, let me know."

"Well, if that's it, I really need to get back to our guest." Kathryn looked towards the open front door.

John glared at the red truck parked with one wheel on the curb. "Uh, yeah. That's it."

"Okay, I'll see you Saturday morning around nine to have your art installed.

Marianne told me she confirmed with you already."

"Yeah, see you then," he said quietly, walking to his jet-black GranCabrio Maserati.

Kathryn shook her head as John peeled out and hurried to the patio where she could hear deep male laughter. The glow from the hurricane lamps flickered in the deep dusk while the sounds of giant palm leaves rustled in the wind. Malibu lights glimmered around a stone path leading through lush flowering hibiscus and orchids. A faint smell of smoke floated in the air.

"I'm so sorry about that scene with John."

"Don't worry about it. I've known Selton for years and he's always been antagonistic, for whatever reason." Mike's smile softened the ice in his eyes.

"Sit down, Kathryn, and have a glass of wine." Richard pulled a cushy, burgundy, rose-patterned patio chair out for her. "I was just telling Mike about our trip to Scotland last year and buying this 1988 vintage from The Glenrothes. The Scots are hardy people. It was raining and sleeting like I've never seen and they're out riding bikes or hiking or playing golf. Marianne and I decided to tour some distilleries and keep out of the weather as much as possible."

Mike swirled the amber liquid around his crystal tumbler before taking another sip. "You certainly found an exquisite Scotch."

"Marianne generally doesn't like this stuff but she was tossing it back like a pro that day."

Kathryn giggled, envisioning her motherly assistant getting loopy. "It must have been the atmosphere inspiring her to keep up with you."

"You could be right. She hasn't touched the stuff since we've been home and we bought ten bottles from various distilleries. But this Glenrothes is by far my favorite."

Marianne opened the screened patio door and said in a mock Scottish accent, "Dinner is served, lady and gents. If you'd be so kind as to follow me, I'll let you fill your plates in here and return to our terrace for further dining and entertainment."

After finishing their succulent salmon followed by dark chocolate Grand

Marnier mousse for dessert, Mike insisted on clearing the table and washing the dishes.

"But you're our guest, Mike," Marianne said, stacking the plates, "you don't need to do anything but relax and enjoy the evening."

"It's the least I can do after the meal you cooked for me. I haven't eaten that well in I don't know how long." He chuckled. "I hate to admit it, but a lot of my dinners come in takeout containers these days."

Kathryn jumped up from the table. "I'll help too. Marianne, you've done so much already you deserve to sit and relax. Can I pour you another glass of wine?"

"I'm fine, dear." She patted Richard's arm. "It is a lovely evening to sit here so thank you for helping out.

Once the dishes and kitchen were cleaned up, Kathryn followed Mike back to the patio and sat down.

"I'd better be on my way," Mike said. "I appreciate your hospitality, Marianne and Richard."

"It was our pleasure having you here," Marianne replied, getting up to give the detective a quick hug. "Let us know what happens with your home. We'll be thinking good thoughts for you."

Mike tapped Kathryn on the shoulder. "Can I show you something out front?"

She cringed. "I'm so sorry, I tried to be careful with the Explorer."

"What happened to my SUV?" Mike drew his eyebrows together. "You weren't in an accident or anything, were you?"

"Uh, no. Just a little curb rash on the rims." She crossed her arms. "I really did try to be careful when I parked."

Mike's deep laugh cut through the night air. "Don't worry about it. That's not what I wanted you to see."

She flashed a puzzled look to Marianne and Richard before following the detective and his dogs out the front door. He motioned her to follow him until he turned to face her, resting his hip on the bright red BMW parked in Marianne's driveway.

"Care to explain how this got here?" His blue eyes darkened as he scowled at her.

"I needed a car to drive, so I stopped by my apartment and picked up the keys." Kathryn turned away from him.

"What?" the detective bellowed. "What were you doing at your apartment? I specifically told you not to go there without me or at least wait until I could get another officer to escort you."

"You don't have the right to tell me where I can't go," Kathryn snapped back. "Your people were done with the crime scene and I wanted to clean it up and get a few things to bring back here. Besides, nothing happened."

"You had no idea if it was safe."

"I am perfectly capable of taking care of myself, thank you very much."

"Uh-huh, and see what's happened to you so far."

"You are an impossible, domineering man!" Kathryn yelled back.

They both paused and looked towards the house as the front door closed. Richard and Marianne could be seen through the large living room plate-glass window, their backs facing the front street. It appeared that their shoulders were shaking.

"Are they laughing at us?" Kathryn asked.

"Probably. Your fault, of course."

"What? You started it by being so bossy!" She stopped speaking when she realized he was laughing.

"My only intention is keeping you safe," he murmured, then surprised her by leaning over and kissing her cheek.

She felt her cheeks turn bright pink and was grateful for the darkness pressing around them. "Thank you. I appreciate your concern and I'm sorry for getting mad."

"Apology accepted."

The silence lingered for a moment before Mike cleared his throat. "Well, I'd better be going. It's been a long day for both of us and tomorrow isn't going to be much easier."

"Which reminds me, would it be okay if I checked into a spa tomorrow? I feel the need to get away and relax."

"I think that's a great idea. But I want you to call me first thing and let me know where you are and then call every hour to check in."

"Have you ever been to a spa? It's impossible to call that often!"

"Come on, Kathryn, don't get angry with me again," he pleaded. "Do you think you can call me every two or three hours?"

"I'm sorry. I'm exhausted, which makes me irritable." She sighed. "Okay, I'll call you in between my treatments. And I hope you have some good news to tell me about your house too."

He leaned over and kissed her on the cheek again. "Thank you again, for helping me today."

Grabbing his hand, she gave it a squeeze. "I'm really glad I was there to help. I truly hope the firefighters can save your home."

After he collected his dogs and left, she stood leaning against her car awhile longer, gazing at the faint stars, wondering what it would feel like to have Mike's soft lips kiss her lips. She remembered the way his hard body felt pressed against her own, when he tackled her to save her from a burning blouse, and then shivered thinking how his fingers had gently brushed her skin as he lifted her shirt to see the burn on her back. It had felt like a caress. She shook her head to clear it before going into the house.

"So did you and the detective make up?" Marianne asked.

"Yes, and I'm so sorry about making a big scene out there."

"That's okay honey, you've both had a long, exhausting day. Why don't you go to bed and get a good night's sleep?"

"You're right, I think that's what I should do." Kathryn paused for a moment. "I thought I might check into a spa for a few hours tomorrow. Do you mind?"

"Why no. I think that's exactly what you need."

"Now that I've found my money, I feel like I need to decompress a bit." She gave Marianne a quick hug. "But I feel guilty having you working so hard while I'm relaxing."

"Don't you worry about me. You've been through so much the last few days, you deserve to rest."

She gave Richard a hug too. "I can never thank you both enough for helping me through this ordeal with Neil."

Kathryn quickly got ready for bed and was about to turn out the light when she saw her birth certificate peeking out of the file folder she had thrown on the bedside table the night before. She pulled it out and studied her mother's maiden name, Evelyn Bailey Stone. An idea started forming in her head, and after powering up her laptop, she logged into Intelius, a person search website.

Forget the spa; I'm going to find my mother's brother tomorrow.

Chapter Sixteen

A long-suppressed yearning for family, combined with seeing her birth certificate suddenly made Kathryn want to connect with her mother's relatives. She had no idea if her uncle was still living or if she had cousins. Seeing her mother's name pop up on the screen made her throat start to close as her eyes teared. She located the page with listed relatives and there was her uncle, Edgar Stone. She did another search using his name and came across one who lived in Bakersfield, California. She vaguely remembered her mother telling her that she had grown up in Bakersfield. After jotting down the address and phone number, Kathryn turned out the light and slept fitfully until the smell of coffee woke her.

After bandaging the worst of the scrapes on her legs and troweling makeup on to cover her bruised face, she dressed in casual black slacks with a crisp white buttoned-down cotton blouse and black strappy sandals. She headed to the kitchen, where she found zucchini bread and coffee waiting for her along with a note from Marianne.

Enjoy your day at the spa and we'll see you this evening. Call me if you need anything, otherwise don't worry about a thing. Please turn the alarm on when you leave. Marianne

Kathryn smiled and decided that she should stop at the bank and then the office before she drove to Bakersfield, even though she knew her company was in excellent hands. It would be better to leave later anyway, to miss the morning rush-hour traffic.

She grabbed the bank statement and dropped it into her new Chanel handbag, along with her sunglasses and her fully charged cell phone, before heading out the door. She hesitated when she saw John standing beside his Porche, parked behind Mike's Explorer.

"Hi Kathryn." He shoved his hands into his blue jeans and walked towards her.

"Good morning." She looked at her watch and saw it was eight-thirty. Too early for a social call. "Is everything all right?"

He hung his head sheepishly. "I was, um, just wondering if you'd like a companion to go to the spa with you. I know a great one out in the Corona area. The Glen Ivy. Have you heard of it?"

"Yes." She slowly exhaled. "John, I feel like doing this by myself today. I need some time alone to assimilate everything that's been going on."

"Okay, if you say so." His voice grew quiet. "But can I take you to dinner tonight? Please?"

"I have no idea when I'll get back." She shifted her handbag to her other shoulder.

"Are you mad at me for last night?" He ran his fingers through his thick hair. "I know I was out of line and I'm trying to apologize. So please let me take you to dinner and make it up to you for being such an ass?"

She tried to frown but her smile took over when she saw the puppy dog face John was making. "All right. Can we meet around seven o'clock?"

His smile lit up his face. "Sure, that will be fine. I'll pick you up."

"No, let's meet. I don't know how long I'll be at the spa and I might come straight to the restaurant from there."

"I don't mind waiting for you here. Just call me if you think you'll be later than seven."

"Okay, I'll do that." She walked towards her car, hoping he would take the hint and leave. "I'll see you tonight, then."

Once John drove away, Kathryn started up Neil's zippy car and headed to the bank.

She walked into the brightly lit lobby and found a generic withdrawal slip on a laminated counter outfitted with pens chained to its surface. Using her own pen, she carefully copied the account number and wrote the amount she wanted to take out on the paper.

Two hundred nineteen thousand and sixty-eight dollars has a nice ring to it. I'll leave Neil one dollar. It's more than he deserves.

She tore up the slip and decided to start with a smaller amount to see if she could pull it off. She had no illusions that she was the Kathryn Landry on the account. Instead, she was certain that the Latina woman, whose face was pasted on her passport, was the one who had opened this account with Neil. Again she carefully copied the bank account number to the withdrawal notice and wrote in five thousand dollars.

Much lower than the checks he's been writing on the account. If this goes well, I'll go to a different branch and take out more.

She waited patiently in the slow-moving line, trying to ignore her heart pounding deep in her belly. When the young teller, with the pierced eyebrow and lower lip, waved her up, Kathryn almost bolted for the front door. Instead she forced her unwilling feet to his window.

You could go to prison for this. She shook her head to dispel the negative thought. *It's your money, so take it.*

She handed the slip of paper to the teller along with her California driver's license. She watched his colorful tattooed hands as he clicked the keys on his computer a few times, then looked at her license, then back at the screen before punching some more buttons. Kathryn's palms started getting slippery and she was ready to grab her driver's license and run.

"Ma'am, I'm afraid you'll need the other signatory, Mr. Landry, to sign for the withdrawal as well."

"Oh, I'm sorry, I wrote down the wrong account number before I left home. Can I have that slip back and I'll call my husband and get the right account number?" The lie slipped from Kathryn's lips before she had time to think about it.

He handed her the driver's license and paper without a second look while waving up the next customer in line. Kathryn rushed back to her car wondering what to do next. She sat in the bank's parking lot for a while with her eyes closed, letting the cascade of thoughts and ideas wash over her. What was the best solution? How could she get around Neil's signature? She finally put her car into gear and drove to her office.

***

"What are you doing here? You should be enjoying yourself at the spa!"

"I know, but I still feel terrible placing the burden of my company on your shoulders all this time. And I told you I would have money for you to pay our vendors, and I suspect your own salary as well."

"It's been my pleasure to help you out. Besides, that's what you pay me for." Marianne smiled broadly. "So you found where Neil hid your money?"

"Yes." She frowned. "I tried to withdraw what we needed but he's set up the account so that he has to sign for it even though my name is on the account."

"That's not good." Marianne's frown mirrored Kathryn's. "I think you should tell the detective and freeze the account so that Neil can't take it again."

"I'm sure you're right. I'll talk to him later today about that."

"Kathryn, you're in a bind and Richard agrees with me. We want to help you out with a loan. Once you're back on your feet, I know you'll be even more successful and will pay us back in no time at all."

"I really appreciate it. However, I think I have a better solution than borrowing your money. It's something I've been giving some thought about for the last few months and I was wondering if you'd consider going into partnership with me? I have some ideas about branching out and expanding the company into staging homes for real estate sales. You know just as much as I do and it would be easy for you to get your certification."

"Really? You would want me as a partner?" Marianne squealed as she jumped out of her chair and rushed to give Kathryn a hug.

"I take that as a yes?" She laughed as she hugged Marianne back. "We can talk to our attorney and work out the financial aspect of this next week, but in the meantime, keep track of any money you put into the company to keep us floating and you will be reimbursed."

I can't believe I let Neil badger me out of taking this step months ago. Marianne is perfect for the expansion.

"I am so excited! I'll call Richard and have him chill champagne for a celebratory dinner tonight."

"Oh, I forgot to tell you that I won't be able to join you for dinner. John wants me to go to dinner with him and I said I would. We're going to meet at your house when I get back from the Glen Ivy."

"Ooh, nice spa!" Marianne pushed her reading glasses onto the top of her head. "How about a glass of champagne to celebrate before you go out?"

"That sounds lovely. Is there anything that needs my immediate attention or has it been quiet?"

"Fairly quiet. Even John Selton has been behaving," she answered. "Of course he's been busy with all your adventures so that might be why I'm not hearing from him much."

"Yes, he has been demanding, but after the art is installed tomorrow morning there shouldn't be too much left to finish on his Newport house." Kathryn laughed. "Then we get to start all over again on his Palm Springs house."

"You're still able to meet the installation people at John's house in the morning?"

"Shouldn't be a problem. Can you send me a text with their name and phone number?"

"Consider it done," Marianne promised. "Now unless my new partner has some pressing issues, she needs to get out of here and start her spa day!"

"Okay, okay, I'm on my way." She paused at the door. "I don't know how I can ever thank you enough. I never would have survived this ordeal without you and Richard."

***

Before Kathryn programmed the Bakersfield address into her car's navigation system, she called the number she had found on the internet the night before.

The shrill voice of a woman answered the phone with a curt "Hello."

"I'm wondering if this is Edgar Stone's residence?"

"It is. Who's this?" The woman's sharp voice grated Kathryn's nerves.

Quickly hanging up the phone, she wondered if the woman could have been her aunt. Maybe there was a reason why her mother hadn't kept in contact with her family. She shrugged off her misgivings, programmed the navigation system and was soon heading north on the 405 freeway. She hummed along with calming classical guitar music as she flowed along in the steady stream of colorful cars, following the wide black asphalt ribbon winding its way through crowded cities lining the road.

As traffic thickened and slowed, Kathryn remembered she was supposed to call the detective.

"Detective Williams here," he answered in a brusque voice.

"Hi, did I catch you at a bad time?"

"No, it's fine," he answered, his voice softening. "Are you on your way to the spa?"

"Uh, yes. And looking forward to it," she lied. "Have you heard anything about your home?"

"There's good news and not so good news."

"Well, give me the good news first."

"They saved the house, although I still haven't heard when I can go back there. The fire isn't contained yet."

"Wonderful! I'm so relieved to hear your house is safe. What's the not so good news?"

"They couldn't save the barn. I'm trying to focus on the fact that I still have my house and my horses and dogs are alive and well."

"Will it be easy to rebuild?"

"Rebuilding won't be difficult but I had a display of antique saddles in the barn that are irreplaceable," he grumbled. "And I'm going to have to board my horses for a few months. I'm worried about the mare when she's ready to foal since I won't be close by."

"I'm sorry to hear that. Is there anything I can do to help? Not that I know the first thing about barns or horses."

Mike chuckled. "Thanks, you were a lifesaver yesterday, but I'll be fine. My horses will be home before I know it and in the meantime the stable has an excellent veterinarian on staff."

"I'm really glad to hear that."

"I need to run. There's another call coming in." Mike was back to all-business. "Make sure you call me in a couple hours."

She disconnected and shook her head as traffic came to a slow crawl. Rush hour apparently wasn't over yet. Inching her way across crowded lanes, she finally reached the right-hand lane, trying to avoid being boxed in. She fiddled with her radio and took a sip of water before applying fresh lipstick. Kathryn watched a man shave himself while his Ferrari crept forward mere feet at a time and a woman read the newspaper while sitting behind the wheel of her Land Rover. She glimpsed flashing red lights ahead and, realizing her path was blocked, began the agonizing attempt to merge into her neighboring lane. The L.A. drivers were relentless though, and kept pushing her back into the blocked lane. Too late she realized there was metal debris from a traffic accident and she rolled over it before wedging her car into a tiny opening between two semi-trucks.

She finally inched around the mangled car and, just as she gained speed, heard the clunk of a flat tire.

"Great. Just great." She pulled over to the shoulder and popped open the trunk.

Cars whizzed by her, anxious to make up for lost time. She wrestled the spare tire from the trunk, then went to examine the flat, thankful it was on the non-traffic side of the car. A jagged piece of metal protruded from the tire wall, which cut her thumb when she tried to remove it. After bandaging the cut she retrieved the jack and the lug wrench, then decided to call AAA Roadside Service.

While waiting for the tow truck, Kathryn sat in her car and closed her eyes, trying to relax and block out the anxiety of wondering if she was doing the right thing in tracking down and meeting her long lost family. She was startled by a sharp rap on her window and, upon opening her eyes, stared straight into a black onyx ring etched with a silver skull and crossbones.

Chapter Seventeen

"Are you all right, miss?" the middle-aged man asked.

Slowly rolling down her window halfway, she noticed shaggy blond hair beneath his black cowboy hat. His beard stubble was half gray and half red, while thick, coarse eyebrows hooded his washed-out blue eyes, which were framed with deep crow's feet etched into sunburned cheeks. A red, frayed, plaid flannel shirt topped faded blue jeans that encased a skinny body.

"Miss, are you all right?"

"I'm okay," Kathryn tentatively answered, trying to see if there was a break in traffic that she could dart into, even with a flat tire. "I'm waiting for Triple A."

"What seems to be the trouble?"

"A flat. But the tow truck should be here any moment."

"I doubt that." His laugh was low and gravelly. "The accident's makin' traffic a bitch. I'd be happy to change your tire for you."

"Thank you, but I don't want to trouble you."

"No trouble at all." He pointed to his SUV parked behind her. "Why don't you get the spare tire and I'll grab my power jack out of my rig. I'll have you out of here in no time at all."

As the cowboy walked towards his Escalade, Kathryn started the car. Before she could put the BMW into gear, he leaned in through her window and jabbed the ignition button. "I think you need to come with me."

"What are you talking about?"

Yanking her car door open, he tried to pull her from her seat. "There's someone who wants to have a serious talk with you about your meddling. So if you come quietly you won't get hurt."

Kathryn clung to her steering wheel but her slippery palms finally gave way. As he half carried, half dragged her towards his vehicle, she bombarded him with blows from her balled-up fists. A sudden loud horn split the air as a boxy blue catering truck pulled in behind her abductor's Escalade.

The man dropped Kathryn, bounded into the cab of his SUV and peeled into the rushing traffic. Cars swerved out of his way; angry honks followed the fleeing vehicle.

"So that's the way to get through Los Angeles traffic," Kathryn muttered to herself, examining the new scrapes on her knees.

Two Hispanic women, wielding heavy cast-iron skillets, rushed to Kathryn. "Are you okay? Did that guy hurt you?"

"I'm fine, just a little shaky." She rubbed a skinned elbow.

"You really shouldn't have a fight with your man in the middle of a freeway, ma'am," the younger of the two women said.

Kathryn wondered if the thin girl was old enough to be out of school yet. Her curly dark brown hair seemed to have a mind of its own even though it was close cropped, allowing a row of ear piercings to glitter in the sunlight. Light brown eyes with curly eyelashes framed a crooked nose that shadowed thin, chapped lips and a chipped front tooth.

Kathryn stared at her in disbelief. "You think this was a domestic quarrel?"

"Yes, ma'am," she answered, staring pointedly at her bruised face.

"I've never seen that man before in my life." Her voice was high-pitched and she started to shake all over again. "I have no idea why he tried pulling me into his car."

"Glad we could help." The girl turned and said something to the older, chubby woman in Spanish, then turned back to Kathryn. "My mom doesn't speak much English. Do you think you should call the cops?"

"I don't know. I didn't get a license plate number. Did you happen to notice it?"

"Naw, sorry. We saw him dragging you around like a ragdoll and that was it." The young woman pointed to her nose and chipped tooth. "My ex did this to me a couple years ago. I want every woman to have a chance to live without violence so if you need a safe place to stay, I can recommend a good women's shelter."

"Honestly, I've never seen that man before in my life." She reached out to shake their hands. "But thank you for rescuing me!"

"So no cops?"

"No, I don't think they'll be able to do anything about it. No license number, no idea who the guy is and only you as witnesses."

"Then we'll be on our way." The young woman pulled her mother towards the catering truck. "Good luck!"

The woman maneuvered the cumbersome vehicle back into the stream of traffic, tooting her loud horn while revving the engine. Cars parted like the Red Sea for them.

"Yet another way to get through traffic."

Kathryn climbed into her car, rolled the windows all the way up and locked the doors until she saw the flashing lights of the AAA tow truck pull in behind her. After looking her up and down the driver quickly changed her flat, took her offered tip and without giving the speeding cars next to him a glance, squealed his tires and joined the rushing stream.

She shook her head, then slowly drove down the shoulder of the road with her left blinker light flashing and waited for a polite driver to wave her into the lane. With cars continuing to move at a steady pace, she made her way through Los Angeles and into the San Fernando Valley, all the while keeping a nervous eye on her rearview mirror, looking for the black Escalade. Kathryn briefly debated calling the detective and telling him about the attempted abduction, then decided he'd only try to make her come home. She checked her navigation screen and saw that, with luck, she'd reach her uncle's within two hours.

Once she started the climb through the Tejon Pass, she let the BMW exercise its horsepower, making up the time lost sitting on the L.A. freeway with her flat tire. As she descended the pass she was dismayed to see brown smoggy air blanketing the valley and wondered if there were wildfires in this area as well.

The drive along the San Joaquin valley floor was a dull ride surrounded by brown, dusty fields and not much else as far as she could see. Following the directions chirped at her by the nasally navigation guide, she finally left Highway 99 and followed a two-lane road for several miles towards the eastern foothills, which were barely visible in the distance. She drove along empty, dusty agricultural fields before she was directed to turn onto an even narrower, gravel-lined road and told to follow it for a mile.

Finally she saw a farmhouse that she assumed had once been painted white. Now it was a dusty tan color, fading into the surrounding empty acres. The wood-framed front door had peeling paint and drooped on its hinges, while the screens on the windows were ripped and rusted. The few plants trying to grow around the scorched crabgrass yard looked parched. An ancient, dusty, paneled Chevy station wagon of indeterminate color stood parked to the side of the house, while a newer Toyota Corolla, probably white under all the dust, was parked behind it. Someone had written "Wash Me!" with their finger on the back window.

She hesitated for a moment, trying to decide if she really wanted to knock on a stranger's door in the middle of nowhere, when the front door was thrown open and a gray-haired woman stepped out onto the sagging porch. Her hair was pulled severely back into an untidy bun and she wore a large pink nurse's smock with blue jeans and white nurse's shoes.

"Are you from hospice?" the woman asked in a shrill voice when Kathryn stepped out of the car.

"No, I'm here looking for Edgar Stone. Is this his home?"

"It is, but who are you?"

"I'm his niece, although I haven't seen or heard from him since I was fourteen."

"Thank God you're here," the woman said, coming to shake Kathryn's hand. "The doctor only gives him a week or so to live."

Stunned, she shook the woman's hand. "What happened?"

"Lung cancer. A smoker for most of his life, so it wasn't unexpected. By the way, I'm Nancy." The woman snorted a laugh. "Nurse Nancy."

"I'm Kathryn," she replied. "My mother was Edgar's sister."

"Come on into the house. I'm sure you didn't come here to stand out in the yard and yak with me," Nancy said, taking huge strides towards the sagging steps.

Kathryn tentatively followed, noticing that puffs of dust swirled around her sandals with every step.

"Are you sure he's up to visitors?"

"He's on pain meds and tires extremely easily. Other than that, I think he'd be happy to see family. Honestly, I didn't think he had any so I'm glad to see you here."

"What about a wife or children? Or at least cousins?"

"Nope, he's a committed, cantankerous bachelor. Haven't heard of any distant relations either."

Kathryn stopped on the threshold before stepping into the darkened living room. "Maybe he'd rather not have me visit then."

"Nonsense. He may be cantankerous at times but he should be happy to know he has someone who cares for him during his last few days."

She followed Nancy through the dimly lit living room, which had yellowing newspapers stacked several feet deep along the walls obscuring the view of any furniture. She raised her eyebrows at the sight.

"He's a newspaper hoarder," Nancy explained. "I've been clearing out the hallway and his bedroom since I could barely squeeze through to tend to him. Some of the newspapers were from the nineteen-forties!"

"He's lucky to have you," she replied, feeling pressed in by the stacks of paper and wondering what possessed her to visit a man she didn't know.

Nancy quietly knocked on the closed bedroom door, then opened it and motioned for Kathryn to follow her. The room was lit by a single low-wattage bulb glowing beneath a frayed lampshade sitting atop a scarred wooden bedside table. A tattered shade covered the window and Kathryn could barely make out a faded rose pattern on nicotine-yellowed wallpaper. The smell of stale cigarette smoke assaulted her nose and made her want to hold her breath. A thin, gray man dozed while propped up on pillows in a twin-sized bed covered in crisp white sheets. His nose, holding the tubes of oxygen, whistled softly with each breath. She saw several metal oxygen canisters sitting on the floor at the foot of the bed, and next to the head of the bed sat a folding wooden chair.

"Edgar, you have a visitor." Nancy gently stroked his skeletal hand.

"What?" he mumbled faintly, after waking up.

"Someone is here to see you."

He leaned up on his elbow and squinted at Kathryn. "Evelyn, you've come home!"

Nancy quietly left the room as Kathryn moved to the bedside.

"No, I'm Evelyn's daughter, Kathryn."

"You look just like her. So beautiful."

"Thank you," Kathryn murmured. "I haven't seen you since I was fourteen."

"You're all grown up now," her uncle feebly said, reaching out to take her hand. "I should have tried to keep in touch, but…"

"I was hoping you could tell me about my mother when she was younger."

"You need to ask her to tell you about it," he growled with a sudden spurt of energy. "Although it will be mostly fiction."

"My mother died sixteen years ago so it's hard to ask," she answered, pulling her hand away from his and crossing her arms.

"I'm sorry to hear that. What about your father? Did he ever turn up?"

"No."

"Harrumph. So I'm the only family you have."

"It would appear." Kathryn walked to the door. "I'm sorry I bothered you. I'll be on my way."

"Just like your mother. Feisty and no patience," he said with a weak laugh. "Come back and sit down. I'll try to answer your questions as best as I can, although I think you would be a happier person if you left it alone."

She opened the folding chair and sat down.

"Where would you like me to start?" Edgar asked.

"Why were you and Mom estranged? Why did I grow up not knowing my grandparents?"

"Are you sure you want to know this? It's not a very pretty story."

"I think it's time I heard the truth about my family."

"As you wish. Once upon a time there was a beautiful little girl growing up on a farm. Her parents doted on her and gave her everything she wanted." Edgar paused for a moment. "And yes, she had an older brother who had to work very hard to earn their approval and get their attention. When this little girl turned sixteen, she decided she wanted to be a famous actress so she ran away to Hollywood. Her parents were devastated and within a month the father had a heart attack. With his poor health, the father couldn't work the farm so their son had to quit college and take over. Her parents spent their entire life savings hiring private investigators to find their precious daughter. When their savings ran out, they took out mortgages on the farm, but to no avail."

"Do you want me to go on?" Edgar gently asked when he saw Kathryn wipe her eye.

"Please, I'll be okay."

"On the daughter's eighteenth birthday, her parents were at another doctor's appointment for the father's heart. The brother was home when the phone rang. It was his long-lost sister. She bragged about all the famous people she was meeting and how exciting her life was with all the expensive gifts she received and the trips she had taken. Not once did she ask how her family was doing. She finally asked if her parents were home. When she found out they weren't, she asked her brother to mail her five hundred dollars but not tell their parents. When the brother refused, she started crying, telling him she'd been raped, was pregnant and needed the money for an abortion."

The old man started wheezing and motioned for Kathryn to hand him the hospital cup full of water. After taking a few sips from the straw he continued. "The brother didn't believe her and called her all sorts of names. He also told her that she had practically killed their father by running away and bankrupting the farm. He made her promise to never call home again because as far as her family was concerned, she was dead."

Edgar stopped talking and stared up at the stained ceiling.

"She grew up," Kathryn whispered. "My mother grew up and into a responsible wife and mother."

He looked at her with sad, tired eyes.

"That can't be the end of the story," Kathryn pleaded. "You saw her again when I was fourteen. What happened to the baby?"

"As far as I know, she managed to terminate it, if she really was pregnant to start with." He sighed. "Don't look at me that way. She may have been a good mother to you but some things never changed with Evelyn. She was always self-centered, willing to lie to get her way. When I saw your mother last, she told me about meeting your dad at a political convention in Anaheim when she was nineteen years old. She was the, ah, um, hostess for one of the lobbyists who was giving a party for several local councilmen and land developers. Your dad was there as a reporter, just starting out. Apparently it was love at first sight."

"They soon married and along you came. She settled into being a housewife and mother and all seemed well. She never told your father about her former life or family. However, about a month before your father left..." Edgar stopped talking as Kathryn rolled her eyes.

"He didn't leave us. He disappeared."

"All right. About a month before your father disappeared, your mother received a visit from a 'ghost from her past,' is how she put it. She claims it was the same man who had raped her when she was seventeen and then periodically early on in her marriage. He had become a wealthy and powerful man."

Kathryn leaned forward. "Who was it?"

"She refused to give me the man's name. Now are you going to stop interrupting me so I can finish the story?"

"Sorry. Please continue."

"She claims he raped her again while you were at school and her husband at work and then threatened to take you, if she ever told anyone. She promised to not tell a soul but somehow your father found out about it. Shortly thereafter your father disappeared. She contacted me, I came to visit and found too many holes in her story to believe she was telling the truth. I suspect she was having an affair and your father found out and hit the road."

"My father would never have left me. I believe my mother's version even if you don't. I'm going to find out the truth."

"Kathryn, if your mother's story is true, then when your father went looking for the rapist, the rapist turned into a murderer."

Chapter Eighteen

"You did believe her, but you were too afraid to do anything about it," she gasped. "How could you make up such vile stories about my mother?"

"You're wrong. I didn't make up how your mother treated her family. What she said happened to her and your father, I can only guess that she, in the very least, embellished the truth," her uncle said quietly. "I know she was a notorious liar as a child and probably continued telling lies into her adult life."

He picked up his niece's damp hand and gave it a squeeze. "Whatever Evelyn's failings were, I can see that she was a good mother. You've turned out to be a caring person."

Kathryn remained quiet, the silence hanging heavy between them.

"I never should have told you this story. Please forgive me." The old man coughed and the oxygen tube hissed even louder. "You have every right to be angry with me, but despite that, I'm glad I had the chance to see you before I pass."

"I'm glad I had the chance to see you too, Uncle Edgar." She handed him the cup of water. "Can I ask what happened to your parents?"

"My father died when he was only fifty years old. A massive heart attack. My mother followed a few years later, a broken woman."

"I wish I'd had the chance to meet my grandparents."

"They would have loved to have known a granddaughter like you." Edgar yawned, his voice getting weaker. "I've been doing all the talking; now it's your turn to tell me about yourself."

Kathryn started telling him about her business, her home and Neil, but cut it short when he dozed off. Tiptoeing to the door, she blew him a quick kiss and started to leave.

"Niece," she heard him say softly, "let the past be. Digging up old things better left buried won't bring your parents back."

Before she had a chance to reply, the old man started snoring. She silently closed his bedroom door and went to find Nancy.

"He's fallen asleep, so I guess I'll say goodbye and start my drive back to Newport Beach."

"You can't stay for a few days?"

"No, I wish I could but I have business that needs to be taken care of. I'll try to visit on Monday or Tuesday, if you think that will be okay?"

"I think that would be a great idea," Nancy agreed. "He hasn't been this lively for a couple months. You did him a world of good."

Kathryn quickly wrote her cell phone number on the back of her business card and handed it to the nurse. "Please call me if there's any change in his status."

After saying goodbye, she started the long drive home. Stopping for gas before beginning the ascent over the Tejon Pass, she checked her voicemail. Ten messages waited for her, five from Mike and five from John, both demanding she call them immediately.

Gritting her teeth, she called the detective first.

"Williams here," he barked.

"Mike, it's Kathryn."

"Where the hell are you? Why aren't you answering your phone?" he yelled.

"Don't yell at me!" she yelled back. "If you've forgotten, I'm at the spa and it's not convenient making and getting phone calls. The reception is lousy here."

"You're feeding me a bunch of BS and we both know it," Mike growled. "Or have you forgotten that I'm a detective?"

"What do you mean?"

"The Glen Ivy has no record of you checking in. They checked their other branches in case I got your location wrong."

"How did you know I was going there?" She quickly switched her phone to her other ear and started pumping gas.

"That's what you told Marianne this morning." He let out an exasperated sigh. "I feel sorry for her, trying to keep track of you all the time since you won't answer your phone."

"Well, maybe I checked in under an assumed name."

"Maybe you checked in wearing a Groucho Marx disguise, or did you forget to think about trying that excuse?"

"Ha, ha," she shot back.

"Well?"

"Well, what?"

"Kathryn, stop playing games. I want to know where you are and why you lied to me." Mike paused for a moment to control his voice. "I've been worried sick about you."

"I'm sorry I worried you," she answered contritely. "I wanted to visit my uncle in Bakersfield. I'm glad I did because he only has a week left to live and he's my only relative."

"Why didn't you tell me in the first place? I'm not an unreasonable man."

"I didn't think you'd let me go, or else you'd insist on coming with me. It's hard to explain but I needed to do this by myself."

"Under normal circumstances that would have been fine. But your life is in danger and something could have happened to you."

"Um, I guess I should tell you that something did happen."

"What?" the detective yelled.

Kathryn held the phone away from her ear until the other end turned quiet.

"Stop yelling at me."

"Stop being so obstinate and start treating me like a friend who only wants to help. I'll try to control my temper if you would just be honest with me."

"I'm fine, just so you know, but somewhere along the 405 freeway in L.A. a cowboy wearing a black ring with a skull and crossbones tried to abduct me."

She held the phone away from her ear while the detective yelled off a string of expletives.

"Are you done yelling?" she sweetly asked.

"I've just started! Why am I just now hearing about this? Why didn't you call me when it happened?"

"Because I knew you wouldn't let me go visit my uncle and I'm tired of being told what I can and can't do."

She heard the detective whispering to himself, "Breathe in, breathe out, relax, relax, relax."

After a moment of silence he asked, "Where are you now?"

"I'm getting gasoline before I head south on the Grapevine."

"So you're at a gas station?"

"Uh, yes, that's usually where you stop to put gasoline into your car."

He noisily exhaled. "Are there any restaurants close to you, where you can hang out until I can line up an escort to get you home?"

"There's a Starbucks right across the street but I think you're overreacting. I don't need an escort!"

"I'm the only person being reasonable here, so let me decide what you need or don't need this time. Go there and wait until I call you back. And Kathryn? Answer your phone this time."

After giving him the exact location, she climbed back into her car. Just as she started the ignition, a black Escalade pulled up behind her. She caught a glimpse of a man wearing a black cowboy hat and without taking a second look, put her car into drive, jammed the gas pedal down and drove as quickly as she could to Starbucks. Parking at a crazy angle, she grabbed her purse and phone, jumped out of the car and ran inside.

Once she felt safe among the milling people waiting for their coffee drinks,

Kathryn watched the Escalade across the street filling up with gas. The cowboy stayed on the far side of his vehicle where she couldn't get a good look at him. After a few minutes the man climbed back into his vehicle, keeping the hat low over his face, then drove into the Starbucks parking lot and parked next to her car. She could see the man talking on his phone, gesturing with his other hand.

Shaking, she backed away from the window while fumbling with her cell phone, trying to call the detective's number. While waiting for the call to go through she looked frantically around the café, trying to find another exit in case she needed to run.

"Williams here."

"Mike, the cowboy might be here at Starbucks. He's sitting in a black Escalade right next to my car. I can't get a good look at him because of the hat, so I'm not positive it's the same guy."

"Whoa, slow down. Do you feel safe right now?"

"Yes, there's a lot of people here right now."

"Okay, stay put and don't try to go out the back exit."

"How did you know?"

"I know these things, trust me. I'm going to hang up now and expedite your escort. Promise me you'll stay put."

"Okay, I promise." She rubbed her arm, trying to erase the goose bumps cropping up.

Within five minutes, Kathryn saw a California Highway Patrol sedan pull up, lights flashing, and block the Escalade. The officer cautiously approached the SUV's driver's side and rapped on the window. The other patrons of the café crowded around the glass doors and windows and watched with her.

The cowboy handed his driver's license to the officer, then stepped from the Escalade and removed his hat to wipe his forehead. Kathryn groaned. It wasn't the right cowboy. This was a young kid. She threaded her way through the crowd staring out the doors and made her way to the officer.

"Hi, I'm Kathryn Landry." She extended her hand. "I'm sorry for the mix-up but this isn't the right man."

"Detective Williams told us about your mishap this morning, so we're happy to help out," the officer said while handing the driver's license back to the frightened teenager. "Just so you know, this is Bakersfield. Farm country. Lots of guys wear cowboy hats. Hell, even I wear one when I'm not working."

"I understand. I guess I was more rattled by the incident this morning than I thought."

As he sent the kid on his way, Kathryn could picture the husky officer in a cowboy hat sitting on a tractor. His forearms were muscled from hard work and deeply freckled by long hours in the sun. Ginger colored hair curled above his ears and his mustache looked like it was tickling his upper lip.

"Are you ready to go?" he asked.

"Go? Go where?"

"I'm part of your escort team," he answered. "Didn't Williams tell you?"

"No, I didn't get the memo. So how is this going to work? Are you driving me all the way home?"

"You'll be driving yourself and I'll follow you until we get to Frazier Park." He put on his aviator sunglasses. "After that, an off-duty sheriff's deputy will follow you the rest of the way home."

"Does that mean I should drive the speed limit while you're following me?"

"Let's just say I'd be more comfortable if you didn't speed more than five miles above the posted limit," he said, giving her a dimpled smile. "Will that work for you?"

"I can live with that." She returned the smile. "Shall I lead the way?"

Once Kathryn got back onto Interstate Five heading south, she set the cruise control for sixty-eight miles per hour and then called John back.

"Where the hell are you, Kathryn?" John yelled.

She sighed. "What?"

"I said, where are you? I've been calling all over the place trying to find you!" he yelled. "And why don't you ever answer your cell phone?"

"Can't a girl have a quiet day at the spa without having to check her phone every five minutes?"

"Don't play games with me. You're evading the question."

"Can we talk about this tonight? I'm driving and there's a lot of traffic I'm trying to pay attention to," she pleaded. "Plus, there's a CHP officer right behind me and I don't want to get pulled over."

"You're still evading my question. Expect a serious discussion about this tonight," he growled. "I'll see you at seven o'clock. Don't be late."

Just as she disconnected the call to John, Mike called.

"I'm glad it was a false alarm. Thanks for letting me know instead of trying to run away from the guy by yourself."

"Thank you for coming to my rescue. I find it very embarrassing, especially when it turned out to be a kid."

"Better to be safe than sorry. You've had too many close calls recently."

"The CHP officer said that after he passes me off at Frazier Park, the sheriff's deputy will be following me home. How did you manage to set that up so quickly?"

"Connections, darlin', connections." Mike chuckled. "However, the deputy will follow you only to Long Beach and I'll meet you there and drive home with you."

"Really, that's not necessary." Kathryn looked at the car's clock. It was going to be a close call getting home by seven o'clock.

"It's something I want to do, Kathryn. I'm anxious to hear about your latest misadventure face to face, and besides that, I still need to pick up the Explorer at Marianne's."

"I'm sure there's nothing I can say to dissuade you, is there?"

"Nope."

"Okay, guess I'll see you in Long Beach."

The rest of the trip to Long Beach went smoothly, with the CHP officer and then the off-duty deputy staying close to her bumper, guarding her the entire distance. Taking the exit in Long Beach, the deputy jumped in front of her to lead the way to where she was supposed to meet Mike. Pulling into the fast food parking lot, Kathryn saw him standing on the sidewalk with his hands shoved deep into the pockets of new blue jeans. His white polo shirt appeared brand new but his cowboy boots were scuffed and looked like they still carried the scent of hot ash. She didn't see his red truck or the government-issued SUV.

"Where did you park?" she asked, climbing out of the car and stretching her legs.

"I had a friend drop me off so that I could drive you home," Mike answered, blue eyes twinkling. "Unless you object to a trained professional driving your BMW?"

"Uh, no, that's fine if you want," she answered, trying to take a casual peek at her watch.

"Are you late for something?"

Kathryn was thankful that the deputy chose that moment to walk up to Mike and shake his hand.

"Thanks for getting Mrs. Landry here safely," Mike said.

"Not a problem," the deputy answered. "Anytime you need a favor, just call. Especially when you have Laker tickets to throw my way!"

They said their goodbyes and watched the deputy drive away.

"So are you late for something or do you have time for a quick bite to eat?" Mike asked, his stomach growling. "I haven't eaten since breakfast."

"I'm supposed to meet someone at seven o'clock for dinner, but please get something to eat before we leave."

"Someone?"

"Um, John. But please get something for the road. I can drive while you eat," Kathryn insisted.

He gave her a long look. "Okay, let me grab a burger, then we can hit the road."

As soon as Mike was inside the restaurant, she called John.

"Don't bail on me tonight," John said as soon as he answered his cell phone.

"That's not why I'm calling. I just wanted to let you know I ran into traffic and am running late."

"Where are you?"

"We can talk about that later," she said quickly. "Let's meet at Fleming's at eight, okay?"

"I'll pick you up."

"No, don't bother. I'll go straight to the restaurant instead of going to Marianne's. It will be quicker that way."

"I want to pick you up."

"No, I insist," she replied through gritted teeth. "Don't be difficult."

John remained silent.

She saw Mike walking towards the front door, toting a large white take-out bag. "I've got to go. I promise, I'll see you at eight tonight."

"Kathryn, you'd better not be with that detective. Is that why you're being so secretive?"

"Bye, John." She disconnected and silenced her phone just as the detective walked out.

"Problems?"

"Uh, no," she mumbled. "Everything's just fine."

"Kathryn, let me give you some advice." He looked her straight in the eye. "Don't get involved with Selton."

"I'm not involved," she answered testily. "It's only business. Besides, it's really none of your beeswax."

"Beeswax?" Mike guffawed. "I haven't heard that since grade school."

Her face turned bright red. "Oh, you know what I mean."

"Yes, I do," he answered, his voice softening. "I just don't want to see you get hurt, is all."

Mike insisted that he could drive and eat at the same time so Kathryn settled herself into the passenger seat. The greasy aroma of burgers and fries filled the car and made her stomach rumble. In between bites of burger the detective questioned her about the attempted abduction.

When there was nothing more to tell about the mysterious man, she told him about the disturbing stories her uncle had relayed that day. He was uncharacteristically quiet and only grunted from time to time.

Once her story was told, she shook her head. "Well, aren't you going to say something, like you'll reopen my father's case and help me find out what happened to him? Or do I have to figure it out on my own?"

Mike pried her left hand from its death grip on her Chanel bag and started massaging her tense fingers. "Don't you think you have enough going on right now? Let's concentrate on your husband and figure out who's trying to harm you. Okay? I promise we'll talk about your father later."

"But what if they're connected? Neil, my dad?"

"I think it's a stretch to say there could be a connection. But I promise, we'll talk about it once we close the file on Neil."

When his cell phone rang, he released her hand and answered, "Williams here."

Kathryn heard a deep male voice rumbling into the phone and Mike's answering grunts before he thanked the man and disconnected. He laid the phone on the console between them and gripped the steering wheel so hard, his knuckles turned white.

"Is everything all right?" Kathryn asked after noticing his clenched jaw and grinding teeth.

"It's, ah, hard to say right now." He kept his eyes focused straight ahead on the road.

"What's wrong, Mike?" she asked, twisting in her seat to look behind them. "Is someone following us?"

"No, we're okay. I just don't know quite how to bring this up." He massaged his tense neck, then suddenly sped up, darting between cars, and took an off-ramp that led to a shopping center.

"What? What's wrong?" Kathryn's stomach started feeling queasy and, when she shivered, she closed her air conditioning vents.

He parked the car beneath a huge pine tree standing lonely in the black asphalt parking lot and opened the door. "Let's get out and walk a bit."

"Mike, what's going on?" She struggled to unfasten her seatbelt and rushed to catch up with him.

"That was my office calling." He blew out a deep breath of air. "A fisherman found a body today. Out by Catalina."

"No, no, no!" Her voice sounded overly loud and shrill in her ears. "I won't look at another dead body!"

"You won't have to. I promise." Mike grabbed her hand again and gave it a firm squeeze. "I need to get the name and phone number of Neil's dentist. There, um, there wasn't much left of the body to ID."

"Wha… What do you mean? Why do you think it could be Neil? How did he get there?" The questions tumbled from Kathryn's lips before she could stop them.

"I'll need to have a team go through your apartment and collect DNA samples."

"Oh god! Why do you think it could be Neil?" Her stomach flip-flopped and she couldn't control her trembling limbs.

"Do you need a jacket?" Mike asked, noticing her shaking.

"No, I'm okay." She pulled her hand from his and hugged her arms close to her body. "Why do you think it's Neil?"

"They determined it was a male Caucasian about the right age. And Neil is currently the only missing person reported in the area."

"So what happens next?" she whispered. "What do I do now?"

"We wait until we get the dental and DNA results back. But first and foremost, we keep you safe."

She found her dentist's name and phone number on her cell phone and gave it to the detective, who quickly called the information in to his office.

"They're going to get this expedited, so hopefully we'll have at least the dentist's input on identification by tonight or tomorrow morning at the latest."

The rest of the drive to Marianne's was a blur. Mike tried to keep a conversation going but she could only answer in monosyllables.

As her car turned down Marianne's street she saw, with chagrin, John's ruby-red Porsche parked behind Mike's SUV and a sherriff's car parked right behind John.

Chapter Nineteen

Kathryn's face burned hotly as she muttered "awkward" under her breath.

"What did you say?" Mike asked.

"Nothing. What's the deputy doing here?"

"I thought it would be best to have a patrol keep watch on you."

"What? No, this is too much."

"Just for a day or two," Mike pleaded. "Please indulge me? We could be looking at two murders now with you in the middle of it."

"I don't know. Let me think about it." She opened her car door when she saw John exit his car.

"I won't have the patrol car follow you to dinner but I want it here at least through tonight. Promise me you'll be careful?"

"I'll do my best."

As John started walking towards her car, she stepped out and turned to Mike. "I guess I'll say goodbye. Call me when you find out about..."

She tensed up when John reached her side.

"Kathryn, thank god you're okay!" John said. "I can't believe someone tried to kidnap you in broad daylight."

"How did you know? Who told you?"

"You always seem to forget that I'm a private detective." He winked. "I have my sources."

Kathryn rolled her eyes.

John sneered when he saw Detective Williams getting out of the BMW. "Williams, I see you're doing another outstanding job solving her case and keeping her safe. Maybe it's time you thought about retiring."

Kathryn's mouth dropped open and she saw Mike with the same expression on his face. "John, that is totally uncalled for! The detective had no idea I was taking off on my own."

"Like I said, it's probably time to hang up the badge." John leaned in closer to the car. "I heard Walmart was looking for security guards. Might be more your speed."

Kathryn could see Mike gritting his teeth, his eyes glacial blue while vein lines rippled along his temples.

"Selton, you are way out of line. But I'm not going to get into this with you now." His voice was low and fury rippled with each word. "If you'll excuse me, Kathryn, I need to collect my dogs and check my property."

She stepped away from John and flushed red. "Mike, I'm sorry. Thank you for arranging for me to get home safely."

"They'll keep an eye on you for a couple days until we can catch the perps." Mike pointed to the patrol car. "And I'll let you know as soon as we get an identification match on the body."

"Body? Are you talking about another body now?" John directed his question at Kathryn.

"Guess you don't know everything, Mister P.I. Guess you'll just have to wait and read about it in the newspapers." Mike turned his back, stomped to the government-issued SUV and drove off.

She silently walked towards Marianne's front door clenching her teeth. John followed behind.

"What's wrong? You're so quiet."

"I'm waiting for you to explode and start yelling at me."

And how do I drop the bombshell that my husband may have been fish food? There's no easy way to do it.

"Ah, you have every right to be angry with me," he said, catching her hand. "Please accept my humble apologies. I was way out of line earlier on the phone."

She stopped walking, yanked her hand from his and turned towards him. "Out of line on the phone? You were way out of line in what you said to Detective Williams! I can't believe you could be that rude to anyone no matter how much you disliked a person."

"I know." He lowered his head and gazed at her through his long lashes. "You're right. I was so frantic worrying about you that I needed someone to blame. And he was with you and I'm, well, I'm just crazy about you. I can't stand the thought of something happening to you."

Kathryn continued to glare at him, arms crossed, pulled tightly against her body.

"Come on, please don't stay mad at me. I promise I won't ever be rude to him again." John reached out and stroked her cheek, then dropped his hand when she backed away. "Come into the house and let's talk about this. I don't like Williams's watchdog looking at us like this."

Just then the front door was flung open and Richard stepped out. "Kathryn, John, come in, come in. Marianne has the champagne chilled and ready to toast."

John raised his eyebrows and looked at Kathryn.

"I offered Marianne a partnership today. We're celebrating."

"That's wonderful," John said. "I think Marianne will be the perfect partner. Congratulations to you both."

She pushed aside all thoughts of Neil and Mike and allowed herself to be pulled along with the tide of celebration. They entered the house and found Marianne sitting on the patio, hurricane lamps flickering in the gloaming, the dancing flames reflecting golden light on sparkling Waterford flutes. A bottle of Veuve Clicquot La Grande Dame champagne sat chilling in an icy silver bucket, beads of water making glistening trails down the sides. Succulent smoked salmon sat in drifts among canapés on a glittering crystal platter. Soft classical music drifted on the breezes, springing from hidden speakers.

"Congratulations, Marianne," John said gallantly.

"Thank you." Marianne's face beamed. "I can't tell you how excited I am about this opportunity."

Richard expertly popped the cork from the champagne and carefully filled the glasses. Once he had passed them around, he lifted his bubbly nectar and proposed a toast.

"To Kathryn, who has filled our life with the treasures of friendship."

She blushed and thanked them before taking a sip. "I'm sorry to cut your celebration short, but John was just leaving. He has another commitment tonight."

"I'm not leaving until we finish our conversation."

"I think enough has been said already," she answered, trying to keep her anger from her voice.

Marianne and Richard exchanged worried glances before Richard said, "Not that we want to stick our noses in where they don't belong, but what's going on?"

John answered, then quickly glanced at Kathryn. "Detective Williams. He's posted a patrol car in front of your house to guard her."

"Why? What happened?" Marianne sputtered. "We thought you were getting a ticket, John!"

Kathryn quickly filled them in on the attempted abduction before John interrupted her.

"I know I can provide better security for you than an inexperienced and underpaid deputy, but you need to trust me and let me arrange it," John smugly said. "One of my uncle's companies specializes in discreet protection and we only hire experts. You'll never even know they're around."

"I don't know. That sounds expensive."

"It's on the Selton family, so don't worry about it."

"I can't possibly let you pay for it!"

"But you're letting Williams pay for it."

"No, I'm not. The city or county pays the salary for its employees."

"Trust me, the county isn't springing for that officer to sit in front of your house." John paused and looked directly into Kathryn's eyes. "You have to ask yourself why the dee-teck-tive would pay for surveillance out of his pocket. How can he afford that kind of money?"

"I have no idea," she whispered. "Maybe he wants to protect me since he thinks I'm a link to Neil's disappearance?"

"Or maybe he wants to keep tabs on you so that you don't have the opportunity to help me find Neil?"

"Why would he do that?"

"All I can say is that he has some ulterior motive." John paused for effect. "He's covering something up and wants to make sure you don't find out what it is."

Kathryn's mind jumped to the description of the man in Neil's novel.

Salt-and-pepper hair. Icy blue eyes. Cruel sneer. Rugged, tan face.

She shook her head. "I think you've been watching too many movies, John. It all seems implausible."

"Think about it, okay? Let me get one of our employees to protect you, even if it's only for a day or two."

"I'll tell Detective Williams to get rid of my guard tomorrow morning but I need to give your offer some thought for a while longer."

Richard cleared his throat. "I might have a solution that should satisfy everyone's criteria. Kathryn is staying with us and I'll be happy to provide protection while she's here."

"No offense, sir, but what are your qualifications for security?" John forcefully asked.

"I don't like to talk about it but I was part of the Special Forces in Vietnam. I still know a thing or two about protection and taking someone down if needed." Richard muttered, "Probably know more than you do."

"Thank you for your suggestion, Richard," Kathryn interjected quickly, leaning over to pat his hand. "I would be happy to take you up on your offer, although I can't let you guard me twenty-four hours a day. That's asking too much from you."

John frowned. "Kathryn's right. You can't stay awake twenty-four hours a day, so what's the point? I strongly recommend letting professionals handle this."

Richard swept his arm in a wide arc. "We have a state-of-the art alarm system throughout the house, including the land. The nights are the easy part. During the day I'll stick close to her side, armed to the teeth."

"Really, you are both going overboard."

Marianne jumped into the discussion. "I have an idea that might make everyone happy. Well, maybe not happy but at least appeased."

Richard leaned over and lightly kissed Marianne's cheek. "My little diplomat. What's your solution?"

"While Kathryn is at our house, you provide security, including following her to wherever she needs to go. When she's with John, he provides the security. And when she's with Detective Williams, he guards her. And with a little tweaking, we can make the office a safe haven without any of you being there."

Kathryn agreed. "I think I can live with that. But just for a few days, okay?"

John was still scowling.

"Come on, John. It's a good compromise," she implored. "I don't want to spend money just to live like a prisoner and I won't accept charity."

"All right, we'll try it your way for a couple days. I would rather not have Williams part of your security team." John narrowed his eyes. "There's something fishy going on and I don't want you caught in the middle of it."

Once they ironed out the particulars for Saturday's schedule, Kathryn fiddled with her champagne flute, then finally cleared her throat. "I have some news, to ah, share."

When she remained silent, Marianne leaned over and patted her arm. "Take your time, honey."

"Mike, uh, I mean Detective Williams, told me they found," she paused and looked at John from the corner of her eye, "they found a man, um, floating in the ocean by Catalina."

Marianne gasped. "You mean floating in a lifeboat or..."

"I'm afraid he was dead. They're comparing Neil's dental records with this person and trying to collect some DNA from my house." The golden champagne splashed on the table as her trembling hands tried to set the crystal flute down. "I really can't believe it could be Neil. It seems surreal."

Marianne leaned over and pulled her into a hug. "I am so sorry, Kathryn. Let us know what we can do."

"He's not going to make you look at the body, is he?" John growled. "Wouldn't surprise me if he did, that insensitive bastard!"

"No, definitely not. Apparently there's not much left of..." The smell of the smoked salmon turned Kathryn's stomach and she pushed away from the table. "I don't think we can do anything until they get positive identification. It's probably not Neil anyway."

"How soon will they know?" Richard asked.

"Maybe by late tonight or tomorrow morning, at least from dental records. I have no idea how long DNA takes."

"We're here for you, honey," Richard leaned across the table and patted her hand. "You're not alone."

"I'm sorry I ruined your celebration, Marianne. Please know that I am thrilled to have you as my partner." She tried to raise her champagne flute to toast but gave up after splashing more on the table.

"No apologies are necessary. I'm glad you're here, safe and sound."

After John left, Kathryn retrieved her handbag to check for voicemails on her cell. She heard an unfamiliar chirp coming from her bag and found Mike's phone lying inside, the message light blinking.

"Uh-oh, he's going to need this."

Kathryn walked out the front door and before she could reach the bottom of the steps the deputy was already exiting the patrol car.

"Evening, ma'am," the deputy said while his eyes darted around the yard and up and down both directions of the street.

"Hi, Deputy..." Kathryn paused, realizing she'd hadn't bothered to find out the man's name.

"Collins, Deputy Collins." He moved closer and she saw he towered at least a foot over her. "Is there anything I can help you with, ma'am?"

"Detective Williams accidentally left his cell phone here. Do you have his home phone number so I can see what he wants me to do with it?"

"I'm pretty sure he only uses his cell phone. No landline that I know of," he answered in a voice that was low and husky.

"I was afraid of that. How do you feel about taking a drive this evening, Deputy Collins? I think Detective Williams is going to want his phone back."

"My orders are to stay with you. There's no way I'm altering that unless I hear from Williams directly."

"Guess that means we're both taking a drive tonight." Kathryn turned towards the house. "I'll let Marianne and Richard know."

"Yes, ma'am."

She quickly told the couple where she was going before retrieving her handbag and the two cell phones. She invited Deputy Collins to ride with her, suddenly glad she had someone with her as the evening darkness deepened. The quiet man gave her directions as she needed them and kept busy watching cars around them and behind them.

When they arrived at Mike's gate, she was happy to see it was open after imagining trying to climb it and walk the long drive to the house in pitch-black darkness. She drove along the tree-lined drive and wrinkled her nose. The smell of smoke seemed to be getting stronger and, as she turned the corner of the drive, she gasped out loud when she saw Mike's house on fire.

Chapter Twenty

As soon as she put the car in park, Deputy Collins bolted from the BMW, Kathryn close behind him. Eight-foot flames licked the side of the house and she saw Mike dragging a long garden hose, spurting water, towards the flames. His dogs ran barking at his heels, their hackles raised.

"Do you have any fire extinguishers?" the deputy bellowed.

Mike finally noticed them, but kept the water aimed at the spreading flames. "There's one in the cargo hold of the Explorer and another one in the garage next to the workbench. But call nine-one-one first!"

Kathryn raced back to her BMW for her cell phone and punched in the three numbers with trembling hands. While waiting for the call to be answered, she ran towards the front door of the house when she saw the deputy already carrying the extinguisher from the vehicle.

Once the dispatcher answered, her voice shook as she gave them Mike's location and the fire emergency information. She disconnected the call after being told that a fire truck was on its way. She frantically threw open doors, hunting for the garage entrance, trying to remember where it was located.

Her breathing escalated with each wrong door until she was almost gasping for air. Finally a large, dark cavern greeted her and, after fumbling for the light switch, she grabbed the heavy red fire extinguisher. She groaned as her muscles complained at the weight, but sprinted as fast as she could to where the men were battling the diminishing blaze.

"Fire Department is on its way." She yelped when a spark landed on her hand but brushed it off, handed Deputy Collins the new extinguisher and took the empty one.

Between the second fire extinguisher and the garden hose spewing out water, the fire was reduced to acrid smoking wood. As soon as he turned off the hose, they heard the sounds of sirens and the roar of large trucks and watched the flashing red strobes light up the night.

"Kathryn, Collins, what are you doing here?" Mike was bent over at the waist and gasping for air. "Not that I'm complaining, because you probably saved my house."

"Somehow your cell phone ended up in my purse and I thought you might need it tonight," she answered while handing him the phone. "Deputy Collins wouldn't leave me unguarded without your permission."

Mike slapped the other man on the back. "You're a good man, Collins."

The firefighters quickly unloaded their hoses and gear and made certain the fire was completely out before the captain came to talk to Mike.

"Williams, I thought we had this fire taken care of yesterday," the steel-gray-haired man said, shaking hands. "Do you think the wind blew up and ignited some dormant embers?"

"I wish that's all it was," Mike answered bitterly, shaking his head. "I'm afraid we've got a loon on our hands."

"What do you mean?" Kathryn shivered.

"Just as I pulled up to the house, there was an instantaneous flash and then the blaze started up. Once I got closer I could smell gasoline. My guess is that you'll find some kind of timer device in that mess."

"I'll call the arson expert out and have him take a look," the captain said. "Lucky you were here when it went off. At least the damage is limited to the exterior."

"Yeah, tell me about it," Mike responded, wiping grit and ash from his face. "It would have been much worse if Collins and Kathryn hadn't shown up when they did."

As the fire crew started packing up their gear, Mike saw Kathryn grimace and rub the back of her hand. "Are you all right?"

She lifted her hand and tried to look at it in the dim light. "A spark landed on me, but I don't think it blistered. I'll be okay."

"Why don't we all go inside and wash up then I'll take a closer look at it." He took her hand.

Kathryn and Deputy Collins followed him into his ranch-style home and Mike directed them to separate bathrooms to clean the ashy grit from their hands and faces. After wincing when the warm water hit the burn, she turned her attention to the cozy powder room, amazed that a man had put so much thought into its design. The palette of charcoals and grays complemented the great room's stone fireplace and the glass vessel sink reflected the light and brightened the room.

She found the two men in the kitchen gulping glasses of iced water and Mike handed her one after she perched on the edge of the leather barstool. She saw a first aid kit had been placed on the counter.

"All right, let's see the burn." Mike gently picked up her right hand and studied the small blister in the bright light before applying ointment and a small bandage. "My prognosis is that you'll live."

"Glad to hear it." She pulled her hand back. "I think we'd better be going. Marianne is probably waiting up for me."

"I can't thank you and Collins enough. You literally saved my home."

"I'm glad we helped. But I think Deputy Collins should come back and guard you instead of me. It looks like you need it more."

"Uh uh, Kathryn. You agreed." Mike shook his head.

"Excuse me, Mike," Deputy Collins cleared his throat. "I think I'll wait out in the car while you two hash this out."

Mike walked the deputy to the front door and shook his hand. "Thanks again, Collins. I'll call you first thing in the morning."

Once the front door was firmly shut, Kathryn crossed her arms. "I had a discussion about my security tonight with the Pattons and Marianne came up with a better idea."

"Oh?"

"Richard will guard me while I'm in their home. He says their security system is state of the art."

"Okay, I can see how that works if he's willing to take on the responsibility."

"Really? You don't think Richard is too old to protect me?"

Mike laughed. "Richard is more than capable. You probably just found out he was Special Forces in 'Nam, but I've known since the day I met him."

"How did you find out? He never talks about it."

"I notice little things, like the small tattoo on the inside of his upper left arm."

"I never saw that. But how did you know what the tattoo meant?"

"My oldest brother had the same tattoo."

"Maybe Richard should get together with your brother and talk about old times," Kathryn suggested. "Marianne would love to throw a party."

Mike pressed his lips together and didn't answer.

She stammered, "I'm so sorry, Mike. I apologize. I shouldn't have assumed…"

"It's okay. It was a long time ago, but I still miss him." He cleared his scratchy throat again. "So what was the rest of Marianne's plan to keep you safe?"

"Richard will either follow me wherever I need to be or drive with me." She hesitated before gushing, "When I'm with John, he'll be responsible for my safety and when I'm with you, you're in charge."

"I like two-thirds of your plan. Selton doesn't have a clue how to keep you safe though."

"His uncle owns a security firm so John wants to hire a couple of their experts."

"Hmmmm."

"I can't afford it and I'm not going to let John pay for it." Kathryn bit her lip.

"I can't let you pay for security either."

"Who said I was paying? Selton?"

"Yes. If you're not paying, why would the county approve money to protect me?"

"I hate to admit it, but Selton is right. This is coming out of my pocket."

"I can't accept your protection then."

"Don't be stubborn."

Kathryn frowned and her voice went up an octave. "Why are you paying for it? So you can keep me under surveillance? Or hope that I slip up and admit I killed Neil so you can wrap up your case?"

"Calm down. It's none of those things. I know you had nothing to do with Neil."

"I am calm," she answered, grinding her teeth. "Why wouldn't I be calm? Being pushed off the road one day, then assaulted the next happens to me all the time. But enough about me… Why are you paying to keep me under surveillance?"

"If I had you under surveillance you wouldn't know it, nor would I tell you about it," he growled. "It's to keep you safe."

"Why? Is this a service you provide for all the victims in your cases?"

"You're making this difficult. It's a complicated answer."

"Then try to simplify it and tell me."

"I, uh, I... Oh hell!" Mike let the silence hang in the air and he stared at the travertine flooring. "I guess what I'm trying to say is that I've come to care about you and I can't bear the thought of something happening to you."

"Oh." Kathryn's cheeks turned bright pink. "I wasn't expecting that kind of answer. I don't know what to say…"

"I never intended for you to find out since this is unprofessional, but you goaded me," he grumbled, refusing to look at her.

Kathryn could hear the embarrassment in his voice as she wondered how to respond. "I know we started out on the wrong foot, but I appreciate all you're doing for me. I've come to enjoy the time we've spent together too."

He mumbled, "I don't want to make it awkward when we're together, so please forget I ever said anything, okay?"

"Actually, I think it's very sweet. Thank you for telling me. You don't have to worry though, I won't bring it up again."

"I appreciate it. I should have let you continue thinking that you were a suspect. Might have been easier working together."

"Oh stop," she laughed. "It will be fine, I promise. Friends?"

"Yes, friends." He coughed again. "Tell me about your schedule tomorrow. I still need to get your flash stick and take a look at Neil's novel."

"I forgot about that," she lied. She briefly wondered if she could convince him that she had lost it. "I have to be at a job site tomorrow morning. The project should take about three hours or so. Can I call you when I'm through?"

"That'll be fine. Make sure Richard sticks close to you."

"I will. So can I send Deputy Collins back here once I get to Marianne's?"

"Fine," Mike growled. "Might as well make him earn his money since I'm paying overtime rates."

***

Gentle knocking on the guest bedroom door dragged Kathryn from a deep sleep and she almost fell out of bed when she saw her clock said eight-thirty.

"Kathryn?" Marianne called in a hushed voice from the hallway. "Are you okay?"

She opened the door. "I can't believe I slept in this late. Thanks for waking me."

"I didn't want to, but thought I'd better since you told John you'd be at his house by nine this morning." She thrust a cup of steaming hot Kona coffee into Kathryn's hand.

"I'd better call him and tell him I'm going to be late," she yawned. "Thanks for the coffee. It's just what I needed."

She left John a quick message telling him she'd be forty-five minutes late, then called the installation company and asked them to be there by ten o'clock. She chugged the coffee before jumping into the shower, and afterwards speedily slathered on her makeup, wondering when the bruises would fade. She chose a floral, ruffled, peach-colored sleeveless blouse with a flared jean skirt, which was long enough to cover the scrapes on her knees. Ballet-style flats accented with peach-colored rosettes completed the outfit.

As she rushed to the front door, Marianne intercepted her and placed a warm brown paper bag in her hand. "Fresh mini blueberry muffins for you, John and Trieste. There are extras for the delivery team."

"They smell delicious. Thanks!"

She jumped into the red BMW, but before she could start the car up, Richard came bounding out of the house and knocked on her passenger-side window.

After she unlocked the door, he opened it and grinned. "Did you forget something?"

"What?"

"Me! I'm supposed to be your shadow, right?"

"Sorry, I forgot. You don't need to come with me though since it's not that far to John's."

"If you want this to work, you have to let me do my job. I don't want either the police or John's people hanging around anymore than you do."

"You're right," she answered with a sigh. "I feel like I'm imposing on your time and I hate doing it."

"I'm an old retired guy. This is kind of fun!"

Kathryn put her lipstick on while she waited for him to open his garage and pull his car out to follow her. She was surprised when she heard the loud growl of a powerful engine being revved, then saw a sparkling deep-blue Shelby Mustang pull up behind her. She shook her head and wondered why men liked muscle cars so much.

The drive to John's house proved uneventful. Pulling up to the curb in front of John's house, she saw a black Bentley parked in the drive. She wondered if John had company and if she should reschedule. Not quite knowing what to do, she slowly walked to the front door, then heard Richard toot his horn before roaring off through the quiet neighborhood.

"Kathryn," Trieste squealed, opening the door before she could ring the doorbell. "My dad said he had a surprise coming for me this morning but he wouldn't tell me what."

She gave the slight girl a hug, then handed her the still-warm paper bag. "Marianne sent these for our snack. Are you hungry?"

"Yes!" She wrinkled her nose and frowned. "My dad made me eat oatmeal this morning. It's disgusting so I threw most of it away when he wasn't looking."

Kathryn laughed. "Oatmeal was never my favorite either."

Together they went to the kitchen and poured glasses of ice-cold milk and placed the muffins on square black stoneware plates.

Just as they had each taken a huge bite, Kathryn heard a loud masculine yell coming from the back of the house.

Trieste giggled when she saw Kathryn's startled look. "Uncle Gerald is with Dad and they're not very happy with each other right now."

She grimaced as more yelling erupted. "I'm sorry to hear that. It sounds awful!"

"Don't worry, they get over it fast. They never stay mad at each other, no matter how much yelling they do," the young girl said with her mouth full of blueberry muffin crumbs.

"I hope you're right."

She studied her muffin in silence, trying not to listen to the argument going on in the back of the house, but she couldn't help but catch some of the phrases being shouted out.

"Gerald, enough is enough!" John hollered.

"I've given you plenty of chances…" the former senator shouted back.

Trieste cut in on Kathryn's eavesdropping. "Hard not to listen, isn't it? I think they'll be done soon."

The men's voices fell to a soft murmur and within a few minutes they were laughing. John walked into the kitchen with his uncle close behind.

"I thought I smelled something delectable. I hope you saved some for me. I'm starving." He grimaced. "I had to eat oatmeal this morning and it was awful!"

"Dad, you're the one who cooked it!"

"I know. Remind me to take you to Starbucks or McDonald's if I ever feel like trying to cook it again."

"Hello, Kathryn," Gerald Selton said. "It's nice to see you."

"Hello, Senator Selton. Would you like a blueberry muffin?"

"Please call me Gerald." He sniffed the air. "They smell delicious, but I'll have to pass this time. Did you bake them?"

"I wish I could say I did, but my assistant, oh, I mean my partner, Marianne, made them."

"She should open a muffin shop and I'd eat there every day," Trieste piped in, placing one on a plate for her dad.

The adults laughed and after John took a bite he agreed. "I think I've found my next business venture: Marianne's Muffins."

"Oh no you don't. I just made her my partner and I'm not going to lose her without a fight."

"I'd better be going," Gerald said, interrupting their laughter. "I have to get to the office."

"On a Saturday?" Kathryn asked.

"Movers and shakers never rest," he answered. "I trust I'll see you tomorrow afternoon for the cocktail cruise?"

"I'm looking forward to it, if you're sure you still want me to come."

The former senator took her hand and bent over to kiss it. "I insist." He then swept his great-niece up into his arms for a big hug and kiss. "Trieste, I promise we'll plan a Christmas Boat Parade party for you and some of your school friends on board my yacht since you can't come to my party tomorrow."

"Can Kathryn come to that one too?"

"You can invite whomever you wish."

"Thanks, Uncle Gerald. You're the best!"

After walking his uncle to the Bentley, John came back to the kitchen and shooed Trieste up to her room to finish homework.

As soon as he heard her door close he turned to Kathryn. "I'm sorry you had to hear the quarrel going on with my uncle."

She shrugged. "It's fine. I guess every family has its own way to deal with disagreements."

"Well, this argument kind of concerns you."

"What? What did I do?"

"I know you hate having people tell you what to do but my uncle is adamant that I do so."

"What do you mean?"

"I have only complained about you spending time with Williams but I'm going to have to demand that you stop all communications with him from here on out."

"John, I know you have your issues with him but you have absolutely no right to insist on that," she answered, stomping her foot.

"I was afraid you would react this way, so I guess I have no choice but to tell you: we have evidence that Williams is on the take and has engineered a cover-up into your husband's disappearance."

Chapter Twenty-One

"I can't believe it!" Kathryn started pacing back and forth. "What proof do you have?"

"You've seen his house, his land, his horses. Where did he get that much money? City employees aren't known for being wealthy."

"Maybe it's family money," she argued. "Just because a guy has nice possessions doesn't mean he's on the take."

"You're right. But my uncle has an informant who would swear on a stack of Bibles that he saw Williams taking cash, big cash, from one of the largest developers in Southern California." He slammed his fist into the palm of his hand. "The informant is certain that another money transfer is going to happen early next week. We're putting surveillance on Williams and we'll catch him red-handed."

"And how does this tie into Neil?"

"Apparently your husband was doing some investigative reporting on corruption in the precinct and city council members when he stumbled on to Williams."

"Are you saying that he killed my husband?"

"Noooo, I wouldn't go that far. We suspect that he knows who did though."

"But you are saying that the body found is my husband?"

"It certainly appears that way."

She leaned her back against the cold granite kitchen island and crossed her arms. "Only a few days ago you were convinced that he ran away with another woman."

"Don't be angry with me. This is all part of investigating. You start out with a hypothesis and the more you dig, the more pieces of the puzzle you find, until you discover the truth." John walked over to her, pulled her into a hug and whispered into her hair, "I know this is doubly hard for you to accept. Finding out your husband has been murdered and then finding out that the man who is supposed to bring the criminal to justice is in bed with the murderer."

"This is too much to process all at once." Kathryn pushed John away and rubbed her temples. "I don't know what to think."

"But you understand now why I have to tell you to keep away from Williams? Promise me?"

"I'll do what I can but until you have concrete proof I'm not going to be able to completely avoid him."

John scowled. "I don't know why the hell not!"

She bit off a retort when the doorbell rang. Sighing, she motioned to the front of the house. "It must be the installers. I'll let them in and get to work."

"Fine, but this conversation isn't over."

Just as Kathryn opened the door for the installers, Trieste came bounding down the stairs.

"Dad said I could watch you work, if it's okay with you?"

"It's fine with me." She smiled and gave the girl a quick hug. "I'm happy to have your company."

After introducing Trieste to Lou and Sam, she directed the burly men to start bringing in the crates and set them in the formal living room. Removing an antique bronze toy carousel, she pushed a heavy square marble-topped coffee table up against one of the platinum-colored silk sofas. Trieste helped her roll the hand-woven Persian carpet up, then spread out felt drop cloths to protect the wood flooring from the crates. A large picture window overlooked a lush green backyard and the golf course beyond that. Two golfers in pastel polo shirts were hunting for a lost ball in the ivy at the edge of John's property.

"My dad said I have to take either golf or tennis lessons next summer." Trieste jumped onto the silk couch and pointed out the window. "I'd rather spend all summer at a dance camp but he wants me to broaden my horizons. What do you think I should choose?"

Kathryn tried not to grimace when she saw the girl jumping on the couch with her shoes still on. "Uh, I really don't know. I never did either of those activities. Wouldn't you be more comfortable, if you took your shoes off?"

"Yeah, then I'll really feel the bounce in the couch!" she answered, flinging her Sketcher Twinkle Toes to the floor. "But seriously, what should I do? Golf or tennis?"

"Does either your mom or dad play tennis or golf?"

"Nope. They're too busy working which is why they want to sign me up for camps. That, and to broaden my horizons." Trieste did the quote, unquote signs with her fingers while rolling her eyes.

"I guess if it were me I'd choose tennis then."

"Why?"

"It seems a lot easier than golf and tennis clothes are so much cuter."

"You're right." The girl giggled.

Just then a crate was brought in and set down with a thud.

"Easy, guys," Kathryn admonished. "Those are extremely fragile."

"Sorry, Mrs. Landry. My hand slipped," Lou grunted. "These are a lot heavier than they look."

While the men retrieved another crate, she cleared chunky mahogany stepped candlesticks from the charcoal-speckled marble fireplace mantel, then carefully picked up a photograph of Trieste housed in a gold-leaf gilded frame.

"I love this picture of you, Trieste," she said. "The colors are so vibrant and you look radiant."

"Thanks. My mom makes me get my picture taken every year around my birthday, in some new location." Trieste walked over to Kathryn and pointed. "That was on Kauai when I was six. We took a helicopter and landed by some waterfalls but you really can't see it in this picture. My mom has a huge one of me sitting next to the waterfall hanging in her office."

"Where did you go this year for your picture?"

"We haven't done it yet because my mom wanted to wait to do a photo-shoot in New England when the leaves turn colors. She said maybe we'd go next weekend if her friend thought the leaves had changed enough."

"Sounds like fun," Kathryn mused, "seeing all these different places."

"It's so boring." Trieste started jumping on the couch again. "I have to sit still so long and just smile. When that part's done we have to go to dinner with my mom's friend - he's the photographer - and the next morning we usually fly back home 'cause my mom wants to go back to work."

"You're right. That doesn't sound like much fun."

The men arrived with another crate, then went back for the last one.

"Come on, you can help me measure where to hang the mirror." Kathryn handed Trieste the end of the measuring tape. "Hold your end against the far wall, high enough so it's above the fireplace mantel."

As the men started opening the crates, she explained to the girl, while they measured, how they would first center and then hang the huge mirror. Once they found and marked the spot where the center bracket would need to be, she let Trieste climb the ladder and hammer in the first nail. After the men finished pounding in the remaining brackets, making certain they were level, they hefted the massive, heavily gilded French antique mirror and gently lowered it onto the awaiting wall.

"Dad, come here and look!" Trieste yelled.

John sauntered into the room. "Nice. I like it. It really opens up the room and makes it seem lighter."

"Dad, I got to pound a nail into the wall to hang it!" Trieste grinned from ear to ear. "Kathryn let me measure and climb the ladder!"

"Sweetheart, I'm sure you did such a good job that mirror will stay hanging no matter how many earthquakes we get."

"I'm going to help with the other two pictures too!"

"Okay, then I'll let you ladies and gents get back to work." John knocked knuckles with his daughter before leaving.

The installers made quick work hanging the remaining art, and once they had left, Trieste gave her father a tour. Kathryn took the opportunity to inspect the damage caused by the water leak. She was relieved to find that the fans and dehumidifier had been picked up, so all that remained was to schedule the carpenter and flooring specialist to repair the damage. Retrieving her cell phone to call Marianne and discuss the details, she saw two voicemails from the detective.

After hearing Trieste's excited chatter to her father coming from the upstairs master bedroom, she picked up the messages from her voicemail.

"Hi, it's Mike. Um, something's come up so I won't be able to pick up the flash drive today," she heard him say in a husky voice. He cleared his throat and the message disconnected.

"Sorry, I don't know why I got disconnected," he said in the second voicemail. "Could I come by tomorrow morning and pick it up around ten? Uh, and if you don't have other plans, maybe we could go to Sunday brunch? Call me when you get this message."

Kathryn sighed. She had a hard time believing the accusations against the detective and it was going to be difficult dodging him while John waited for his surveillance photos. She needed to see concrete proof.

She quickly called Marianne and confirmed the upcoming schedule for the contractors to repair the damage.

"Did Mike get a hold of you, Kathryn?"

"He left a voicemail."

"Poor dear. I hope his horse is okay."

"Oh no! What happened? He only said he wouldn't be able to stop by today."

"The fire and move must have been too much for the mare and it looks like she might go into labor." Marianne tsked. "Those arsonists cause so much pain and suffering."

"I'm so sorry to hear that. Is there anything we can do?"

"No, I asked. The poor dear though. He's had so many terrible things happen to him in such a short time."

It's going to get a lot worse if John has his way.

"Marianne, I've got to get back to work. I'll call you if I hear anything new."

"All right dear. Would you like Richard to come follow you home or will John bring you?"

"I'll have John follow me. I don't know how much longer I'll be here though."

"Don't worry about it. If we're not home, call my cell and we'll meet you there."

Kathryn quickly disconnected when she heard Trieste and John coming down the hallway.

"So, what do you think?" she asked when she saw John's smiling face.

"I think the pieces are perfect additions to your work," he answered. "They complement the design even better than I envisioned when you picked them out."

"I'm pleased to hear it." She stooped down and looked into Trieste's eyes. "Thanks for being my assistant today. You worked hard and helped me a lot!"

Trieste's smile beamed and she tugged on her father's hand. "Dad, I've got an idea. Can we all go to the beach and rent bikes to ride around, then go to lunch at Ruby's on the Pier? Pleeeeze? Kathryn, pleeeeze say yes?"

They both laughed before Kathryn pointed to her skirt and shoes. "I'm not really dressed for biking."

"You can change, can't you?"

Kathryn looked at John and saw him chuckling. "What's so funny?"

"Trust me, you're no match for a seven-year-old. You might as well give in now."

"Does that mean you're okay with this plan?"

"Yep, count me in."

"Kathryn, will you pleeeeze come?" Trieste begged, tugging on her hand.

"Okay, as long as you don't mind dropping by my apartment for a minute so I can change clothes."

Trieste started dancing around, giving them both high-fives. "This is going to be so awesome!"

John interrupted her celebration. "Before we go, you have to put on sunscreen and find your shoes. I'll go pull the car out, so hurry."

As soon as Trieste bounded up the stairs towards her room, John took Kathryn's hand and pulled her close. "Thank you for spending time with Trieste."

"She's fun to be around and seems like she's really interested in my work."

Kathryn abruptly pulled away when she heard Trieste pounding down the stairs yelling, "Dad, where are my shoes?"

Kathryn laughed. "You left them in the living room."

"Oh yeah, I forgot."

"I'll meet you two girls out front, okay?"

"Okay, we'll be there in a minute."

***

After leaving her car in the parking structure, Kathryn hurried towards John, who had deftly parked his car next to the circular curb in front of the apartments.

"You can wait in the car for me," Kathryn said, leaning in his open window. "I won't be long."

"I don't think that's the security agreement we have," John said. "We'll all go up and I'll make sure you stay safe."

Kathryn muttered "out of control" under her breath, but led the way into the lobby.

"Mrs. Landry!"

"Hello, Tommy. How's it going?"

"Good. I wasn't sure how long you'd be gone so I've had the manager put your mail in your apartment every day."

"Thanks."

"Oh hey, Mr. Selton. And Trieste, what a surprise. My, you've grown!"

"Hi Tomas!" Trieste squealed, running around the reception counter to knock knuckles with him.

Kathryn looked from the doorman to Trieste, then back to the doorman. "Aren't you Tommy?"

The man laughed. "Nope. Trieste is one of the few who can tell us apart."

"I have no idea how she does it," John interjected. "Where's Tommy?"

"We swapped stations today. Change of pace keeps things a little more interesting." Tomas hesitated. "You won't tell the manager on us, will you?"

"Don't worry, your secret is safe," John answered, winking at Kathryn.

"Dad, can I stay down here with Tomas, uh, I mean Tommy?" Trieste giggled.

"It's fine with me as long as Tommy doesn't mind."

"I'm good with it, Mr. Selton."

"We won't be long." John pulled Kathryn towards the elevators.

After Kathryn unlocked the front door, John swept in ahead of her and looked through the apartment. "All clear."

"I knew it would be," Kathryn huffed. "I'll be just a minute if you want to go wait with Trieste."

"I'll wait here."

"Fine," she answered before firmly closing her bedroom door.

After changing into black cropped yoga pants and an aqua-colored tank top, Kathryn applied sunscreen to her face and shoulders, then pulled her hair into a baseball cap. She grabbed her running shoes and a light sweatshirt before joining John in the living room. He was gazing out the window towards the mirrored apartment opposite hers.

"Hard to believe you can really see into the apartment over there," he gestured.

"I wouldn't have believed it either had I not seen it with my own eyes. Makes me wonder if Neil's novel was based on facts and if it had any bearing on his murder."

"What do you mean?" John asked sharply, still looking out the window. "I thought I told you I discovered he was writing an exposé on corruption in the precinct."

"I know. But maybe his novel, Helene and that apartment are all part of the corruption?"

"I guess we'll never know since Neil's laptop was stolen."

"Um."

John quickly spun around and faced her. "What do you mean by 'um'?"

"I thought I told you," Kathryn tried explaining when she saw his face turn red. "I copied the novel onto a flash stick."

"No, I think you neglected to tell me that useful bit of information."

"Over breakfast at Shady Canyon? I'm sure I said something."

"And I'm sure you didn't." His eyes narrowed. "Maybe you're confusing me with the other guy you've been hanging around."

"Don't start making this ugly because you're jealous."

"You're right, I'm jealous." He turned around and looked out the window and took a deep, prolonged breath. "I apologize for reacting this way."

"I'm sorry too, for neglecting to tell you about having a copy."

He kept his back towards her, his voice icy. "Who else knows you have a copy of the novel?"

Chapter Twenty-Two

Kathryn kept silent, chewing on the bottom of her lip, not understanding his quiet anger.

"I see. So the detective knew and I didn't," he said harshly. "Did you give him a copy?"

"No. He wants it, but with everything happening I keep forgetting to."

"Where is the flash drive?"

Kathryn glanced at her purse. "It's locked in my desk at my office."

"Is that the safest place for it?"

"I think so. My office is alarmed and the building has a security patrol come by every couple of hours."

"I think we should stop by and pick it up this afternoon. I'll keep it in my safe at home."

"It'll be fine where it is. I'm planning on working at the office on Monday anyway, so I'll make a copy and courier it over to you."

He turned to face her, a scowl on his face. "I don't trust Williams. If he knows about it, you can bet he's going to try to destroy the evidence against him."

"But it's only a novel. It can't be considered real evidence, can it?" Kathryn scowled back. "Besides, it probably has nothing to do with Detective Williams."

"It doesn't matter. I want to make sure he can't get his hands on it."

"John, I think you're making too big a deal about this." Kathryn's voice softened. "The flash stick is safe where it is and I'll make sure you get a copy of it on Monday."

"What about Williams?"

"What about him?"

"You are not giving him a copy, understood?"

"I understand."

"Please make sure you remember that."

"Okay, I'll do my best," she answered irritably. "Maybe we should cancel the beach? You've obviously got more important things to worry about than having a fun afternoon."

John gave her a long look before laughing. "We can't disappoint Trieste, can we? Shall we rescue Tomas and hit the beach?"

Kathryn knitted her brows together. "I think that's a good idea."

They entered the lobby and found Trieste perched on the counter, eating a lollipop. Tomas was on the phone and scribbling notes furiously while another phone was ringing. He waved to them as they walked back into the sunshine.

"Sheesh, what took you guys so long?" Trieste complained, grabbing Kathryn's hand while they followed John back to the car. "Was my dad trying to kiss you or what?"

Her face flamed bright red and she could see the tips of John's ears turning scarlet. "Uh, no, we just had a lot to talk about. I'm sorry we made you wait."

"Trieste, that wasn't a polite thing to say," John admonished. "You should apologize to Kathryn."

"Okay, I'm sorry. But can we go already?"

John looked over at Kathryn, rolled his eyes and mouthed "sorry" when he loaded them into the vehicle.

The rest of the sunny afternoon flew by in a delightful blur. Kathryn was relieved that John's mood seemed to have turned around and he never mentioned the detective or the case. She wanted to keep a wary distance, but his warmth and silly playfulness with his daughter drew her in, and she all but forgot about the earlier incident. After spending a couple hours in the sun, biking along the asphalt path that bordered the wide sandy beach, with fresh ocean breezes cooling their faces, they were more than ready to walk the length of the Huntington Beach pier and eat at the red tiled roof that housed Ruby's. They all had cheeseburgers, fries and chocolate milkshakes and ate until their plates were clean.

As the sun made its way westward over the ocean, the three strolled along the long pier and watched surfers catch waves before plunging back into the gray, foam-flecked water.

"Dad, can I go to surfer camp instead of tennis or golf next summer?"

"I don't think you're old enough yet."

"Aw, Dad. How old do I have to be?"

"I'm not sure, but I know you have to be at least nine to try out for the Junior Lifeguard program. Maybe we should look into that when you're older."

"But I really want to try surfing now."

"How about we go to Hawaii on Christmas break and take some lessons where it's warm?"

Trieste squealed and hugged her father. "Yes! I really want to do that! Can Kathryn come watch me?"

John looked up at Kathryn with a smile on his full lips. "She's more than welcome to come."

"Will you pleeeeeze come, Kathryn? Pleeeeze?"

"Trieste, I would love to watch you surf, but I can't promise anything right now. Let's talk about it when Christmas gets closer, okay?"

The girl gave her father a jab with her elbow and whispered out of the corner of her mouth, "Dad, if you'd kiss her, she'd come!"

John threw his hands up in the air. "Okay, on that note I think it's time to head home."

On the drive back to Newport Beach, Kathryn convinced John to drop her off at her apartment and let her stay instead of following her to the Pattons' home. Richard would meet up with her later and follow her back to his house.

"This goes against my better judgment," he said. "But I trust Tommy, or Tomas, not to let anyone in that doesn't belong there."

"Thank you for understanding. I need some time to go through my mail and pay bills without anyone hovering over me. I can't believe the pile that accumulated the few days I've been at Marianne's."

"I can trust you not to take off on your own, can't I?"

"I promise I'll stay in my apartment."

"And Williams isn't coming to visit?"

"No, I'm avoiding him."

He smugly smiled. "Glad to hear it."

After leaving Trieste at the front desk with Tomas, John once again searched Kathryn's apartment. Finding it safe, he pulled her into his arms and kissed her lips.

She pushed away from him and frowned.

"What's wrong?" John brushed a lock of hair away from her cheek.

"While I had a wonderful time with you and Trieste this afternoon, I just don't…" Kathryn shrugged her shoulders.

"Come on," he said, taking her hand and stroking her palm. "You have to admit there's something happening between us. You can't ignore it."

"I'm tired of having to walk on eggshells around you, every time something comes up about Detective Williams."

"I know, I know." He sighed and entwined his fingers through hers. "You don't realize the impact you have on me. I've never had this happen to me before with any other woman and I go crazy thinking about you with him before I can stop myself. Can you forgive me?"

"Why can't you understand that there's nothing going on between me and Detective Williams, and there shouldn't be anything going on between me and you?" Kathryn's stomach started doing flip-flops, very aware of the sensations John was creating by stroking her palm. "It's too soon. I need to have closure on Neil and put all this behind me."

"But you're looking at a man who's falling in love. And I know you feel the same way." He stepped closer to her, entangled his free hand in her hair and brought his lips to hers.

She started to pull away but the demanding passion of his mouth brought her back and she melted into him.

"Dammit, I wish I didn't have to go," he murmured into her hair. "Tomorrow night, after the cocktail cruise. Promise me I can spend time with you then."

"I don't know." Kathryn sighed, then gave in to another kiss as his lips hungrily sought hers.

He groaned when his cell phone rang with a Justin Bieber tune.

Breathing heavily, he answered his phone. "Hello Trieste."

"Daddy, have you kissed her yet?" Kathryn could hear the girl's high-pitched voice asking.

"I'm standing at the elevator waiting to come down," he answered. "Can't you entertain yourself for two more minutes?"

"You didn't answer my question, Dad!"

"Polite young ladies should know better than to ask questions like that. I'll see you in a minute, Trieste."

He put his phone away and pulled her close again. "Now where were we?"

"Heading out the door to catch the elevator," she answered, ducking out of his arms. "You can't make your daughter wait any longer."

Catching her hand, he held it tightly while walking to her door. "I'll pick you up at four o'clock tomorrow, all right?"

"Sounds good," Kathryn replied with a husky voice, unable to keep her hands from trembling.

She closed the door behind him and leaned against the wall, her knees weak, ready to give out.

Get a grip, Kathryn. It's not like you've never been kissed before. Yeah, but it's been years since Neil's kissed or held you like that.

She gave herself a few moments to relive the passionate kiss before wobbling to the pile of mail stacked on the kitchen island. She separated it into organized piles, discarding junk mail, advertisements and catalogs. After opening utility bills first, she quickly wrote checks to mail out once her account was replenished and placed the receipts in a folder to file later. She fingered through Neil's mail, curious about the number of credit card statements. She was certain they only had two Visa credit cards with no balances, but there seemed to be three additional statements. She ripped into the American Express envelope first and was stunned to see it was a Platinum account with a balance of over eighty thousand dollars.

Blood drained from her face and she gripped the counter to keep upright. There had to be a mistake. She frantically scanned the charges. Over thirty thousand dollars for two first-class tickets to São Paulo, Brazil for passengers Kathryn and Neil Landry. Over fifteen thousand dollars spent at Louis Vuitton on luggage. Thousands upon thousands of dollars more spent at various boutiques on Rodeo Drive earlier in the month.

Blindly, she staggered to her husband's office and pulled out the file drawer where she had hidden their passports. Opening Neil's, she quickly found the official visa needed to enter Brazil. It had been obtained two weeks before. With trembling hands, she opened her passport and found the Brazilian visa, then flipped to the front page and stared at her name, Kathryn Evelyn Landry. The photo of the unknown raven-haired beauty stared back at her.

Tears finally coursed down Kathryn's cheeks. Her mind whirled, darting from scene to scene of their eleven-year marriage, wondering how she had missed the signs. Lots of men had affairs, but most never stole their wife's identity and then left her saddled with mountains of debt when running off with their mistress.

She grabbed a tissue and wiped her eyes before retrieving the American Express bill and the two other unopened credit card statements. Trying to remain calm, she examined the charges for the flight to Brazil, hoping to find the flight date. They were scheduled to depart Los Angeles International Airport on October twentieth and return November twenty-fifth. That was almost two weeks away. She'd have to call American Airlines and pray she could cancel the flights and be reimbursed. She tore into another charge statement, holding her breath. A Platinum Mastercard. Shaking, she wondered how much liability she had for the ten-thousand-dollar cash advance Neil had taken. There was also an eleven-thousand-dollar charge for a deposit at the Brazilian Ponta dos Ganchos Resort for a two-week stay at the beginning of November. Another phone call to make.

The last statement was for a Visa Black card. Had she not been heartbroken, she would have laughed when she whispered "Reasonable" after seeing the only charge was one thousand dollars for a room deposit at a hotel in São Paulo.

She was startled when the phone rang and she struggled to her feet on leaden legs. "Hello."

"Mrs. Landry, Richard Patton is here to see you."

"Thanks, Tommy. You can send him up."

Kathryn grabbed another tissue, wiped some of her streaked makeup from her face and wished she could do a touch-up, but all her makeup was at Marianne's house. She hastily opened the door just as Richard rang the bell.

"What's wrong? It looks like you've been crying."

She waved him in and tried to calm her trembling lips. "I opened Neil's mail. I don't know what to do. He had so many expensive purchases and I can't afford to pay them."

"I'm sure something can be done since there's a police investigation going on. You certainly can't be held liable for his charges."

"But you don't understand." She paused as a sob escaped. "He gave another woman my identity and they were heading to Brazil. I'm left holding the bills."

"Surely you're mistaken?"

She handed him her passport. "There's my name but someone else's photo. There's a Brazilian visa in the back and over on that table is the American Express statement for two first-class tickets to São Paulo."

Richard scratched his gray head. "Have you told Mike about this? He needs to know right away."

"N-n-no. I didn't want to tell him before because I was afraid he'd call it spousal abandonment. But now that they might have found his body, they're going to think I killed him."

"It's not going to look good, hiding this," Richard said as gently as he could. "You have to tell Mike."

"But I made it even worse." She hiccupped before continuing. "There's the money."

"What money?"

"Didn't Marianne tell you I found all the money, plus more, that Neil took from our accounts?"

"No, she failed to mention that to me." He rubbed the stubble on his cheek. "Why is it going to make it worse?"

"Because he opened the account with this woman, under my name," Kathryn whispered, "and I tried to withdraw some of it. Now there are several reasons for the police to suspect me."

Chapter Twenty-Three

"This is way beyond either of us. You have to call Mike. Maybe the woman had a jealous boyfriend or husband?"

"I don't know," she said, sniffling. "I'm going to be the most convenient suspect. Can't I wait until tomorrow or Monday to talk to Detective Williams? I need time to think about how to make sure I don't look suspicious."

"I don't know why you're being obstinate." He raised his eyebrows. "It's going to look much worse waiting to tell him."

Chewing her lip, she shrugged, reluctant to tell Richard about the accusations against Mike.

"Come on, you have to do the right thing." He pulled his black cell phone from the back pocket of his blue jeans and handed it to her. "Do you have his number?"

Sighing, she nodded, entered Mike's number from memory and heard his voice after the first ring.

"Hello, Richard," Mike answered.

"It's Kathryn. I hope I didn't catch you at a bad time?"

"Actually, I'm really glad you called. I have a huge, huge favor to ask…" His voice faded away and she could hear him answering someone in the background. "My mare looks like she's going to give premature birth."

"Oh no, I'm sorry to hear that." She shook her head at Richard when she saw him circling his index finger. "How can I help?"

"I've been here at the stable since four this morning and it doesn't look like I'm leaving anytime soon." He cleared his throat. "I hate to impose on you, but could you go to my house and pick up some insulin for me?"

"Insulin?"

"Yes, I'm diabetic. Had it my whole life. Usually I'm prepared with an extra dose, but I didn't think I'd be away from home for so long today." Mike gave a quick humorless laugh. "Doesn't help that all I've eaten today is junk food."

"Of course I can bring it to you." She was relieved she could postpone telling him about the passport and bank account for at least a while.

***

Richard eased his Shelby into the space next to Mike's red truck. Rows of squat, narrow stables lined dusty walkways and several horses had their head hanging over half-opened dutch doors. Kathryn opened the car door and grabbed the insulated bag containing insulin.

"I'll wait here for you." Richard rolled his window down and turned off the engine. "I know you don't want to tell Mike about the passport, but you've got to do it."

Horses gently nickered as she walked past, sniffing towards the sack, hoping for a treat. Horse manure and green hay scents lingered in the air while the early evening breeze felt cool against her skin. As she approached stall number ten, she began to hear loud groans and Mike's soothing murmurs. She slowly pushed the door open and dim light revealed a large, swollen mare lying on her side amidst mounds of golden straw. The horse groaned again and began thrashing her hooves.

Mike knelt at the tail end, his arm plunged elbow-deep into the glossy brown mare. "Shhhh, it's okay, Sierra. Your baby is almost here."

Another man squatted by the horse's head, holding the halter. His forehead was beaded with sweat and half-moon glasses were in jeopardy of sliding off his pudgy nose.

Kathryn was mesmerized as Mike began pulling long, thin legs covered with a white film from the mare.

"Quick, hand me those scissors." His commanding voice broke her focus. "There, on top of the vet's bag."

She stumbled across the straw and handed gleaming, stainless steel scissors to him. He quickly cut through the white sac, picked up a towel, which he wrapped around the foal's two legs, and began to gently pull once again.

Mike tore his eyes away from his horse for a brief moment and looked at her. "Perfect timing. Bet you've never seen a foal birthed before, have you?"

"No, this is definitely a first."

He pointed his chin towards the other man. "This is my vet, Jacob. Jacob, this is Kathryn."

She started to acknowledge the introduction, but was distracted by another loud groan from the mare and the appearance of the foal's slippery black head, followed quickly by the rest of his body and back legs. Mike rested the colt's body against his mother while the vet grabbed more towels and began drying the soft, silky baby off.

"He's a preemie, so we've got to keep him warm," Mike explained. "We're not out of the woods yet. So many things could still go wrong."

Instead of calming down after labor, the new mother seemed more agitated and, before Mike could stop her, she struggled to her feet, snorting. The umbilical cord snapped and red blood began gushing from both the mare and her colt, staining the trampled straw.

Kathryn jumped when Mike grabbed her arm and guided her hand towards the mare's halter. "Hold her still."

The vet handed Mike clamps, which he attached to the foal's cord while the vet did the same for the mare. While the vet sutured the mare and ascertained that the colt's cord had stopped bleeding, Mike began wrapping the baby in warm blankets.

Jacob stepped away to set up heat lamps while Mike stroked the newborn's neck and looked at Kathryn. "Would you like to name him?"

"Me? You'd let me name him?" She could barely get the words past the tight constriction in her chest.

"Sure, just as long as it's nothing too sissy."

"His mom is Sierra, right?"

"Yes."

"How about another mountain name?" She pulled her cell phone from her pocket and Googled. "How do you like Thunderbolt? It's part of the Sierra mountain range."

Mike bent over his new colt and whispered into his floppy ears, "What do you think little guy? Do you like the name?"

The foal weakly nuzzled Mike's hand. "I think he likes it! Thunderbolt it will be."

The stable door swung open and Richard popped his head in. "I was wondering what was taking so long. Congratulations, Mike!"

"Thank you, and thanks for bringing my medication." Mike struggled to his feet and tied the haltered mare to a feeding trough, away from her baby. "It's been a long day and I'm not sure when I'll make it home."

The vet knelt back down by the colt and pressed a stethoscope to the horse's chest. He glanced up at Mike and shook his head. "There's some respiratory distress. I think we'd better be ready with the resuscitator."

Mike grabbed a bright yellow zippered tote and extracted a clear plastic bell-shaped dome, clear tubing extending from the end and attached to an inflated blue bag. "Kathryn, Richard, you should probably head home."

"Isn't there anything we can help you with?" Kathryn couldn't tear her eyes away from Thunderbolt, willing him to keep breathing.

"Nothing, but pray for this little guy." Mike looked down at his dirty hands, then walked to the sink and scrubbed them vigorously with soap and water.

Before he could dry his hands, the vet began frantically fitting the plastic bell onto the colt's nose. Mike rushed to his side and began compressing the inflated bag while the vet pulled a vial and syringe from his medical bag. Jacob quickly gave the colt an injection, set a timer on his watch, then listened for heartbeats with his stethoscope. Mike paused compressing and looked at the vet, who shook his head. Furrowing his brows, Mike began the compressions again, his lips silently counting out a rhythm.

Richard put his arm around Kathryn and they stood quietly together, watching the two men fight for the life of the colt, the sound of rushing air filling the stable every few seconds. The mare stood placidly at her feeding trough munching hay, ignoring the crisis her newborn was immersed in. When the shrill beeping timer went off, the vet filled another syringe and injected Thunderbolt again. This time, when Mike paused from forcing air into the small lungs, Jacob smiled and removed the dome. Kathryn could see the small chest rising and falling on its own.

"That was a close call," Jacob said, slapping Mike on the back. "I'll call my assistant and have him come down so we can take turns monitoring tonight."

Mike rubbed his whiskered cheek, then noticed Kathryn and Richard standing next to the door. "I thought you'd already gone."

"No, we couldn't leave until we knew Thunderbolt was going to start breathing again," Kathryn said. "I'm so scared for him."

"Jacob's the best vet there is, so I have confidence he'll make it." Mike stood back up and shook Richard's hand, but looked into Kathryn's eyes. "I can't thank you enough for coming. I'd better take my med while I have the chance."

"Not a problem," Richard replied. "Marianne sent some snacks for you as well. Keep us posted on how Thunderbolt is doing and if there's anything else we can do to help."

***

Richard summoned Marianne from the darkening garden, where she was putting away her gardening tools into the shed, and updated her on Mike's horses before telling her about the passports and credit card statements. Once he completed the recital of the facts he left for a run, giving the women privacy to talk about Kathryn's anguish.

"I am so sorry, my dear." She rushed to give the younger woman a hug. "I'm shocked!"

"I'm in shock too. I just want a couple days to assimilate this before giving it to Detective Williams. I am so afraid I'll be the prime suspect. You know, the wronged wife avenging the cheating husband?"

"Uh oh." Marianne looked into Kathryn's eyes. "Why the formality? I thought it was 'Mike.'"

Kathryn turned away. "I'd rather not talk about it just yet. But my reluctance to share this information with him stems from that reason. I just need a little more time."

"Is it something John said?"

"Yes." Kathryn tried to hold back a sob. "Oh Marianne, I'm so confused right now. When I'm with John, he convinces me that Mike can't be trusted, and when I'm with Mike, he makes me question John. John says he will soon have proof that Mike is on the take."

"That's a serious accusation. I don't believe it for a minute."

"I don't want to believe it either, but what if it's true? That's why I have to stall giving him evidence. John thinks it could all be connected to Neil's disappearance and murder. And if it's true, then the detective is going to make everyone think I'm the guilty one."

"I think that's a far-fetched theory." The older woman sighed. "There's probably a very logical explanation for whatever it is John thinks is going on. I hate to say it, but I think John is most likely responding to a jealousy factor rather than actual facts."

"That entered my mind, but when he said he would be able to supply photographic proof, it made it seem real."

"We're going to have to tell Richard about this."

"All right, if you think I must." Kathryn rubbed her gritty face. "I think I'll take a shower before he gets back from his run."

"I think that's a good idea. Take your time. We can talk about this over dinner."

She gave the older woman a hug. "Thanks, Marianne."

After Kathryn took a long, hot, soothing shower, she dressed in soft white cotton drawstring beach shorts and a coral-colored tank top. Not willing to talk to Richard yet about the accusations, she took the flash stick from her purse and copied the contents to the hard drive on her laptop. She wondered about her reluctance to share the novel with either John or Mike, but then shrugged it off, too tired to even briefly analyze her feelings. After stashing the copies of the passports and charge statements deep into her suitcase, she returned the originals and flash stick to her purse, determined to lock them safely in her office.

Next she decided to call Nurse Nancy and check on her uncle.

"Hello?" Nancy's shrill voice answered curtly.

"Nancy? It's Kathryn Landry." She felt guilty that the kind-hearted woman's voice grated her nerves. "How is my uncle doing today?"

"Honey, it's like he's been given a reprieve since you visited yesterday. He's much stronger and even ate his meals without me having to nag him."

"I'm so happy to hear that! Can you let him know I called?"

"Of course. I'd let you talk to him but he just fell asleep."

"That's okay. I'm still planning on trying to get back up there next week. I'll call Monday and let you know which day I can make it."

"He'll be thrilled," Nurse Nancy replied. "Thanks for calling. It will mean so much to Edgar."

Kathryn hung up her cell phone and plugged it into the charger. She dallied in front of the mirror, examining her fading bruises, and applied Neosporin to her various cuts and scrapes, grateful that they no longer stung. Finding nothing else to occupy her time, she shoved her feet into turquoise-colored flip-flops and went to face Richard.

"We're out here on the patio." Marianne's voice echoed through the hallway.

She found the couple sitting in glowing candlelight, quiet music playing in the background. Richard looked freshly showered and comfortable in jean shorts and a t-shirt advertising a pirate bar at the river. Marianne, dressed in a casual black knit dress, looked subdued and more than a little worried.

"We're trying a new wine tonight. It's Conundrum. A blend from Caymus winery." Richard deftly poured a glass for her. "It's a little sweeter than Chardonnay but I think you'll like it."

She swirled the golden liquid in the oversized wine glass, then took a sip. "I think you've found a keeper. I like it."

"I was just telling my wife that we need to take a long weekend trip up to Napa Valley and Sonoma next spring. We haven't been for a few years and it's a nice way to discover new labels for our cellar."

"Sounds lovely. You more than deserve a vacation after putting up with me this week."

The three fell into an awkward silence, each slowly sipping on their wine. Finally Richard cleared his throat and patted his wife's hand. "Marianne has been telling me about the terrible accusations against Mike. I'm shocked, to say the least."

"I know. It was a shock to me too."

"But you must believe it to be somewhat true, which is why you're not keeping him informed?"

"I don't know. I'm so confused right now." Kathryn started wringing her hands and twisting her mother's ring before looking towards Marianne. "I know John wouldn't make something like that up out of spite or jealousy. He said that his uncle had an informant who saw Mike taking a lot of cash from one of the largest developers in Southern California. They were going to put surveillance on him and photograph the next time he accepted cash, which they thought would be sometime very soon."

Kathryn paused to take a sip of wine. "John also said that my husband was investigating a story on corruption within the precinct and city council members, and that Neil discovered Mike was on the take."

"Is John insinuating that Mike might have been involved in Neil's disappearance?" Richard asked skeptically.

"No, but he said Mike knew who killed Neil."

"That must be why all these crazy things are happening to you," Marianne squeaked. "Whoever it is must think you know something."

"I don't know anything though," she answered, massaging her temples. "Then you throw in the mystery woman stealing my identity and my husband and I get even more confused."

"Why did you think to look at your passport when you saw the statement today?" Richard asked. "Maybe Neil was planning the trip as a surprise for you."

Kathryn pursed her lips together, hoping they wouldn't notice her pink cheeks. "I, um, found the passports hidden in Neil's office when I was cleaning up the mess on Wednesday."

"And you kept that information to yourself?" Richard practically exploded. "This is important. Mike needs to know about it."

"I can't explain how devastating it is to be told that your husband or your father abandoned you, when you know that's not the case," she cried. "Detective Williams was involved in my father's investigation and even though he's apologized and gave a very convincing story of why he gave up, I can't quite trust him to not do the same thing this time with my husband. Especially now that John has come up with these allegations."

Marianne patted Kathryn's hand and tried to soothe her. "I understand, dear. I think what Richard should be trying to say is that you can't keep everything bottled up, especially something so distressing as finding out your husband is in the middle of planning to leave you for another woman. I want you to feel free to share with us, like family, and then make your decision if you need to go to the authorities. Right, Richard?"

"Yes, absolutely right," Richard said, patting Kathryn's other hand. "I'm sorry if I sounded judgmental."

"I know you mean well," she answered. "It's been so long since I've been able to trust anyone. I almost don't know how."

"We're both here for you, honey. Please remember that," Marianne said, swatting at a lone mosquito. "I'd better get some citronella candles going before we have a swarm attacking us. And it's about time to think about dinner."

"I can help you with the candles," Kathryn volunteered. "Just tell me where to find them."

"They're in the pantry, but I can show you while I start dinner. How does seared Ahi sound with coconut-scented Jasmine rice?"

"Absolutely delicious!"

She lit the citronella candles and placed them on the patio table while Marianne started the rice and Richard busied himself chopping salad ingredients after lighting the gas barbecue grill. Their doorbell rang and Kathryn hurried to answer it since she wasn't involved in the food prep. Opening the door, she came face to face with a frowning Detective Williams.

Chapter Twenty-Four

"Mike, what's wrong?" Kathryn asked with trepidation, seeing his dejected face.

"You should have checked to see who was at the door before opening it," he said, his voice hoarse. "May I come in?"

"Sure. Marianne and Richard are in the kitchen." She opened the door wider and stepped aside. "What's happened? Is Thunderbolt okay?"

"He's going to make it. The vet's assistant is there now to give me a break." Mike's scowl disappeared and the tension in his shoulders relaxed. "I wanted to share the good news with you in person."

"I am so happy for you," she answered, reaching out to hold his hand. "I know how hard you worked to save him."

He gripped her hand tighter and looked at the floor. "Today made me realize how much being able to confide in you means to me."

Just then Richard came down the hallway. "Hello, Mike, nice to see you again. Can I pour you a Scotch?"

"Thanks, Richard, but I don't think I'll be staying." He looked at Kathryn, who had abruptly pulled her hand away from his. "I wanted to let you know that Thunderbolt is doing well."

"No, please stay. At least for a while?" She put her hands into her pockets.

"I'm happy to hear about your colt. I was sure you and Jacob had a good chance of saving him." Richard gestured towards the patio. "Come sit down and I'll bring you a Scotch."

"Thanks, maybe I'll stay for a drink. Better make it a short one though; I'm pretty wiped out already."

"Will do. I'm sure Marianne has plenty of Ahi too, so unless you have other plans you can stay and eat with us."

"That's very kind of you." Mike rubbed his stubbly cheek tiredly.

No sooner had Kathryn and Mike sat down on the comfortable patio cushions, than Marianne came bustling out with a large platter of cold cuts, cheese and vegetables. "You poor dear, such a long, exhausting day. I am so happy to hear about the baby horse. How's the mama doing?"

"She started bleeding a bit, but she seems to be okay now." He grimaced. "The vet left his assistant to monitor Sierra and Thunderbolt this evening, so I know she's in good hands."

"That's good to hear. Richard said you haven't had much to eat today. You'd better have some appetizers before he brings you the Scotch. I told him to pour you a short one to start out."

"Thanks, Marianne. I appreciate it," he answered, scooping up a large piece of meat with cheese. "I didn't realize how hungry I was until I saw this."

Marianne bustled back to the kitchen just as Richard brought out an amber Scotch in a vintage Waterford crystal glass. "Here you go, buddy. I'll be in the kitchen helping Marianne, but let me know when you need a refill."

"Thanks. I think this will be more than enough."

Richard hurried back to the kitchen and they were left in awkward silence.

"Ah, Kathryn." Mike put his whiskey down and turned towards her. "One more time you've had to come to my rescue."

"I didn't do much." Kathryn looked towards the bright lights shining from Marianne's kitchen. "I'm happy I was there to see Thunderbolt's birth."

211

He reached out and brushed a strand of hair from her cheek. "It meant a lot to me that you were there and named him."

Kathryn looked down at her wine glass and listened to crickets chirping.

Mike sighed and turned back to his Scotch. "With everything going on at the stables, I forgot to ask you why you called."

"It's nothing, nothing important right now." She took a sip of wine.

"I'm getting the feeling you'd rather not have me here." Mike set his glass down and turned back to face her. "Is it because of what I said yesterday, about my feelings?"

"No, no. It's not that." She looked off into the garden, anywhere except into his blue eyes. "I'm a bit distracted, is all. Did you find out about the dental records yet?"

"No. Apparently your dentist took the entire staff to Hawaii for a week." He shook his head. "They won't be back until late Monday night."

"Oh." Kathryn twisted her cocktail napkin between her fingers.

"Is there anything else wrong?" He gently turned her head so she was forced to look at him.

"I, ah, had some upsetting news today." She finally made eye contact.

He looked closely at her eyes. "Yes, I can see you've been crying."

"Really? How can you tell?"

"Your eyes are a bit puffy and kind of red." He grinned. "Goes well with the purple-and-green shiner."

"Great, just what a woman wants to hear. Puffy red eyes," she answered with a smile, "that complements the bruising."

"You're still beautiful."

She blushed. "Thanks."

"What was your bad news about?" he gently asked.

"Nothing that I need to talk about right now. Why don't you tell me about the rest of your horses?"

He gave her a long look before plunging into a detailed story about his animals. While he was talking, Marianne and Richard brought dinner to the table and the conversation turned to the wildfires and the loss of property and animals.

"Sad, sad, sad," Marianne commiserated. "I hope they catch the arsonist who started the fire. He's caused nothing but terrible grief for so many people."

After they polished off dinner, Kathryn jumped up to clear the dishes. Richard followed close behind her to the kitchen, where they started loading the dishwasher.

"Did you have a chance to tell Mike about the passport and charge accounts?" he whispered.

"No. The poor guy doesn't need to know yet," she whispered back. "He's been through enough today."

"You've got to tell him soon. Especially about the accusations flying around."

"That would be like kicking a guy already on the carpet."

"You mean 'don't kick a man when he's down'?"

"Yeah, that's what I meant."

"That's a nice sentiment but he's going to be more hurt if he gets blindsided by this."

"Okay, I'll tell him tomorrow." She hesitated. "Or Monday at the latest."

Mike came into the kitchen. "I'm going to head back to the stables and check on Sierra and Thunderbolt before getting a hotel room. I'm dead on my feet."

"I'm glad you stopped by." Richard shook his hand. "Let us know if there's anything we can do."

"I appreciate it." Mike gently took Kathryn's elbow and pulled her towards the door. "Can you see me out?"

They walked silently to his red Dodge truck with its one wheel perched on the curb. Mike turned to her, looked down at the ground, scuffing his dusty boot back and forth. "You really haven't responded to my, uh, feelings one way or the other. I need to know where to go from here."

Before Kathryn could talk herself out of it, she flung her arms around his neck and pulled his lips to hers. His kiss was tender and sweet, the promise of passion as his arms encircled her waist, sending heat waves down to her belly.

She pulled back and looked into his surprised face. "I've wanted to do that ever since you tackled me in your front yard."

"Mmmm, I liked that," he said, lowering his lips to hers. The kiss was even sweeter than the first as he gently stroked her silky auburn hair.

All too soon, he pulled away and smiled. "I really have to go but I'm happy we have this dialog going on."

"I am too. Let me know how your horses are doing tomorrow."

"I will. I'm meeting with the contractor for my new barn in the morning. Do you think I can see you tomorrow afternoon?"

"No, I'm sorry. I already have other plans that I can't get out of."

"All right. I plan on coming by your office Monday to pick up your flash stick. How about lunch then?"

"Sounds good. I'll see you then."

He gave her another kiss then whispered into her hair as he hugged her close, "Stay safe, Kathryn."

***

She slept fitfully that night, tossing and turning, wondering if she should have kissed Mike, but glad that she did. She found his willingness to talk about feelings, and his protectiveness when it came to her safety, endearing. The accusations against him hung over her head and she wanted to believe there had to be another explanation, but John had a strong argument too.

The morning light came too soon and she stumbled out of bed and into the shower still unsure how to proceed with the detective. She shook her head when she saw dark circles under her eyes, adding shadows to the puffy eyelids and leftover bruises. She chose a golden taupe-colored silk blouse with a flared black wool skirt to wear for the cocktail party aboard the Selton yacht that evening. The blouse complemented the Chanel sunglasses John had given her and she was grateful she had them to help hide her fatigue and bruises.

She found Marianne and Richard sitting at their breakfast nook table, reading the Sunday paper, sipping coffee.

"Good morning, Kathryn." Marianne yawned. "I hope we didn't wake you."

"No, I didn't sleep all that well last night, so I've been awake since the sun came up."

"Have some coffee. There's warm quiche in the oven for you too."

Kathryn shook her head in amazement. "Richard, does she always feed you like this?"

"Yep. That's why I took up running."

"I'm going to have to tag along with you and get back in shape for the half marathon or my clothes aren't going to fit before long."

"You two are being silly." Marianne giggled. "'All things in moderation,' as my father always said."

"I like that saying. I'm going to have to remember it." Kathryn frowned. "But I still need to find time to train for the race. I'm worried I'm not going to be able to cross the finish line."

"How many miles have you worked up to?" Richard asked.

"My last long run was ten miles."

"Then no problem, you'll be able to finish," Richard answered. "You can count on adrenaline and team spirit to carry you part of the way too."

"That's what everyone keeps telling me, but I still worry."

Richard handed her a section of paper. "Bring your food and coffee over here. You can catch up on the news with us and worry about your race later. Right now the most important thing is for you to stay safe and being out on the street running would only make you an easy target."

"I know you're right, but I'm still not happy about it. I feel like I'll be letting so many little girls down if I can't complete the race."

"I know your determination to cross the finish line will make it happen, even if you have to walk part of the way," Marianne added, patting Kathryn's hand.

"Thanks, I appreciate the encouragement."

They sat in companionable silence, sipping coffee and rattling pages of newsprint. Kathryn finished eating then got up, loaded the dishwasher and wiped down the counters.

"You really don't have to do that," Marianne told her.

She turned towards her partner and placed her hands on her hips. "You have to stop treating me like a houseguest and let me contribute to helping with the workload. Like family would."

Richard chuckled. "She has a point, dear. You're always telling her that she's family."

"Can I vacuum, sweep or dust for you today?" Kathryn asked.

"Oh goodness, no!" Marianne exclaimed. "My housekeeper comes tomorrow. There are better things to do with our Sunday than housework."

"We were thinking we could all go to the office and I can work on the safety locks and alarm system," Richard interjected. "I want you to be able to go about business as usual tomorrow morning."

"Sounds like a good idea. I have some things I want to lock in my desk and I'm sure there's a huge pile of mail to go through."

"I'll go to Home Depot first and pick up some supplies for the project. Can you girls be ready to leave in about an hour?"

"Sure," they replied in unison.

"I need to water my garden but that shouldn't take me long," Marianne said.

"While you do that, I should call my uncle and see how he is today."

Kathryn went to her room and unplugged her charged phone. She saw a voicemail waiting for her.

"Hey, it's John. Just thinking about you and wondering if you wanted to spend the day with me since Trieste went to her mother's this morning. Call me."

She started calling John, then disconnected before the call when through, unsure what to say to him. After sharing sweet kisses with Mike, she didn't know how to proceed with either man.

Instead she called her uncle's house and was rewarded when Nurse Nancy said he was up to taking her phone call.

"Hello, Uncle Edgar, this is Kathryn."

His voice was shaky but sounded stronger than when she had seen him.

"Hello, Niece. I was afraid you were angry and would never talk to me again."

"No, I'm not angry with you."

"I'm glad to hear it. It's kept me worrying." He coughed and gasped for air. "I shouldn't have told you those stories. It only brought more pain. I'm sorry for that."

"Please don't worry anymore. Whether or not I believe those stories are true doesn't matter. I'm glad you shared with me and gave me a glimpse into my family."

"Take care of yourself, little Kathryn," he said, his voice getting tired and trailing off.

"Goodbye. I'll try to visit you next week."

As soon as she disconnected the call, another call came in.

"Kathryn, it's Mike." His voice sounded haggard. "I hope I didn't call too early."

"No, it's fine. I was up early today. Is everything okay?"

"I've been up since three this morning. My mare took a turn for the worse and started hemorrhaging."

"Oh no! Is she going to be all right?"

"Jacob thinks so but it was touch and go for quite a while."

"Is there anything I can do?"

"No, but it means a lot to me that you asked. I'm going back to my hotel room to get some shut-eye." He tried to stifle a yawn.

"Get some rest and I'll see you tomorrow."

After saying goodbye she disconnected and another call came through. Shaking her head, she wondered if her cell battery was going to survive the barrage of calls.

"Good morning. Did I wake you?" John said, a boyish bounce in his voice.

"No, I've been up for a while."

"Oh. You didn't answer my call."

"I just got your voicemail and you called before I could call you back."

"How about I come pick you up? We can come back to my house for some R and R." He whispered into the phone, "I have the Jacuzzi heated and ready

217

to go."

"John…" She sighed and started pacing her room, trying to find the words to explain her reluctance. "Please don't be upset with me but this is moving too fast. You say you understand and that you'll give me time to come to terms with Neil's disappearance. But in the end you seduce me into starting something that I'm not ready for."

There was nothing but silence from the phone.

"Please don't be mad at me. I enjoy being with you. Spending time with you and Trieste yesterday was one of the best days I've had in a very long time."

"I'm not mad at you. Just disappointed."

"I'm sorry."

"Yeah, but not as sorry as I am." He blew out a long breath. "Would you rather skip going with me to the cocktail party?"

"No, not at all. Unless you'd rather I not go."

"Nope, I definitely would like you there. Shall I pick you up at four o'clock this afternoon?"

"Yes, that sounds good. I'll see you then."

As soon as she disconnected, she heard Richard returning from Home Depot.

"Are you girls ready to get going?" he hollered down the hallway.

Kathryn grabbed her purse and cell phone and met them at the door. "I'm ready."

When they arrived at the office, Marianne disarmed the security alarm and checked for voicemails while Richard unloaded supplies from their Honda Pilot. Kathryn opened her office door and stopped short. File cabinets were hanging open, manila folders were dumped on the carpet and piles of white paper lay in haphazard heaps around her desk.

Chapter Twenty-Five

"No, no, no!" Kathryn shrieked. "This has to end!"

"What's wrong?" Marianne dashed to the recently opened door, saw the mess and screamed. "Good lord, what happened here? I should call the police!"

"No, I doubt there's anything missing."

"How can you tell with this mess?"

"What happened?" Richard said, breathing heavily right behind them.

Both women jumped at the sound of his voice and, as they turned to look at him, they screamed in unison. A gun was held tightly in his hand, ready for action.

"What's wrong? Why are you screaming?" Richard asked while his eyes darted around the office.

"I didn't know you brought a gun." Marianne nervously licked her lips. "You didn't have to sneak up on us either."

"I didn't sneak up on you. I ran in as fast as I could when I heard you scream." He stepped into Kathryn's office and surveyed the scattered files.

219

"Looks like my effort to safeguard your office came a little too late. We'd better call the police."

"I don't think there's anything missing. I have a very strong suspicion that what they were after has been in my purse all along." Kathryn pursed her lips.

"What would that be?" Richard asked.

"My flash stick." She paced around the piles of papers in her office. "And I only told two people that my flash stick was in my office desk. John and Mike."

Marianne plopped down onto the soft sofa. "I still think we should call the police."

"I don't think that will be necessary," Kathryn argued. "Especially if nothing is missing."

"But they might be able to pick up some prints to identify who did this," Richard said, pulling his cell phone out of his pocket.

"They won't find any. Whoever did this is probably the same person who broke into my apartment and took Neil's computer. There wasn't a trace of fingerprints from anyone who didn't belong there."

Except for John. I wonder if Trieste really was with him all night or if her mother picked her up yesterday instead of this morning like he said.

Richard gestured towards the file-strewn floor. "I'd feel better if you at least called Mike and let him decide what to do about this mess."

"I hate to bother him. He's exhausted after being up practically all night and day with his horse."

Or was he? Should I call the stable and verify that he was there last night?

"It's your decision," Richard conceded. "But I would suggest you thoroughly check everything to make sure nothing is missing. And you too, Marianne. Check your drawers, petty cash, credit cards and client files."

"Whoever did this was a professional. The alarm was still on when we came in, wasn't it?" Kathryn asked.

"Yes, it was," Marianne agreed. "Somehow they disarmed it and then reset it. Otherwise the alarm company would have called security and then called us."

"Marianne, call the alarm company and see if they can tell us when it was disarmed last. I guess this could have happened Friday night just as easily as last night. I'll start sifting through the papers in my office."

Richard appeared deep in thought until Marianne poked him in his ribs. "Don't you think you should get to work beefing up our security here?"

"That's what I was thinking about. I'm not sure my efforts are going to do much good. I think the only thing I can do is stand guard at the office with you gals until this gets resolved."

"No, that's asking too much of you," Kathryn protested.

"Now that Marianne is your partner, you'll probably need to hire a new assistant? I'm that guy. Just call me Guy Friday."

"Huh?" Kathryn looked puzzled.

"You're dating yourself, Richard," Marianne laughed. "It's Girl Friday. It's an old-fashioned term describing an assistant who does anything and everything for her boss. I think I can handle you being my Guy Friday."

"*His Girl Friday* was a great movie too," Richard said, poking Marianne back. "Cary Grant. They don't make actors like that anymore."

Kathryn looked from Marianne to Richard, then back to Marianne, before throwing her hands up in the air. "I think I'm going to lose this argument, so I'll gracefully give in. Marianne, as my new partner you can negotiate a salary with our new Guy Friday while I clean up my office."

The rest of the morning flew by as Kathryn straightened her office, re-filed the strewn papers and went through the mail. Although she tried to concentrate on the job at hand, she jumped at every little noise and felt like hidden eyes were peering at her. She wondered if she'd ever feel safe in her home or her office again.

She was impressed how thoroughly Marianne had taken care of all the pressing matters and there wasn't much that needed her attention. Richard interrupted her once, to let her know that the alarm company verified that the alarm had been disarmed the night before, between the hours of two and four a.m. He also complained, with a grin, that the "new boss" was working him to death, trying to train him so that he'd be up to speed by Monday morning.

Once she was satisfied with her office being clean and organized again, she stuck her head out her door. "Marianne, could you... Oh, I mean, Richard, could you please find me the phone number for OC Stables in San Juan Capistrano?"

He raised his eyebrows. "Sure, but do you think it's really necessary?"

"I'd feel better doing what little I can to at least rule out the possibility. After all, there were only two people I told where I had the flash stick."

"But it wasn't here. You lied to both John and Mike?"

"I guess that's what I did." Kathryn twisted her mother's ring, her cheeks flaming. "They both wanted Neil's novel for whatever reason, but I was, um, embarrassed by it. Even though Neil doesn't deserve to be shielded from criticism, I guess I kind of wanted to protect him. People are going to think he's a pervert."

"It can't be that bad."

"I'm not a prude but this was more than I could stomach. I don't want anyone else reading it."

Richard sighed. "Okay, I'll get the phone number but let's go eat lunch first."

"Sounds good to me," Marianne said. "How about In-N-Out Burgers?"

"I haven't had one of those in years." Kathryn's mouth watered and she swallowed noisily. "This is going to be a treat!"

After a satisfying lunch of double doubles, french fries and vanilla milkshakes, they drove back to the Patton residence. Kathryn took the stable phone number from Richard.

"You've done enough for me already," she insisted. "I feel terrible wasting your Sunday working. Go relax with your wife and enjoy the afternoon."

"Marianne's idea of relaxing is weeding her flower garden," he grumbled. "I was looking forward to doing some detective work even though I don't think it's necessary."

Kathryn laughed. "Making phone calls isn't detective work. It's boring work."

She went to her room and called the number Richard had found. The phone was answered by a cranky old man who sounded like he'd forgotten to put his dentures in that morning. He informed her that he was not a horse stable and he was sick and tired of getting their phone calls. Kathryn called information and was given the exact same number that Richard had given her. No wonder the old man was cranky.

When the doorbell rang, Kathryn jumped when she saw it was four o'clock already. Hastily checking her reflection in the mirror, she decided there wasn't much more she could do to fix the bruises, so she jammed the Chanel sunglasses onto her face and hurried out to open the door for John.

"Hello." His voice was sultry and he looked as if he'd just stepped from a cover of a men's fashion magazine.

"Come in. I need to let Marianne know I'm leaving. I think they're out back gardening."

John followed close behind her and Kathryn's knees went weak when she smelled his familiar masculine scent and remembered the last time he had held her close. She stumbled as she crossed the threshold to the patio and John quickly grabbed her arm to steady her.

He let his fingers linger on her arm as he whispered into her ear. "Are you okay? You seem distracted."

"I'm fine. Just a klutz as usual."

"John, nice to see you again!" Richard boomed across the lawn.

"I wanted to let you know we're going now," Kathryn said. "We'll be back around seven or eight o'clock."

Richard removed his gardening glove to shake John's hand. "Make sure Kathryn tells you about our excitement this morning."

"What happened this time?" John asked incredulously.

"I'll tell you on the way to the party," she answered. "I'd hate for you to be late."

"Okay, but I want to hear all the details. And I do mean all."

John drove his 911 Turbo Porsche more slowly than usual as Kathryn told him about her office being broken into.

"What did they take?" he asked, keeping his eyes on the road.

"Nothing. That's the strange thing. Marianne's computer was still there, as well as our petty cash box and company credit cards."

"What about your flash stick? Did they find that?"

"No, I had it well hidden. Do you think that's what they could have been after?" she coyly asked.

"Kathryn, you're playing games that you're no good at. Of course that's what they were after." He gave her a hard look as they came to a red stoplight. "Aside from me, who else knew you had it at the office? Oh, never mind, I know the answer. Williams."

"I don't think he did it. I'm checking into his alibi though, to be sure."

The light turned green and John revved the engine and gritted his teeth. "And why would you know what his alibi is for the middle of the night?"

"He, uh, called this morning to let us know about his horse."

"What?"

Kathryn sighed. "His horse—mare—gave premature birth and there were complications. He was quite upset."

"I'm sure."

"He mentioned he had been at the stables with the mare from three o'clock in the morning on. The alarm at my office was disarmed from two to four."

"How convenient. Offer an alibi before anyone even thinks to start asking."

"I'm sure it's not like that. Besides, why would he make up such a sad story about his horse?"

"To get the sympathy vote, and it sounds like he's reeled you in."

"Give the guy a break. He's had some unlucky things happen to him the last few days."

John didn't answer and Kathryn could see the muscles in his jaws clenched.

"Can we please not argue about this?"

Another stoplight turned red and he turned to her. "Next I'll be finding out that you suspect I broke into your office. Do you need to talk to Trieste about my alibi?"

"No, I wouldn't think that. I trust you."

"You're a terrible liar." He laughed suddenly. "Actually, I think having you suspect me is pretty funny."

"You do?"

"I'll have Trieste call you tomorrow after school and verify that, yes, she spent the night at my house last night. Will that work?"

"It won't be necessary. I really didn't think you did it."

Chapter Twenty-Six

He pulled into the parking lot at the Balboa Bay Club and Resort and handed his car keys to the valet attendant. Leading the way down to the marina, he told her that in addition to the resort hotel, the club leased apartments and slips at the marina and had been operating since 1948. His uncle had leased his apartment for entertaining clients for over thirty years and had berthed a boat for as many years. John grew animated telling her about spending time on the ocean while growing up.

Kathryn took in the dizzying array of colorful boats gently swaying on sparkling water directly behind the Mediterranean-style hotel with its stately arches. Some were small boats, holding but a few passengers, while others seemed to have more square footage than an average house. They walked up the gangway and boarded a ninety-foot yacht, where they were met by a uniformed waiter holding a tray of crystal flutes filled with bubbly golden champagne.

John handed her a glass and clinked it with his. "Cheers. Thanks for coming with me."

No sooner had they taken a sip than Gerald Selton came rushing up to them, larger than life. He had on navy blue European-cut trousers with a white silk shirt unbuttoned far enough for Kathryn to see a heavy gold chain lying against his gray-haired chest.

"Welcome to my domain, dear Kathryn," he gushed while clasping her hand to his lips. "I'm so delighted you could join us this evening."

"The pleasure is mine, Senator Selton."

"Please, I must insist you call me Gerald."

"Thank you, Gerald," she answered. "You have a gorgeous yacht."

He waved his hand dismissively. "It does its job. Gets me where I need to be and entertains my guests."

"I've heard all boats have names. Does yours?"

"Of course, my dear. She's *Il Gioco*."

Kathryn gave John a puzzled look.

"It means 'The Game' in Italian," Gerald explained. "Come, meet my other guests and have some hors d'oeuvres. I'll tell the captain to cast off before joining you."

Gerald walked towards the staircase that led to the bridge, then turned around. "Make sure John gives you the grand tour before the evening is over."

She followed John down a passageway lined with thick, plush, ivory wool carpet. Golden walnut paneled the walls and subdued bronze sconces were spaced evenly, lighting their way. Entering the dining room, Kathryn was surprised at the open, airy feel. A large round table was the central focal point, while a white marble wet bar divided the room from a gleaming stainless steel galley and cozy salon. Spacious windows on either side of the table looked out onto the bay.

The grand table held a carved ice swan and was piled high with delicacies from the sea. Oysters on the half shell, sashimi, calamari, jumbo shrimp and abalone. Other platters held mountains of a rainbow assortment of fresh and grilled vegetables and tropical fruit. There were enough artisanal cheese selections to make a gourmet deli jealous. Baskets brimmed with crackers, toast points and bruschetta. Her eyes lingered on the dark chocolate mousse, crème brûlée and chocolate-covered strawberries. An attentive uniform-clad waiter hovered at their elbows, waiting to refill their flutes with Cristal Champagne.

As Kathryn filled a plate with shrimp and vegetables, she glanced around at the small groups mingling over food and drink. There seemed to be about eighteen people total, half men and half women. She didn't recognize anyone.

"Don't worry, they're not all boring," John whispered behind her. "I'll introduce you to the fun ones as soon as we get something to eat."

He led her to a group of three men who were standing next to one of the windows. All of a sudden Kathryn felt light-headed and grabbed John's arm. He chuckled. "They've got the yacht underway. You'll be fine as soon as the captain straightens it up."

She looked out the window and saw that they were moving. "I hope you're right. Did I mention I get motion sick?"

"We're staying in the harbor so there's nothing to worry about."

He quickly introduced her to the men. Two were San Diego city councilmen and the other an anchorman for a Los Angeles news broadcast.

"Landry… Landry… Landry…" Andrew, the anchorman, said while snapping his fingers. "Are you any relation to Neil Landry?"

"I'm his wife."

Andrew gave John a quick look. "I loved the sports column he used to write for the *Register*. That guy is so humorous. I was sorry when they stopped the column."

"Thank you. I know he was disappointed when they discontinued it as well."

"What's your husband up to these days?"

John smothered a cough.

"Freelancing. Mostly working on whatever sounds interesting to him at the moment."

"Let me give you my business card. Have him call me. I think I have something that he might be interested in sinking his teeth into."

"Thank you," she answered, tucking the card into her Chanel handbag. "I'll be sure to pass it on."

John pulled Kathryn's elbow. "If you'll excuse us, my uncle insisted I give Mrs. Landry the grand tour."

John handed their plates and crystal flutes to the waiting attendant before leading her down another hallway, their footsteps muffled by the thick carpet. He pulled her into the master stateroom and closed the door, then turned to face her.

"I take back everything I said earlier. You are one smooth lady." He grinned and gathered her into his arms and nuzzling her ear. "I had no idea you could lie so convincingly. I might have to be worried."

She playfully pushed him away. "I'm waiting for the grand tour. Somehow I don't think this is what your uncle had in mind."

"All tours end up here so I thought we could skip the boring stuff."

"Honestly, I do want to see where they drive the boat."

He laughed and pulled her back into his arms. "We'll see that soon enough, but for now I want to take advantage of some private time alone with you."

"This is hardly private, John. There's a lot of people on the boat with us."

He locked the stateroom door. "It's private now. No one is going to interrupt us this time." He wrapped his arms tight around her and kissed her eyelids, then her earlobe, along her jawline, then crushed his lips against hers.

Kathryn pushed him away.

A loud knock made them both jump and Kathryn stepped farther away from John.

"Mr. Selton? Your uncle would like to see you on the bridge right away," a timid male voice said.

John cleared his throat. "Tell him I'll be there in a minute."

When they could no longer hear the man's footsteps, John reached for her hand. "Now where were we?"

"I'm so sorry. I'm really not ready for this." Kathryn lowered her eyes and her cheeks blazed. "There's so many reasons why this is a bad idea right now. Besides, your uncle is waiting for you."

He clenched his jaw, then leaned over to stroke her cheek. "I'm not giving up, Kathryn. One of these days we'll be together. You can't deny what we feel."

After Kathryn had reapplied her lipstick, they walked back down the hallway, John pointing to various rooms. "Here's stateroom number one, here's stateroom number two, yadda, yadda, yadda."

"The yacht doesn't look that big from the outside. It's amazing how much room there is and it's all so beautifully appointed."

They climbed the steps up to the bridge, where they found Gerald talking to the captain.

"Come in, come in. Let me introduce you to Captain Shelby. He's been with me for twenty years now? But we've known each other since our tour in 'Nam."

"Yes sir," the captain answered. He removed his white captain's hat and ran his hand through thin black hair, long enough to comb over his bald spot. His deep black eyes twinkled. "And this is the best ship you've ever had me command."

"It is impressive," Kathryn agreed. "Do you mind if I take a closer look at how you maneuver this?"

"I'd be happy to show you." Captain Shelby pointed at the electronic-packed console, which sat beneath windows that gave a bird's eye view of the bay. "It's all computerized like an airplane. Here's the screen that shows depth and this one shows power output on each of the engines."

Kathryn looked down at the captain's dark, sun wrinkled hand pointing at the console and saw a white outline of where a ring had recently been worn. The face of the ring had been large and square. Almost identical to the shape of the onyx skull-and-crossbones ring she had seen on the freeway in Los Angeles.

Kathryn felt her face flush then drain of all color. Her head buzzed and her knees started to buckle.

John caught her before she fell. "What's wrong? You looked like you were going to pass out."

Gerald barked out some commands and helped John ease her onto a soft sofa. A waiter appeared with a glass of ice water, a small bottle of ginger ale and a plate holding black and green olives along with crackers.

"I got dizzy for a second, is all. I think I'm feeling better. I guess I'm more susceptible to motion sickness than I thought."

"Eat a couple olives and take a sip of ginger ale," Gerald ordered.

"Olives? Thanks, but I'm not a huge fan."

"Try to eat a couple anyway. They help combat queasy stomachs from motion sickness."

Kathryn decided to let them think she was motion sick and chose a green olive. She tentatively bit into it, grimacing at the briny bitter taste. Quickly swallowing, she rinsed down the lingering saltiness with ginger ale. "I'm fine now. I'm sorry I worried you."

"John, take her downstairs and sit on the stern patio. Some fresh air will help." Gerald patted her hand. "The higher you are above the water, the more movement you'll feel. Do you want to try to finish our harbor cruise or should we head back to the dock?"

"I don't want to disrupt everyone's evening. I'm feeling much better so please don't worry about me."

John took a firm hold of her arm and helped her down the stairs. Kathryn thought she heard the captain say "landlubber" and Gerald laughing before he closed the door to the bridge.

John settled her into an overstuffed club chair and whispered instructions to the attendant who had followed them there. Once again the waiter quickly produced a bottle of ginger ale and a plate filled with olives and crackers. The young man placed the drink and food on a glass-topped cocktail table before retreating back to the party.

"I am so embarrassed," she whispered, rubbing her face.

"Nonsense. You're not the first person on board this ship to ever get seasick."

"Yeah, but I'm probably the only person to do so after getting only ten yards away from the dock."

"Well, I can't argue with you there." John chuckled. "If it makes you feel better, we were at least a hundred yards from the dock."

She groaned. "Thanks, I feel so much better now."

"Stop worrying about it. We can sit out here and enjoy a gorgeous sunset. No one is going to care one way or another."

She twisted in her seat and looked across the bay to the west. The sun was rosy red, slowly lowering itself behind the houses lining the far shore. Golden yellows and light purples danced at the edge of the sky while a formation of pelicans spread their wings against the rays of the dying sunlight. Cool ocean breezes blew across them, ruffling Kathryn's hair.

"It is beautiful."

"And so are you," he murmured, taking her hand and stroking her palm.

She abruptly pulled her hand back when she heard the glass sliding door open and footsteps coming onto the deck.

"Kathryn, my dear. How are you feeling?" Gerald sat down next to her. "Your color is much better."

"I'm fine. Thank you for asking."

"I was just talking to one of my other guests about astrology and palm reading and how she thinks it shapes our personalities and destinies. It made me curious about you." Gerald leaned over, picked up her hand and opened her palm. "See, your life line is very long. Wait, I think I've got it confused with the love line. Maybe I should have paid more attention to her."

Kathryn laughed and took her hand back. "I really don't know about any of that stuff. I'd rather think I was in charge of my destiny."

"Hmmm, you must be a Leo."

"Yes, how did you know?"

"Just a lucky guess, but it fits, especially with the color of your hair," Gerald answered with a smile. "When's your birthday?"

"August first. I never liked having a summer birthday because I missed out on class parties in school."

"Do you mind if I ask how old you are?"

"Uncle, really, that's too personal," John barked. "I'm sorry Kathryn, he's usually not so nosy."

"Settle down, John. I'm merely curious, given the subject the young lady inside told me she was working on. She is trying to see how our zodiac signs relate to the Chinese zodiac signs and if there's a correlation between the two and personality development. As we know, Westerners are given a sign according to their birth month, more or less. Chinese are given a sign according to the year they were born."

"I just turned thirty-four," Kathryn volunteered.

"You don't look a day over twenty-four," the former senator said with a silky voice. "Let's see, that would make you a… hmmmm… I guess that would make you an Ox."

"An Ox. That sounds kind of like an insult." Kathryn laughed. "Not that I think you're trying to insult me."

"Actually, an Ox and a Leo are very similar. Both are strong, leader types." Gerald cocked his head at John. "Maybe I should get her into politics. What do you think?"

"I think you should go have a cocktail and entertain the rest of your guests with your crazy hypothesis," John said, pointing at the dining room. "While you're at it, could you have the waiter bring me a vodka on the rocks?"

"You're right, I need to go schmooze with the movers and shakers for a while. What vodka do you want?"

"I saw you had Crystal Head. I'll take that."

"You got it." Gerald picked Kathryn's hand back up and lightly kissed it. "As always, Mrs. Landry, it was a pleasure chatting with you."

"Crystal Head? I've never heard of it," Kathryn said after Gerald left.

"Dan Aykroyd, the actor, founded it. The vodka is sold in glass skulls. It's pretty cool looking."

She shivered. "Ugh, I don't care for skulls."

"I'm sure the waiter won't bring the bottle so you don't have to see it."

After being served his drink, John talked about his family and how his Uncle Gerald had practically raised him after his father had been killed in a car racing accident in Italy when John was just six years old. His older sister lived in San Francisco, was divorced and raising two teenage boys on her own, so his mother spent most of her time helping his sister out.

"So Trieste doesn't see much of her grandmother?" Kathryn asked.

"No, but it's not my mother's fault. My ex hasn't let Trieste stay with me much in the past." He rubbed his cheek thoughtfully. "It's only been the last few months that I've seen my daughter on a somewhat consistent basis. There must be a boyfriend in the picture."

The glass door slid open again and high heels clicked on the teak deck.

"John, you've neglected to introduce your guest to us," chided a brassy blonde woman of indeterminate age with obvious plastic work.

"Brenda and Becca, this is Kathryn Landry. Kathryn, this is Brenda and Becca Pirraney."

Kathryn rose to shake hands with the women and saw they were identical twins. "Nice to meet you both."

Brenda pointed to the ginger ale and crackers. "Ah, I see why you're sitting out here. Our mother gets seasick just taking a bath."

"I'm much better now but I'm not sure about going back inside," Kathryn admitted.

"It's a lovely evening," Becca piped up. She started to say something else, but then grabbed her sister's arm and pulled her towards the door. "We just wanted to say hello before getting another glass of that divine champagne. Right, Brenda?"

"Uh, right. Nice to meet you, Kathryn."

As soon as she heard the sliding door slam shut, Kathryn looked at John and raised an eyebrow. "That was a little awkward. I wonder why they rushed off like that."

"I gave them the evil eye."

"You didn't. Did you?"

"I cannot confirm or deny." He brushed a lock of hair from his forehead before pointing to the deck. "This isn't the first time I've had to remind them to stay off the teak. Their stiletto heels have caused extensive damage before but they insist on wearing them anyway. Besides, they know I don't like them."

"Why not? They seem nice, kind of vapid, but nice."

"Don't let their act fool you. They're piranhas waiting to tear into anyone or anything that crosses their path."

Over the next hour and a half, the yacht slowly circled the bay. In between guests coming out to chat with them, Kathryn told John about finding the airline tickets to Brazil and the other woman stealing her identity. She showed him the copy of the passport that she had in her purse and he asked to keep it.

"I'll run this through my computer and see if I can come up with an identity," he promised. "I'll make sure you're not liable for any of the charges as well."

Their conversation moved on to other things and John told her more about the adventures he'd had sailing with his uncle as a young boy. By the time they docked and said their goodbyes Kathryn had all but forgotten her uneasiness over the captain's ring tan, convincing herself that her imagination was triggered by motion sickness.

After retrieving his car from the valet, John headed south on the Pacific Coast Highway with a sexy saxophonist playing jazz on his satellite radio. "Can I convince you to have a nightcap at my house?"

"John, that's not a good idea."

"Pleeeze?" he asked, imitating his daughter's voice.

She laughed. "As hard as it is to say no, that has to be my answer."

"Are you sure? What can I say to change your mind?"

Kathryn crossed her arms. "Why do we have to keep having this same conversation every time I see you? I'm tired of telling you that while I enjoy your company and care about you, I'm not ready to take it further than that."

"You're right. I'm sorry," he grumbled. "You're just so damn beautiful I can't help myself."

"Ha, that's almost funny. Black eye and all."

"It wasn't meant to be funny. It just gives you... character."

They rode the rest of the way to Marianne's house in silence. When they turned onto her street, John muttered, "Oh hell. That guy's gotta get a life."

"What are you talking about?" Kathryn asked.

"Williams. That's his truck, isn't it?"

Chapter Twenty-Seven

Kathryn looked up and saw that Mike's red truck was parked in front of Neil's red BMW.

"Great, just great," John said vehemently as he pulled in behind the car. "I think you need to reconsider that nightcap."

"I can't do that. I need to go in and see what's going on." Kathryn nervously bit her lower lip. "Richard must have told him about the break in or maybe there's news about the body."

"I don't like it one bit," he growled. "I thought you were going to avoid the dee-teck-tive."

"Kind of hard to do when he shows up at the house I'm living at, especially since he's still in charge of the investigation." She paused, looking at the porch light shining in the dark night. "Have you heard anything from your informant about photographic proof yet?"

"No, but I think Gerald was supposed to be meeting with the informant tonight." John gently touched her cheek, pulling her back towards him to look into his liquid chocolate eyes. "He wanted me in on the meeting but I told him

I had more important plans this evening."

She cleared her throat. "I guess you can go to the meeting now, right?"

"Naw, I'd rather get the condensed version tomorrow morning."

She kissed his cheek before opening the car door. "Thanks for the evening, John. I really did enjoy myself."

"That's all I get? A peck on the cheek?"

"For now," she answered.

He grumbled. "Promises, promises."

She waited for him to drive off before entering Marianne's house. She heard low voices coming from the patio and, following the sound, found Richard and Mike smoking cigars and drinking Scotch. As soon as Richard saw Kathryn approaching, he stubbed out his cigar and hurried into the house without saying a word to her.

Mike's face was rigid with controlled fury. "Did you have a nice evening with the Seltons?"

"It was entertaining," she answered cautiously. "You seem very upset. Did I do something wrong?"

"Let's see, where shall I start? Maybe withholding evidence? Does that ring a bell?"

Kathryn looked towards the house. "I guess Richard's been talking to you."

"Don't blame him. I stopped by for a reason having nothing to do with the case," he snarled. "Using my deductive detective powers I could tell something was bothering him, and using my uncanny ability to interrogate people I was able to get the truth from him. Something I'll be damned I haven't been able to get from you."

A tear trickled down Kathryn's cheek. "I'm sorry, I've been so confused. I don't even know which way is up or down anymore. Or who to trust."

Mike threw his hands up in the air. "Don't start the tears. It's not going to work with me this time." Kathryn sniffled and he handed her a cocktail napkin before continuing. "Yes, let's talk about trust. You heard I was on the take. From Selton, right?"

She nodded.

"So you decided to believe him instead of finding out my side of the story." His voice raised an octave. "I am a damn good detective and your case isn't my only one. Did it ever cross your mind that maybe, just maybe, I was operating a sting? That I'm for law, order and justice? And let's not forget the American Way! And you kissed me. What the hell did that mean anyway? You couldn't trust me, but you could kiss me?"

Kathryn was quietly crying into the palms of her hands. The cocktail napkin had disintegrated to bits.

"Aw, hell," he swore, getting up and stomping to the house. Moments later he returned with a box of Kleenex, which he slapped down in front of her.

She grabbed a handful and wiped her eyes. "I'm sorry. I am so, so sorry, Mike." She grabbed another handful and repeated the process. "John made it sound so convincing, especially after I saw your ranch and home."

"It's nobody's business how I can afford my ranch and horses, but to set the record straight, I have a sizeable trust fund from my grandmother." He sat quietly for a moment, then awkwardly patted her knee. "I needed to blow off some steam and you set yourself up perfectly for taking it. I still don't understand how you could make such irrational choices though."

"You'd think I was blonde under this red hair, huh?" She tried to laugh, but choked.

He gave her a sharp look. "This isn't a joking matter."

"I know. I'm just nervous."

"I need to ask you some questions and I need God's honest truth, okay?"

"Okay."

"Can you tell me verbatim what Selton said about me being on the take?"

"I don't know about verbatim but I can be pretty accurate."

"Before you start, I need to record our conversation. And please, please stick with answering only the questions I give you." He pulled out his cell phone, launched a recording app and muttered, "Last thing I need is for my captain to find out I kissed you."

He started out by having her identifying herself. Then he led her through her conversation with John Selton about the accusations, the money and the informer. Next he asked her to identify, if she could, people who had been on the yacht that evening. When he asked if she had anything else to add about the subject matter, she answered that Gerald Selton was supposed to be meeting with the informant that night.

Mike turned off his phone. "You did good. This is exactly what we were looking for. I need to get to the office with it right away."

"I'm glad I could help."

"Don't start thinking I'm finished with our conversation yet, because I'm not. Not by a long shot. We have a lot of withholding evidence issues to discuss, among other things," he growled. "I'll see myself out."

He strode to the door. "And Kathryn, stay away from Selton. He's in on this."

Before she could say anything, he was gone. She sat in the semi-darkness trying to stop the jumble of thoughts swirling around her head, wondering how everything in her life had turned into shambles. She finally stood up and started clearing the crystal tumblers, taking them to the kitchen to wash. Marianne and Richard joined her there.

"I'm sorry I put you in an awkward position," Kathryn began.

"No need to apologize, dear." Marianne gave her a hug. "It'll work itself out, you'll see. Mike won't stay mad long."

"We should tell you the reason he stopped by here in the first place," Richard said, pacing the kitchen. "The vet did a toxicology report on Mike's mare and got back the results late this afternoon. Someone shot her full of drugs to make her miscarry. Thunderbolt is very fortunate to have survived, although he may have lingering health issues."

Marianne jumped in when Richard paused for a breath. "That's why he was so angry. Not because he was mad at you, but furious because someone tried killing his horses and tried to burn down his house."

"Well, I think he's pretty mad at me too."

"I'm having a real hard time trying not to say, 'I told you so,'" Richard said quietly.

"I deserve it, so say it if it'll make you feel better."

He gave her a hug and a kiss on her forehead. "Get some sleep, kiddo. I believe my wife when she says it'll work itself out."

Kathryn ended up tossing and turning half the night and finally, around dawn, fell into an exhausted slumber. Her ringing cell phone pulled her reluctantly from the depths of a deep sleep.

"Hello," she answered with a croaky voice.

"Kathryn? It's John. Sorry I woke you."

"What time is it?"

"Seven o'clock. I thought you were going to the office this morning."

"I am, just not this early. What's up?"

"I think I found out the identity of the woman using your passport."

"What? Where?" Kathryn bolted from her bed.

"Meet me at the Starbucks across from Fashion Island. Can you be there at nine o'clock?"

"Yes. Absolutely."

"Okay, I'll see you then."

She sped through her shower, barely bothered with makeup and jammed herself into jeans and a pale pink v-neck tee. She opted for comfortable Mary Jane shoes instead of the strappy sandals she usually wore with jeans.

She found Marianne and Richard sitting at the breakfast nook, gray heads bent over the morning paper, floral-etched coffee mugs in hand.

"John called. He said he's found the woman who was using my passport and my husband," she excitedly told them, pouring coffee. "I feel wired. I probably shouldn't be drinking this."

"Did he say who she was?"

"No. He wants me to meet him at Starbucks across from Fashion Island at nine this morning." Kathryn started pacing. "I wonder if she knows what happened to Neil. I wonder what she's like. I wonder how John found her so fast."

"Calm down." Marianne stood up and placed a warm lemon and raspberry muffin on a plate along with a slice of sweet, ripe honeydew melon. "Sit down and eat some breakfast. You'll find out soon enough."

Kathryn ate but didn't taste anything. She kept her eyes glued to the digital clock marking time on the microwave and, at eight-forty, jumped up. "I think I'll go now even though I'll be early."

Richard cleared his throat. "Aren't you forgetting something?"

"What?"

"I need to follow you there, right?"

"Oh yes, I forgot again. Can we leave soon?"

"Sure, if you really want to. I guess we can always go in and have more coffee while we wait for John."

She grabbed her purse and her cell phone and sped to the BMW after telling Marianne she'd call her later and tell her when she'd meet up at the office. She impatiently waited for Richard to pull his Mustang out of the garage and line up behind her before driving towards Fashion Island. At each red light she cursed under her breath, trying to ignore her pounding heart.

Pulling into the Starbucks parking lot, she saw John standing next to his BMW X5. He waved her into the empty spot next to his car, then waved to Richard, who tooted his horn and drove off. Kathryn got out of her car and ran to him, struggling to catch her breath.

"Where is she, John? How did you find her so quickly?" Her words tumbled over each other.

"Whoa, slow down. How much coffee did you drink this morning anyway?"

"Probably too much. Is she here?"

"No, but we can drive together to where she's at."

"The suspense is killing me," she wailed. "Let's go."

"I'm going to let you drive my vehicle since I need to go over paperwork for a meeting with my uncle today."

"We can take my car if you want."

"No, I already have my briefcase and tablet set up in my passenger seat." John winked at her. "I trust your driving."

"You probably shouldn't, I'm too hyper. But, if you really need me to..." she answered while trying to squeeze herself between John's SUV and a white delivery van that had parked too close.

As she opened the BMW door, she heard the sound of a heavy metal door rolling back on its tracks behind her. Rough hands grabbed her shoulders and yanked her backwards into the bed of the van. Before a black cotton bag was jammed over her head, she caught a glimpse of a black onyx ring with a skull and crossbones. She tried to scream but the hand with the ring quickly covered her mouth. She couldn't get enough air into her lungs to make another attempt. The van's engine roared to life and she heard the sliding door shut with a bang and then the front passenger door slammed shut.

Chapter Twenty-Eight

Kathryn frantically tried to suck air into her gasping lungs but the heavy black cotton bag encasing her head made it difficult. Her heart was pounding in her chest.

"Go, go, go! Get us out of here now!" she heard John yell.

Her body went rigid. Too late, she remembered Mike's warning: "Stay away from Selton. He's in on it."

Aside from the driver and John, Kathryn felt two other men in the back with her. One pinned her legs down and the other kept her head still. She tried to moisten her lips but her mouth was parched.

"John?" she croaked. "Where are you taking me?"

"Shut up, Kathryn. It's your own damned stubborn fault. You had to go around asking questions instead of listening to me."

"Please take the bag off my face. I can't breathe," she begged, her words coming out in ragged gasps.

"Can't do it, so don't ask," he snarled.

She tried to quiet her anxiety by breathing in slowly, holding and letting it out slowly. Didn't work. "Remember how I panic? It's happening to me now, John. If you ever cared for me at all, please let me get some air. Please?"

She heard him grunt and then she was turned over, face down and the bag yanked from her head.

"Your uncle's going to be pissed," Foot Holder said.

"I'll worry about that later," John growled back. "Kathryn, keep your head down or I'll have to put the bag back on."

"Okay, I promise."

She had no idea how long they travelled, but some of it was on a curvy, twisting road. Minutes seemed like hours and hours felt like days as her body shivered uncontrollably, worrying about what awaited her. Eventually she felt the van slow and turn onto a poorly paved road. They drove cautiously, bumping across potholes, which jostled and bruised her bones as she lay on the hard metal surface of the van. At last they stopped.

The side door slid opened with a bang. She heard Gerald bark, "Get that bag back on her head, now!"

Foot Holder muttered, "It was John's idea."

"I don't care whose fault it is." His voice was low and menacing as he accentuated every word. "Get. It. On. Now!"

The bag was roughly shoved back onto her head before she was half carried, half dragged out of the van. Her feet had fallen asleep so her legs gave way when she tried to stand and she fell to the gravel. Sharp stones abraded her knees. When she cried out in pain, an unseen hand struck her across her face.

"Shut up."

She bit her lower lip until it bled, trying to keep from sobbing. Foot Holder and Head Holder grabbed her by each arm and started dragging her across a grassy area and then up five steps. She heard a horse whiny in the background. The men shoved her into the cool interior of a house.

The smell of lemon furniture polish and coffee tickled her nose and she suppressed a sneeze. They had her walk thirty steps across tiled flooring before stopping. She heard keys jingling, a click in a lock and a deadbolt thrown back, before a door creaked open. The two men tried to help her climb down stairs, but she balked, not able to see where she was going. One of them swung her up and over his broad shoulder and carried her down, fireman-style.

Kathryn was dumped unceremoniously onto a small, hard bed and heard the men stomp back up the stairs, slam the door and slide the deadbolt back into place. Ripping the hated black bag from her head, she used it to wipe her eyes and nose. Her eyes slowly adjusted to the dim lighting provided by one single bare low-wattage bulb hanging from the rough lumber ceiling and took in her surroundings.

Aside from the bed the only other items were a sink, toilet, a small refrigerator and a glass-topped cocktail table, identical to the one she had sat at the evening before on Gerald's yacht. Kathryn slowly crept up the wooden stairs, cringing each time one of the steps creaked beneath her weight. Only fifteen steps separated her from the outside, from freedom. Realizing she had been holding her breath, she made herself inhale deeply and exhale slowly to calm herself. Knowing it was hopeless, Kathryn tried to open the door anyway. She pulled and pushed to no avail. Pounding on the heavy door with both fists, she was startled when it flew open.

"I wondered how long it would take you to try to get out." John wouldn't look her in the eye. "The basement is escape-proof so you might as well give up."

"John, please help me."

"It's no use. Go back downstairs and wait for my uncle."

She tried to force the door open farther to make a dash for freedom.

John roughly pushed her back. "Listen to me. There's no escaping, Kathryn."

She limped down the stairs and threw herself onto the bed. She could feel the cold prickles of panic edging down her neck towards her back, and hear the dull black roar filling her ears. Shooting stars edged the corners of her vision and she couldn't get enough air.

"Breathe deep, breathe slow!" she tried telling herself to stall the panic attack. "Think of a beach; think calm; think about Mike."

After a few minutes, Kathryn stood on shaky legs that felt as if they could be blown over with a single puff of a gentle breeze. Since she couldn't escape up the stairs maybe she could find another way out of the basement. She inched her way around the walls, hunting for a small opening, any small hole she could use to claw her way out. But the walls were plastered with thick, rough concrete that scraped her shaking, groping fingers. She pulled the small refrigerator away from the wall, the contents spilling onto the charcoal-gray travertine floor. A green glass bottle of Perrier cracked, then exploded, spraying her with cold, fizzing, foaming water. A yelp escaped her firmly clinched lips when a shard of glass cut her ankle. Limping back to the hard bed, she tripped over Godiva chocolates, the gleaming golden box barely reflecting the dim overhead light.

A closed straw basket rested at the foot of the twin bed. She tentatively opened it and saw a jumble of red, pink and black lace. Her panties, stolen from her apartment.

Kathryn shuddered and tried, unsuccessfully, to push visions of her body being violated from her mind. Her stomach churned and she wondered how her mother had coped for so many years.

At the bottom of the basket she found two framed photographs. One was a picture of her father and mother on their wedding day. The other was of Neil. Stunned, Kathryn dropped the photographs.

What did Gerald have to do with Neil? How did he know my parents?

Bits and pieces of her uncle's story about her mother being raped crowded her mind. It couldn't be. Gerald couldn't have been the man who had terrorized her mother. Could he?

The deadbolt was shoved back and the door thrown open with a bang. Her knees started trembling again, as she waited to face the man who had made her life a living hell.

"Kathryn, how nice of you to accept my hospitality," his loud voice boomed while he descended the stairs.

"Please, please let me go." Kathryn tried to steady her voice. "I won't tell anyone about this. I swear!"

"A little late for that, don't you think?" Gerald Selton slowly descended the stairs, a smug smile on his face. "Think of this as your new home for the time being. I've tried to make it comfortable for you."

"What do you want from me?" Kathryn whispered. "I want to go home."

He set his briefcase on the glass table and looked at the shattered green bottle lying in puddles and the trampled box of chocolates. "I see you've been a naughty girl. Tsk, tsk. I'll have to teach you how to be a better houseguest."

He took two quick steps and pulled Kathryn's hand into his own. She jerked away from him and backed up until she was stopped short by the rough, cold wall.

"Now, now, my dear, there's no need for you to treat me like that," he scolded her. "You can see how much trouble I went to make your room pleasant for you during your stay with us. Even stocked up on chocolates since John said you liked them so much."

Kathryn rubbed her shivering arms, her eyes darting towards the fifteen steps to freedom. "You'll never get away with this. People will be looking for me."

Gerald gave a thin, cold laugh before stepping between her and the stairs. "We're not amateurs. Marianne will find an expertly forged letter from you, sweetly explaining that you're in love with John and have decided to run away to Brazil with him. Ironic, since that's where your husband was heading with his beautiful Latina mistress, wasn't it?"

"What do you want from me?"

"Want from you? Why, nothing. I won, you lost. End of game." His cold blue eyes remained passive. "You asked me the name of my yacht. *Il Gioco*. The Game. That's all this is."

"What? A game? With other people's lives?" Kathryn's voice raised an octave, indignant that her life had been reduced to nothing more meaningful.

"Yes, what else? Well, there might be a few million dollars riding on your interference. I had Tomas start you out on my trail by giving you Helene's charge statement. John was against me bringing you into the game but it's made it so much more interesting." The former senator reached down and picked up his briefcase, placing it on the glass table. He retrieved a plastic Ziploc bag and took out a cotton swab before stepping towards her. "Now if you'll allow me to swab your mouth. This won't hurt a bit, I promise."

"What's that? Why do you want a ..." Kathryn inhaled sharply. "Oh my god! You're the one who was raping my mother."

"I knew you were intelligent. Much more than your insipid mother." His eyes gleamed close to her face. "She was very beautiful, wanting to please me no matter what. Then she met that nosy newspaper nut. After she married him, it was like she found religion and wanted nothing to do with me. No one ever says no to me. Ever."

"So that's why you were asking about my birthday," Kathryn said, stifling a sob, remembering the harsh slap across her face earlier. "You raped my mother and I came along about nine months later."

"Rape is too harsh. I took what belonged to me. Now give me the swab or I'll have to call my men to hold you down."

She reluctantly opened her mouth and allowed him to swab her cheek. He took the Q-tip back and placed it into the bag. Snapping his fingers, one of his men rushed down the stairs. "Get this Fed-Ex'd out today. And pay for the rush processing. I want to know if this pretty little thing is my daughter or not."

Kathryn shuddered and tried to pull away as he stroked his fingers across her cheek, but it only made him push her harder against the wall, his body pressing into hers. "Actually, it wasn't until I saw you and John together that I put two and two together. You have the same bone structure and nose shape. Pity he had to fall in love with you. It's been quite a shock to him finding out he was seducing his own cousin."

Gerald finally released her and went back to his briefcase. "Actually, I don't think finding out you're his cousin was quite as upsetting as finding out you're a whore, just like your mother."

"What are you talking about? I never..." The words caught in her throat when she saw the photographs of her embracing Mike.

"My photographer tells me you're the one who initiated the kiss. Interesting, especially since John specifically told you that Williams was an enemy." Gerald strode towards her, his hand held high, his mouth twisted in a cruel grin. "I ought to teach you a lesson for breaking his heart."

Kathryn's eyes darted back to the stairs and the door, which Gerald's man had left open. When he finally turned back to his briefcase, she made a dash for the stairs. Her body felt like she was in a dream, swimming against a strong current, moving in slow motion. Before she had traveled even halfway across the room, unseen hands grabbed her from behind and threw her roughly onto the ground. Unprepared for the sudden force, her weight landed on her right arm and she heard her watch shatter. Her right knee took the rest of her weight and cracked against the cold travertine. Shooting pain traveled straight to her spine, making her head spin, and a moan escaped her lips.

"Don't you ever try that again," Gerald commanded in a low growl.

His quiet, icy voice sent chills through her veins as she struggled to turn to face him. He briskly walked back to his briefcase, slammed it shut, then stooped in front of her until their faces were inches apart. "I'm very disappointed with your behavior, Kathryn. You've been a naughty girl so I'm going to leave and let you contemplate your actions."

After Gerald stomped up the stairs, slammed the door shut and jammed the deadbolt into place, Kathryn hobbled over to the bed and started massaging her swelling, bruised knee. Just as she started looking at the scrapes on her arm and the broken watch, the single light switched off, plunging her into total blackness.

"No, please don't!" Kathryn shrieked, her voice echoing in her ears long after she had ceased to scream.

Chapter Twenty-Nine

Lying curled up in the fetal position in the inky darkness, Kathryn rocked herself, willing her mind to avoid a meltdown panic attack. Whenever a sob threatened to escape her lips she bit down even harder until she tasted her metallic, salty blood. The only sound she could hear was the fierce beating of her own heart. Even the refrigerator had been silenced by the hand that had switched off the basement electrical breaker.

Kathryn thought about her mother being terrorized by Gerald and wondered how Evelyn had managed to cope. Was it the love she had for her husband and daughter that had gotten her through the worst days? Somehow her mother had survived at least until her husband had been murdered. Kathryn was certain her father was dead. Gerald would never have allowed him to live.

He'll never allow me to live either. What are you going to do, Kathryn. Are you going to give up? Or are you going to fight and live to find justice for your mother and father?

She sat up and started listing reasons why she should fight. Why she should live. Kathryn was surprised when Mike's name was the first reason that popped out of her mouth. Despite Neil's betrayal, she still wanted to find love and be loved. And despite the friction between herself and Mike when they first met, she had grown to admire him and care for him. Could she be falling in love?

Kathryn thought back to meeting Neil. She thought she'd been in love with the handsome young student but now she realized he had controlled and manipulated her from the very beginning. She was always trying to be better, be thinner, be successful to gain his approval. That wasn't love.

I want the chance to find real love. I deserve the chance to find it!

The dim light switched on and off at random intervals and Kathryn lost track of time after her watch shattered during her fall. The terrifying darkness pressed against her, preying on her mind, but each time she thought she would succumb to panic, thoughts of Mike calmed her. And each time the light suddenly switched on, her hopes raised that she might find a way out, only to be dashed into panic when the small basement room plunged back into darkness.

After what seemed hours, the light was switched on and the door thrown open. Kathryn squinted against the light, trying to see who was stomping down the stairs. John finally came into view carrying a tray with sandwiches, fruit and bottles of water.

"I thought you might be hungry," he said quietly as he placed the tray on the small cocktail table. "Gerald is in a meeting, so if you want to eat, you'd better do it now before he comes to check on you."

"You mean before he comes back to terrorize me?" Kathryn spat out, her panic fueling her fury. "I can't believe I ever trusted you or thought I could care about you."

"Just eat something so I can get this out of here before Gerald comes back."

"How did you ever get involved with kidnapping and murder, John?" She moved towards the food, eyeing the weight of the tray.

"It's complicated."

"You have a captive audience, so try to explain." She fingered a peanut butter and jelly sandwich and silently prayed for John to turn his back.

"You wouldn't understand."

"Try me. Maybe you can convince me you're not a monster like your uncle."

"He practically raised me, you know. Gave me everything my mom couldn't. It didn't start out with kidnapping and murder, it was more like: 'John, I have a small problem I think you can help me with.'"

He sighed, picked up half of a sandwich and took a bite. "And each time the problem was a little bit bigger than the last. So here I am."

"Why didn't you walk away? Or were you addicted to his money, his power?"

"In the beginning it was probably the money, the power, but then…"

Kathryn let the silence linger for a few moments. "But then what?"

"Trieste." He ran his fingers through his wavy black hair, a gesture Kathryn had come to know well. "He threatened to harm Trieste if I ever so much as thought of leaving his organization. That's the real reason Amanda left me. She couldn't stomach Gerald anymore and I couldn't get out because he would have found Trieste no matter how far we ran."

"What kind of sicko would do that to their family?" Kathryn shivered suddenly and her voice almost squeaked. "Even if I am Gerald's daughter, he's going to kill me, isn't he?"

John shrugged. "I've given up trying to understand my uncle. He'll do whatever he damn well wants to do."

"You have to help me get out of here!" She grasped his arm. "You can't let me die!"

He pushed her away. "I won't jeopardize Trieste. There's nothing I can do."

Kathryn turned and covered her face with both hands. She let a sob escape and didn't try to keep her tears from sliding down her cheeks.

"Dammit, tears aren't going to change my mind." John chewed on his lower lip. "If anything, it's only going to infuriate Gerald, so get a grip."

"What does it matter? He's only going to kill me." She suppressed a hiccup. "Might as well get it over with."

John shook his head, then looked anxiously at the stairs. "Do you want the sandwich or not? I need to get out of here."

"No, but can you put an apple and water into the refrigerator for me?"

He gave her a long look, then picked up an apple and water bottle and turned towards the mini refrigerator. Kathryn quickly picked up the tray and swung it at his head. As soon as she felt the tray hit his body, she let it go, spun around and rushed for the stairs. The sound of the crashing tray and plates hitting the stone floor echoed in the confined space and she heard John grunt when he tripped over the tray, lost his balance and fell.

After racing up the wooden steps, Kathryn was temporarily blinded by the dazzling sunlight as she burst into the kitchen. She paused for just a moment to find the best way out of the house and then she rushed out the back door, down stone steps and into the backyard. She heard John yell at her, but it only spurred her to run faster towards the avocado orchard bordering the lush green lawn.

Before she could leap over the low stone wall and into the orchard, rough hands stopped her mid-stride, picked her up and slung her over a broad shoulder, her face pointing towards her escape route. She started kicking and screaming but John suddenly appeared in front of her and clamped his hand tightly over her mouth.

"Shut up, Kathryn." His dark eyes looked like an angry ocean storm, but his voice sounded terrified. "If Gerald finds out about this, not only will your life be a living hell, but you'll jeopardize Trieste. You've got to help me protect her."

She stopped fighting and limply nodded her head. "There's got to be a way out of this for both of us. Please? Help me?"

John glanced at the man still carrying Kathryn across the broad lawn towards the house and brought his index finger to his lips, then winked. "There's nothing I can do, except pretend like this never happened. And if you're lucky, Gerald won't find out about your escapade. Right, Edward?"

The large man grunted and shifted Kathryn's weight as he began climbing the stone steps.

"You're a good man, Edward," John answered, clapping him on his free shoulder. "Let's get this lady back where she belongs and everyone will be happy. Well, almost everyone."

After being unceremoniously dumped onto the small bed in the basement once again, John and Edward quickly cleaned up the broken pottery, squashed sandwiches and the tray. They trudged up the stairs, bolted the door and plunged her back into darkness, leaving her to wonder what John's wink meant.

Kathryn resumed her fetal position on the bed and kept her eyes closed against the inky blackness. Too soon the light was thrown on and she heard Gerald stomp down the stairs and make his way to her side. She felt him plop himself onto the bed and noticed his clean scent. The same one John used.

"How are we feeling now?" He pried her hands away from her face and peered into her red, puffy eyes. "Are you ready to be a good girl and apologize?"

Let him think you're weak and broken. Patience. Wait for the perfect opportunity to run for it.

"I'm sorry." Kathryn sniffled and rubbed her eyes. "I panicked. Didn't John tell you I'm claustrophobic?"

"Yes, he did. That's what makes this hidey hole so perfect for you. Either it will make you stronger, which a Selton should be, or break you."

"I was accidentally locked in a car trunk playing hide-and-seek when I was four years old. It took hours for anyone to find me." Kathryn shuddered. "I'm not sure how much longer I can stand being in here."

But you survived that and you survived Neil's locked closet punishments when he was angry.

"Get a grip, Kathryn. You're an adult now." He patted her knee before walking over to the glass table and opening his briefcase. "Now where were we, before you so rudely interrupted me?"

He went back to the glass table, pulled out a small flash stick and held it up. "I'm sure you have so many questions, but, being my daughter, let's see if you have my intelligence and can figure it out with a few hints. Why was Neil's novel so important that I had to make sure no copies existed?"

She fumbled for words, her mind going blank.

"Come on, you can do better than that! You led my nincompoop nephew on a merry wild goose chase so I know you figured some of it out."

Kathryn chewed the inside of her lip for a moment, giving herself time to figure out what Gerald wanted. "I copied Neil's novel on to it before you had his laptop stolen. But no one knew."

"Yes, go on." He was breathing heavily.

Her mind raced, trying to remember the details of the novel. "Neil was the voyeur! He wrote what he was seeing. And you were the man across from our apartment with the prostitute."

"Very good!"

"I'm not done yet. Neil figured out who you were. Somehow he either planned on exposing you..." She stopped talking when she saw his head shaking. "Or he was trying to blackmail you? So you had to stop him?"

"Brilliant, my dear, just brilliant. I'm sure you're my daughter now. Maybe you should join our family business instead of making me decide on how to dispose of your body."

How does Gerald want to see me? As a weak, broken woman? No, I'm not sure. Think, Kathryn. What does Gerald want? He doesn't have any other children. Does he want a daughter?

"What's wrong, Kathryn?" he sneered. "Did you lose your voice?"

"I wish my mother had told you that I was your daughter when I was little." Kathryn tried to steady her voice, to sound sure. "It would have solved so many of my problems, like Neil."

Gerald studied her for a moment. "Yes, I can see how I could have given you a much better life than your mother's husband. He was a weak man, just like Evelyn. I can't believe the squalor they raised you in."

Forgive me, Mom and Dad. I have to do this to survive. Gerald detests weakness. I can see that now.

"I know, and they never taught me to stand up for myself. That's why someone like Neil could come along and victimize me." Kathryn sighed. "I guess I should thank you for getting rid of him for me. I've wanted to kill him many times over the last eleven years, but didn't know how to accomplish it without spending the rest of my life in prison."

"You're welcome, my dear." Gerald chuckled. "I think I might be able to find a place for you in my business after all."

"I would like that opportunity. But can you tell me what Neil was blackmailing you over? Was it the prostitute?"

Keep him talking, Kathryn. Get him to let down his guard.

"Your husband turned out to be quite an accomplished hacker and found a way to breach my legitimate businesses and track my other activities. He encrypted the paths into his novel. He was blackmailing me over that. Not over a common hooker. She had to die too, you know. Neil decided to use her to pass messages to me and then she wanted in on the action."

He dropped the flash stick and slowly ground it into pieces beneath the heel of his highly polished John Lobb shoe. "That's the end of that little problem."

"How did you ever end up in the apartment across from me in the first place?"

He batted his eyelashes at her. "True love brought us together."

Kathryn thought long and hard. "I'm not following that hint."

"Oh come on, Kathryn. Look at that handsome young man at the top of the stairs pining away over what might have been."

"I wouldn't call it true love. Maybe mutual attraction."

"Either way, I have a dilemma to solve, my dear," he answered, sitting down close to her. "If we welcome you to the family business, I need to bind you to us, so to speak, so that you have an incentive for staying loyal and not running back to that detective you can't seem to stay away from."

Chapter Thirty

"I swear I'll be loyal!"

Gerald's laugh was harsh. "Ah, I'm sure you would be until the first opportunity to escape came along. Let's see, Trieste has worked well for keeping John with me. A pity you don't have a child of your own."

Gerald slowly stroked her arm, then moved his hand to the top of her thigh, ignoring her shudder. "Maybe we can do something about that. What do you think, my dear?"

Kathryn tried to pull away, but instead was pulled closer into his body and held tightly. "You're my father! You can't do something like that!"

His fingers entwined themselves into her hair and he brought his lips to her ear, breathing heavily. "We don't have the DNA answer yet, so maybe I can."

She struggled to push him away but his grip on her hair tightened and he pushed her on to the bed. Kathryn tensed and tried to kick and flail her arms against him, but it only made him yank on her hair harder, making her want to scream in pain. Instead, she bit harder on her lower lip to hold it in, and waited for the right moment to knee him in the groin and make another run for freedom.

Gerald shifted and loosened his grip on her hair. She threw her head forward as hard as she could and connected with his nose. He grunted and blood began flowing and dripped onto her cheek. When he raised his fist to hit her, she wedged her knee between his legs and kicked.

Fury filled his eyes but, before he could hit her, his weight was lifted from her body and Gerald hit the floor with a thud. Kathryn sat up quickly while looking towards the stairs, wondering if she had the chance to run.

"Stay away from her, Gerald." John was panting hard and placed himself between his uncle and Kathryn.

Gerald picked himself up from the floor and wiped blood from his face. "You'll pay for this, Kathryn."

"You've crossed the line this time, Uncle! Stay away from her."

"I wasn't actually going to harm her. I only wanted to see what your reaction would be. See if you loved her enough to risk Trieste."

John backed away. "What are you talking about? This has nothing to do with Trieste."

"Anytime you cross me, you put your daughter at risk." Gerald crossed his arms and glared at John. "You should know that by now."

"Please, please leave her out of this," John whispered. "You can do whatever you want with Kathryn."

"A little late for that, don't you think, Johnny Boy?" Gerald gave another humorless chuckle. "Like I said, I wanted to see your reaction. Seems to me you're a man in love, ready to defend his damsel in distress. And the damsel seems to like you too. Or at least she used to."

"What the hell are you talking about?" John inched closer to Kathryn.

"Do you really think I can easily kill my one and only child?" Gerald shook his head. "I need assurance that Kathryn will remain loyal, so I propose that you marry her. Once she gives birth and bonds with the baby, she'll have her freedom."

"What?" Kathryn screeched. "You can't force me to marry John and have a baby!"

"You're not paying attention, my dear." He glowered at John, who immediately moved out of his way, then sat back down on the bed next to her. "I said I couldn't easily kill my child, but if I have to in order to protect myself, I will."

Kathryn interlaced her fingers and tried to stop her hands from shaking, her mind trying to find another way out.

"I take it you have no further objections?" Gerald stroked her cheek. "Good! I'll have my ship's captain make plans to sail tonight. We'll have a ceremony once we're underway. John, get a bottle of champagne and let's toast your bride-to-be!"

Once John had pounded up the stairs and was out of sight, she turned and looked Gerald straight in the eye. "It won't be a legal marriage. You know that, don't you? And if John is my cousin, we shouldn't have children together."

"Where we're going, none of it will matter, my dear." He stood up and walked to his briefcase sitting on the glass table. "While we're waiting for that champagne, is there anything else you want to know?"

Kathryn eased from the bed and edged towards Gerald, keeping the stairway in her sight. "Besides where you're taking me?"

"Right. You'll have to wait until we get there to see."

"Why did you have to kill my father and then make Neil disappear the same way?"

"These family reunions are so touching, aren't they?" Gerald affected wiping a tear away, then leaned close to her face and raged. "Don't you ever call that man your father again. I'm your father!"

"What would you have me call you? Daddy Dearest?"

The blow came out of the dim darkness, striking her full on her mouth. "Don't you ever disrespect your father again! Do you hear me?"

Kathryn whimpered, trying to staunch her bleeding lip.

"Stop that noise. I detest females who aren't strong. And stop bleeding. You're a Selton after all."

"Yes, sir."

Gerald seemed distraught, unfocused by her whimpering and blood.

Now's the time, Kathryn. You can do it. Find a way to escape. Keep him unbalanced.

She inched closer to him. "I'll admit I am so much like you. No wonder John and I argued all the time."

He turned towards her quizzically.

"What would you like for me to call you? Father? Dad? Daddy?"

"I like 'Father.' It sounds so… authoritarian." A cruel smiled played on his thin lips.

"Then Father it is." Kathryn inched closer, whispering, drawing his face closer to her own. "Then how does my father like having his…"

She drove her knee as hard as she could into his groin. Before he hit the floor, she bounded up the fifteen stairs and burst into the house. Without pausing, she shoved John and the bottle of champagne out of her way, almost fell down the stone steps, before running as fast as she could towards the avocado orchard. The sun was setting in the west, directly in her eyes, causing her to trip over an unseen sprinkler. Ignoring the pain in her twisted ankle, she picked herself up and limped as quickly as she could towards the sound of a horse whinnying in the distance. She hoped she could find the horse and ride away.

"Stop, bitch." Gerald was standing at the door of the house, one hand clutching his lower abdomen, the other pointing a pistol. "I don't care if you're my daughter or not. You're dead. Now!"

She backed up, then crouched down when he chambered a round into the pistol. Her hands closed around something hard. Something solid. Rising up, she launched a garden gnome towards the demented man.

Hearing the sharp crack of the gun being fired and an answering shot, she closed her eyes, waiting for the bullet to hit. Instead she heard the groan of a man, then a second moan and two bodies hitting the ground. A searing pain ran through her left arm; warmth trickled to her hand. She wasn't sure she should open her eyes. She didn't want to see death coming. Instead she heard masculine yells coming around her and then warm, tender arms swept her up.

"Kathryn, Kathryn! Thank god I found you!" It was Mike and his face was full of joy.

"I threw the gnome but I was afraid to see what happened. I thought I was going to die," she cried. "He was going to kill me just like he killed Neil. I thought I'd never see you again and tell you…"

"Shhh, it's okay now." Mike turned away from her and yelled, "Guys, get a paramedic over here now! Forget about the dead guy."

"Dead? Who's dead?" She shivered, teeth chattering.

"I shot Gerald Selton." He ground his teeth. "He was trying to kill you."

Kathryn looked around and saw John lying on the ground, cursing the paramedics who weren't being overly gentle with him.

Mike yelled at the paramedics tending to John. "I need one of you to take care of this woman. She's been shot too."

"Did you shoot John?" she whispered, her mouth suddenly parched.

Mike helped her sit down on the damp grass as her legs gave way, and held her bloody arm. "The bullet just grazed you after going through Selton. You probably won't even need stitches."

"But did you shoot John? I need to know."

"No. He wasn't endangering you. In fact, he saved your life. He took the bullet his uncle intended for you." He gave her a long look. "Are you in love with him?"

Before she could answer, a paramedic inserted himself between them and began bandaging her arm after examining the graze.

"Doesn't look like you'll need stitches, ma'am," the uniformed medic informed her while fitting a blood pressure cuff to her uninjured arm. "But we'll take you to the hospital and have a doctor examine you."

"I've got to get back to work." Mike looked towards the house, stood up and started walking away without looking back at her. "Take care of yourself."

As she opened her mouth to call out to him, the paramedic inserted a thermometer and told her to close her mouth. She watched Mike's shoulders sag as he climbed the five stone steps and disappeared into the house. Several uniformed officers followed close behind him while several others strung crime scene tape around the property line.

Once the thermometer was removed, the paramedic helped her to her feet and tried to escort her to a waiting ambulance. They walked towards a small group of officers whose heads were close together. Even though the men were talking in hushed voices, Kathryn could still overhear them.

"Yeah, me and Adams were staking out the house, waiting for the slime bag to show up, when out runs this real pretty redhead and two goons chasing her." The officer puffed out his chest a little bit more. "We didn't know if we should blow the stakeout or what. Adams called it in and they tell us to sit tight, even though it's killin' us watching those guys manhandle her."

Kathryn made sure she was hidden behind the paramedic as they walked by, embarrassed to be caught listening to their conversation.

"Forty-five minutes later Williams roars up and man, he's goin' crazy! You can always count on him being steady-eddy, but not this time. He's cursing the SWAT team for not going in, then tellin' em they'd better make sure the woman stays unharmed if they go in. I think the lead guy was ready to deck him."

She felt a tug on her arm. "Ma'am, it's time to go."

"I'm not ready to leave yet," she told the young man in a quiet voice. "I need to speak to Detective Williams first."

"I don't think that's possible, ma'am." The paramedic shifted his heavy medical bag to the other hand and tried to guide her towards one of several ambulances parked around the perimeter of the lawn. "That's a crime scene and they're not going to want you trampling over any evidence."

"But aren't they going to want to talk to me since I was kidnapped and held here? Aren't I evidence?"

"Yes, ma'am, but I was told to transport you to the hospital and someone will be in contact with you there."

She saw John being loaded into one of the ambulances, two uniformed officers guarding the stretcher. "Can I talk to him for a moment?"

"I'm not sure that's allowed." Her escort looked uncomfortable and tried to steer her away.

Kathryn ignored him and instead walked to the side of John's stretcher. His eyes were closed and he was whiter than the sheet he was lying on. An IV was trailing from his arm, attached to a plastic bag filled with clear liquid, while a steady beep emitted from the machine monitoring his vital signs. Kathryn reached out and squeezed John's hand.

A burly policeman pulled her aside. "Please stand back, miss."

A quiet grunt escaped John's lips when the two medics collapsed the legs on the stretcher and rolled him into the back. Kathryn's view was blocked by the policeman and she heard the sound of the ambulance's door slam.

When she turned to go to her own ambulance, she noticed Mike standing at the top of the steps watching her, his head hung low. As soon as she started walking towards him, he disappeared back into the house.

"Ma'am, I have to insist we go now."

Kathryn gave the house one last look, then allowed herself to be placed in the back of the ambulance.

***

Marianne and Richard both showed up at the hospital to take Kathryn home. Marianne fussed over her bandaged arm, which the emergency room doctor decided needed eight stitches after all.

Neither of them commented on how uncharacteristically quiet she was, nor did they ask additional questions after she gave them an abbreviated version of her ordeal. And when she said she needed to go to bed, they each gave her a hug.

Long after all the lights were out in the house, Kathryn lay awake remembering the hurt look on Mike's face right before he turned away from her. She crept out of her room and called his cell phone using Marianne's landline.

She sighed when the call went directly to voicemail but left a message anyway. "Mike, it's Kathryn. I think there's been a terrible misunderstanding and you need to know I'm in love with you, not John. I think my cell phone is at the… at Gerald's house, so I'm calling from Marianne's landline. Please call me tomorrow."

Kathryn barely slept the rest of the night. Nightmares woke her and the gunshot wound started throbbing in the early morning hours. When she heard Marianne rustling in the kitchen, she got up.

"I'm sorry if I woke you, dear." Marianne gave her a worried look. "Were you able to sleep?"

"A little. I think I need to take another pain pill as soon as I eat something."

"I'll heat you up a pumpkin cream cheese muffin." Marianne opened the refrigerator and started taking food out. "Just sit down and make yourself comfortable."

"You don't need to wait on me. I can fix my own breakfast."

"Nonsense, it's the least I can do while you're injured and…"

Kathryn let the silence linger and focused on the microwave counting down the seconds to a warm muffin.

"Would you like me to stay home with you today?" Marianne's voice intruded on her wandering thoughts.

"What? No, I think it's best if I come to work today." Kathryn ran a hand through her hair and immediately thought of John. "I need to get back into the routine of things, get back to my life."

"It won't hurt for you to rest today." Marianne gave her a quizzical look, then went back to loading the dishwasher. "But if that's what you want, then you can ride with me."

"Oh, I forgot. I don't have my car, do I?"

"I think Mike said he had it towed. You can call him and ask where it is."

"Um, yeah, I'll do that."

"Kathryn, I can't begin to imagine the trauma you endured yesterday, but what's going on with Mike?"

Before she could respond, the house phone rang. Kathryn's heart started pounding and her palms turned sweaty. She hoped it was Mike calling her back.

Marianne answered the call. Within a few seconds Kathryn could tell it wasn't him. Instead, their company attorney was confirming an appointment for signing their partnership papers the following day, then wanted to know all the details of the Selton scandal. Marianne rolled her eyes and made circle motions with her index finger, mouthing the word "Sorry."

Dejected, Kathryn tuned Marianne's voice out and wondered if Mike would ever call or if she'd ever see him again. The ringing doorbell made her jump, and since it appeared their attorney was not going to end the call anytime soon, Kathryn trudged to the front door and opened it.

A huge bouquet of red roses was thrust into her face and, before she could react, familiar arms encircled her waist and a low, gravelly voice whispered in her ear, "Can you ever forgive me? I was such an idiot."

Kathryn pushed the flowers to the side and flung her arms around Mike's neck. "I was so afraid I'd never see you again. I'm not in love with John, I'm in love with you!"

Chapter Thirty-One

Kathryn breezed through the swooshing automatic doors, Mylar balloons proclaiming "Get Well" trailed behind her on colorful ribbons. She clutched a fluffy pink teddy bear to her chest while the elevator took her to the ninth floor and deposited her on a quiet corridor.

The officer guarding the hospital room gave her a brief nod before opening the door for her. John's usual tan face was still drained of color and almost blended into the white sheets. IV lines snaked from a plastic bag and wrapped themselves around his shoulder and down his arm before disappearing under gauze. He smiled when he saw her and raised his bed into an upright position.

"Hey cuz, is that pink teddy bear for me?" His voice was stronger than he looked.

"I saw this and thought of Trieste." She held the bear up and pointed to its pink tutu and ballerina slippers. "I'm meeting her for lunch in a few minutes but wanted to see you first."

"Then the balloons must be for me?"

"How'd you guess?" Kathryn tied the balloons onto the railing of the bed.

"I don't think I'll ever be able to repay you for saving my life, John."

"Guess that's what family's for." He coughed and reached for his water cup. "Besides, it made me look like a hero. I just wish you could have been a little more patient and waited for me to get you out of there. I would have rather avoided Gerald's gun altogether."

"I'm sorry." She walked to the window and looked down at the cars whizzing by on the Pacific Coast Highway and the ocean glittering beyond the roadway. "I hear you're working with the D.A. and cutting a deal for reduced time in prison."

"Yes, thanks to Williams, uh, I mean Mike, they've been willing to work with me. I guess I have you to thank for softening them up?"

"Guess that's what family's for." Kathryn turned, looked at John and smiled. "I'm curious though, why did Gerald's man run me off the road? Was he trying to kill me? Mike says you're not talking about that."

"This will stay just between us, right?"

"Yes, if that's what it takes to find out."

"That idiot was only supposed to scare you, and when I found out what he'd done..."

"And?"

"You get the picture, Kathryn. Let's just leave it at that." He scowled, then shook his head. "You're involved with a cop and, believe it or not, I don't want to say anything that could come between you and him. You deserve some happiness."

"Thanks, I appreciate it." Kathryn looked at her new watch, a gift from Mike. "I'd better go so I'm not late for lunch."

"Can you pass a message on to your beau for me?"

"Sure! What is it?"

"I'm really sorry that Gerald tried killing his horse and burning his house down." John's face flushed. "I didn't know anything about it until you told me. I just don't want Mike to think I had a hand in something like that."

"I'm just glad that both Sierra and Thunderbolt survived and have recovered, otherwise..."

267

"Yeah, I know, he never would have forgiven me, right?"

Kathryn smiled. "I really do need to leave for lunch, but I'll be sure to pass your message along."

"Give Trieste a huge hug from me, okay?" John quickly swiped his eyes with the hand not hooked up to the IV. "Amanda says she wants to work on becoming a family again after I finish my sentence."

"I'm happy for you! And Trieste will be so happy too!"

"Aw, get out of here and give both my girls a hug from me."

Kathryn walked into the cafeteria located in the hospital's basement and immediately saw Amanda, Trieste and John's mother sitting at a table for four. Amanda's platinum blonde hair was pulled back into a ponytail, her makeup was subdued and she was dressed in casual jeans. Mrs. Selton's eyes were red-rimmed but she flashed Kathryn a smile before running a hand through her white-streaked black hair. The same gesture John often made.

"Over here!" Trieste yelled, then hopped from her chair and ran towards Kathryn with her arms outstretched. "Did you see my dad? What did he say? How is he?"

She laughed and gave Trieste a big hug before handing the slight girl the ballerina teddy bear. "He said to give you a huge hug! So here's one from me and here's one from your dad."

"Is it true? Are you really my cousin?"

Kathryn looked towards Amanda and Mrs. Selton, who both nodded their heads in unison.

"Yes, it's true. Is that okay with you, if I'm part of your family?"

Trieste spun around and did a couple pirouettes with her bear. "That's my happy dance! I'm so glad you're my cousin!"

Kathryn hugged her again, then grabbed her hand and walked towards the table. She nodded to the two women. "Mrs. Selton, Amanda, thanks for agreeing to have lunch with me today."

"Now dear, you just call me Aunt Deirdre," the older woman said as she got up from her seat and hugged Kathryn. "The family is appalled, absolutely appalled by Gerald's actions. We will never forgive him for the crimes he's committed against you and your family but we'll try to make it up to you as best as we can."

They sat down at the table and Kathryn pursed her lips together. "I was afraid you'd blame me for his death and, well, John going to jail."

"I thought I raised John better than that. And Gerald, I've known Gerald since we were in kindergarten together, and to think he was capable of evil and corrupting my boy just boggles my mind." Deirdre tsked and shook her head. "No, dear, you're an innocent victim and I'm happy to have you as part of our family, if you'll have us."

Amanda reached over and held Kathryn's hand. "If it weren't for you, Trieste and I probably never would have had the chance to get John back as a husband and full-time father. We're very grateful."

Kathryn spent the next hour answering questions about her childhood and learning about her new family. Before saying goodbye, she made plans to meet for another lunch date with the women and a playdate with Trieste.

Stepping into the warm sunshine, a white Ford Explorer pulled up and ran over the red-painted curb before stopping right in front of her. The passenger door popped open. "Your carriage awaits, your highness."

Kathryn hopped into the seat, leaned over and kissed Mike. "How did you know I would be here?"

"I'm a detective, remember?"

"How could I forget? You're my hero!" She gave him a big smile. "But what's up? I thought I wouldn't see you until dinner tonight."

Mike pulled away from the curb and eased into the line of cars exiting the hospital lot. "As usual, someone doesn't answer their cell phone or check for messages."

"Ugh, I had to turn it off when I saw John and completely forgot to turn it back on." She reached into her handbag and turned the phone on.

"When you didn't answer your phone, Nurse Nancy called your office and left a message with Marianne, who called me and asked that I find you."

Before Mike could get another word out, Kathryn gripped his hand. "Has something happened to Uncle Edgar?"

"Not yet, but Nancy doesn't think he has much time left. And he's asking for you."

"I need to go back and get my car so I can go see him." She twisted in her seat and pointed back to the hospital.

"Relax, sweetheart, we're going to Bakersfield together right now." At the stoplight he leaned over and kissed her cheek. "I had Marianne pack a bag for you, and if she missed something we can always buy it when we get there."

"Really? You're actually willing to go with me to see my dying uncle?"

"Of course. Isn't that what you do for someone you love?"

***

Leaving Mike perched on the edge of Edgar's threadbare sofa, Nurse Nancy quickly led Kathryn into her uncle's bedroom, which was quiet except for the hissing sound coming from the oxygen tubes dangling from his nose. She sat in the wooden chair next to his bed and gently touched his hand.

"Uncle Edgar, I'm back," Kathryn whispered close to his ear.

He slowly opened his eyes and he gave her a smile.

"I'm sorry it took me so long to see you again." She gently patted his frail hand. "I finally found justice for my parents and wanted to tell you their story."

Edgar's voice was so faint she had to lean closer to hear him. "I'm glad to see you're safe. That's all that matters."

"But it matters to me what you think of my mother, even after all these years." Kathryn paused, trying to organize her thoughts. "I think she made a foolish mistake running away as a young girl of sixteen but an evil man made her pay for that mistake for the rest of her life. If it weren't for him, I think she would have returned home almost as soon as she left."

Edgar's eyes turned red and his lower lip trembled. He pointed to the cup of water sitting on his bedside table and Kathryn helped him take a sip from the straw before continuing.

"This evil man murdered my father and my husband, but justice was done and he won't ruin anyone else's life again."

"Are you blaming me for turning my back on your mother when she asked for help?" His quiet voice barely registered above the hissing oxygen.

"No! The only person I blame is that evil man." Kathryn couldn't bring herself to say Gerald's name or acknowledge him as her biological father. "I would feel better knowing you forgave my mother and understand that, once he got ahold of her, she didn't have any way to escape from him."

"I never stopped loving my sister. Your mother." Edgar stopped talking and wiped his nose with a corner of the sheet. "It was easier to pretend she never existed than to admit I missed her."

"So you forgive her?"

"Yes. I've always forgiven her." His shaking hand found Kathryn's hand and he gave her a gentle squeeze. "I'm looking forward to seeing my sister soon. I'll be sure to tell her that she can be proud to have such a wonderful daughter."

She leaned over and kissed the old man's whiskered cheek and held his hand until he fell asleep.

Chapter Thirty-Two

A cheery fire sparked and crackled in the gray river-rock fireplace. A deep cocoa-brown leather couch was pulled close to the cozy warmth and a half-eaten pepperoni pizza, still in the cardboard box, lay on the hearth next to two glasses of rich red Cabernet Sauvignon. Kathryn had her head cradled in the buttery soft leather, her eyes closed.

"What are you thinking about? You have a frown line right here." Mike gently touched between her eyebrows.

She opened her eyes and smiled. "I thought I was relaxing so well, but you're right, I can't stop regretting not finding my uncle sooner."

"But at least we had two days with him before he passed."

"I know. I'm glad I had the chance to tell him the real story of what happened to my mother." Kathryn sighed. "How she was betrayed by Gerald."

"Thanks to the copy of Neil's novel you have on your laptop, the whole world is going to know how you and your family were betrayed by Gerald. We've been able to penetrate most of his illegal enterprises." Mike leaned back and puffed out his chest. "We've made a lot of arrests these last few days, including the Pirraney sisters, who were running Gerald's prostitution service. Helene's address book is proving to be invaluable tracking down their clients, who will have a strong incentive to testify against them."

"Did you ever find out what happened to my father? Gerald practically bragged about murdering Helene and Neil, but he wouldn't say a word about him."

"John confirmed that his uncle had your father murdered and forced your mother to overdose on the sleeping pills." He rubbed the light stubble coating his cheek. "We're still hunting for the captain of Gerald's yacht, but several of the crew members are ready to testify that they had used the yacht to dispose of a few bodies deep at sea."

"I'm glad I finally have most of the answers and it's over." Kathryn snuggled into his arms. "I wish we could find out who Neil's mistress is. I'm afraid she's going to use my identity and leave me paying the price one of these days."

"I'll never let that happen, Kathryn." He leaned into her and brushed a stray strand of hair from her face before gently kissing her lips.

Scottsdale, Arizona

Dark eyes, hidden behind Louis Vuitton sunglasses, watched a group of golfers skirt the edge of the infinity pool and head towards the bar for after-game cocktails. The eight men were mostly middle-aged and mostly fit and two of them stopped mid-sentence and mid-stride to stare at her lying on her lounge chair beneath the cabana. She lifted a chilled, juicy strawberry to her mouth and took a bite, sucking at the juices released, and waited for their reaction.

One of the men watched her a few moments longer than the other before turning back to catch up to his pals. He paused at the door to the bar, turned back to give her another long look, before entering the building.

She raised a well-manicured hand and flagged down a passing cocktail waitress.

"Yes, Mrs. Landry? Would you care for a cocktail?"

"No thank you, Collette." Her thick Latin accent hung in the hot air. "I'm in need of some information."

"Information? Shall I have the concierge contact you?"

Ruby-red nails slipped a twenty-dollar bill into the young waitress's hand. "This is between you and me. Sí?"

"Gracias, Mrs. Landry. What can I do for you?"

She glanced around and made certain no one was within hearing distance. "There's a gentleman who just entered the poolside bar. He's wearing white shorts and a red-and-black striped shirt. He's about fifty years old and his blond hair is thin on top. Not bald, just thin."

The waitress shifted her tray and looked towards the bar, then back at her customer. "Do you want to buy him a drink?"

"No, not yet. What I want from you is his name, his casita number and how long he's staying here. If you can find out if he's married or not, there will be another tip for you."

"Consider it done." The girl turned and started towards the bar.

"Collette?"

"Yes, Mrs. Landry?"

"Remember, this is between you and me. I would rather he not find out that I'm inquiring about him."

Once the waitress was out of sight, she leaned back into the soft lounge cushions and furrowed her delicately arched brows.

This has to work. My funds are getting low and I need a new identity. Curse that Landry woman. How did she find out where Neil opened our bank account anyway? I shouldn't have wasted so much time on him even though he kept promising that we were going to hit pay dirt. I'll never make that mistake again. Stick to the game plan, Juliana. Take the money and run.

The waitress came sashaying out of the bar, her bright tropical-patterned sarong skirt flapping against her thin, bird-like legs, which were much too pink from being in the sun too long. Her thin arms balanced a drink on a tray that wobbled as she stooped to place a frozen margarita next to Mrs. Landry. Beads of moisture began running down the side of the glass and pooled on the table.

"Compliments of Mr. Huxton."

"Mr. Huxton?"

"Yes, Paul Huxton. Apparently the gentleman is just as interested in getting to know you as you are him."

"Married?"

"Going through a very nasty divorce. His friends think he needs a distraction, thus the golf trip. He's here for another five days."

Mrs. Landry peeled another twenty-dollar bill from her bag and handed it to Collette. "Casita number?"

"I can do better than that," she answered, handing a napkin with writing on it to the scantily clad woman. "Here's an invitation to join him for dinner, starting with champagne in his villa. The Saguaro Villa."

"Excellent," Mrs. Landry purred. "And does he know about my inquiries?"

"No, I never had to open my mouth. He was practically waiting by the door and couldn't wait to start asking questions about you."

"Thank you, Collette. Would you be so kind as to tell Mr. Huxton that I'd be delighted to join him this evening?"

"Yes, Mrs. Landry. Is there anything else I can do for you?"

"That will be all for now. You did an excellent job."

An excellent job indeed.

The End

RECIPES

Lemon Poppy Seed Bundt Cake with Lemon Glaze

Ingredients

Cake

>1 yellow cake mix
>1 3.4 ounce box instant lemon pudding mix
>Zest from 1 lemon
>1 cup sour cream
>1/2 cup vegetable oil
>1/2 cup sherry (or whole milk)
>4 eggs
>1/4 cup poppy seeds

Glaze

>1 cup powdered sugar
>2 tablespoons fresh lemon juice (or more as needed)

Instructions

Cake

1. Preheat oven to 350 degrees (F).
2. Heavily grease a bundt pan with vegetable shortening (not butter) and sprinkle with granulated sugar.
3. In a large bowl whisk the cake mix and instant pudding mix together.
4. Add the lemon zest, sour cream, vegetable oil, eggs, and sherry (or milk).
5. Using an electric mixer (either handheld or stand), beat until the batter is smooth, about 2 minutes.
6. Stir in the poppy seeds.
7. Pour cake batter into prepared baking pan and bake for 40-50 minutes until a wooden skewer inserted comes out mostly clean. A few moist crumbs clinging will be okay.
8. Allow to cool in the pan 10 minutes before inverting cake onto a serving platter.
9. Allow to completely cook before drizzling with glaze.

Glaze

1. Whisk the powdered sugar and lemon juice together until smooth. If the mixture is too thick to drizzle, add lemon juice, 1/2 teaspoon at a time, until desired consistency is reached.
2. Drizzle glaze over completely cooled cake.
3. Store at room temperature, covered, for up to 3 days.

Banana Chocolate Chip Muffins

<u>Ingredients</u>

1/2 cup butter, room temperature

2/3 cup granulated sugar

2 medium ripe bananas (about 1 cup mashed)

1 egg, room temperature

2 teaspoons vanilla extract

1/3 cup milk (2% or whole)

1 cup (4.3 ounces) all-purpose flour

1 cup (4.3 ounces) whole wheat flour or white whole wheat flour

1-1/2 teaspoons baking powder

1/2 teaspoon baking soda

1/2 teaspoon salt

1/2 teaspoon ground cinnamon

1 cup mini chocolate chips

Optional: Coarse sparkling sugar

Instructions

1. Preheat oven to 350 degrees (F).
2. Line a 12 cup muffin tin with paper liners. Set aside.
3. In a medium-sized bowl, whisk together the flours, baking powder, baking soda, salt, and cinnamon. Set aside.
4. In a large mixing bowl, beat the butter and sugar together until creamy.
5. Mix into the sugar mixture the egg, banana, vanilla extract, and milk, beating well after each addition. Mixture will appear curdled which is normal.
6. Add the flour mixture to the banana mixture and beat until mostly smooth.
7. Stir in the mini chocolate chips.
8. Divide the batter between 12 muffin cups and top with sparkling white sugar if desired.
9. Bake for 20 – 22 minutes or until a wooden skewer inserted into the center of the muffins comes out mostly clean. A few moist crumbs clinging to the skewer is okay.
10. Allow muffins to cool in the pan for 3 minutes, then transfer to a wire rack to continue cooling.
11. Serve warm and store completely cooled muffins in an airtight container for up to 2 days at room temperature.

Tips
- Lightly spoon flour into measuring cup and level to measure.
- If you wish to freeze leftover muffins, allow to cool completely then wrap individually in plastic wrap. Place muffins in a freezer-safe Ziplock bag and freeze up to 2 months. Allow to defrost at room temperature, keeping the muffins wrapped. When ready to eat, gently reheat the muffins in the microwave for a few seconds until warmed.

Chewy Chocolate Chip Oatmeal Cookies

Ingredients

5 tablespoons unsalted butter

1 cup (5 ounces) all-purpose flour

1 teaspoon salt

1/2 teaspoon baking soda

3/4 cup dark sugar, packed

1/2 cup granulated sugar

1/2 cup vegetable oil

1 egg plus 1 yolk

1 teaspoon vanilla extract

3 cups old-fashioned rolled oats

1 cup chocolate chips

Instructions

1. Don't preheat the oven as these cookies need to chill first.
2. Brown the butter in a medium-sized skillet over medium-high heat. Stir butter constantly until the butter turns golden brown. Pour butter into a large heatproof bowl and allow to cool while you collect the rest of the ingredients.
3. Whisk the flour, salt, and baking soda together in a small bowl. Set aside.
4. Add brown sugar, granulated sugar, and oil to the bowl containing the browned butter. Whisk until smooth. Add the egg, egg yolk, and vanilla and stir to thoroughly combine.
5. Stir in the flour mixture until no white streaks remain.
6. Stir in the old-fashioned oats and chocolate chips and mix until thoroughly incorporated.
7. Allow the cookie dough to chill in the refrigerator for 60 minutes.
8. Remove dough from refrigerator and then preheat oven to 375 degrees (F).
9. Drop dough by rounded tablespoon on to a parchment-lined baking sheet, 12 cookies to each sheet. Leave room between the cookies as they will spread.
10. Bake for 8 to 10 minutes, rotating pan halfway through baking.
11. Cool cookies on baking sheet for 5 minutes then transfer to a wire rack to cool completely.
12. Store leftovers in an airtight container for 3 days.

Dark Chocolate Grand Marnier Mousse

<u>Ingredients</u>

Pudding

    1/2 cup granulated sugar

    7 tablespoons unsweetened cocoa powder

    2 tablespoons Grand Marnier

    1/4 teaspoon orange extract

    1/2 teaspoon vanilla extract

    1/8 teaspoon salt

    1 (12.3 ounce) package silken tofu, drained

    1 (12.3 ounce) package reduced-fat silken tofu drained

    3 ounces dark chocolate, chopped

Garnish

    Whipped cream

    1 small can mandarin oranges, drained and patted dry

    Chocolate curls

Instructions

1. Place the chopped dark chocolate in a small microwave-safe heatproof bowl. Heat for 30 seconds at 80% power. Remove and stir. Repeat for another 30 seconds, remove and stir. If chocolate isn't melted, heat in 10 second intervals, stirring until melted. Set aside.
2. Place sugar, cocoa powder, Grand Marnier, orange extract, vanilla extract, salt, and tofu in the bowl of a food processor or blender. Process or blend until completely smooth.
3. Add the melted chocolate to the pudding mixture and process until completely incorporated.
4. Divide the pudding between 6 serving dishes and refrigerate for at least 1 hour.
5. Just before serving garnish with whipped cream, orange wedges and chocolate curls.

．．．

For additional recipes mentioned in the book (and for many others), please visit my blog:

Cinnamon, Sugar, and a Little Bit of Murder
https://cinnamonsugarandalittlebitofmurder.com/

About the Author

K. A. Davis lives in Southern California with her husband, near wildfire country. During the Portola Hills fire in October 2007, she had to evacuate her two young granddaughters, one of whom has Rett Syndrome, as a wall of one hundred foot flames crept towards their home. Thankfully, due to the brave efforts of firefighters, their neighborhood was spared and no loss of life or property occurred.

She writes the Cinnamon, Sugar, and a Little Bit of Murder blog and has had several children's articles published in *Cricket*, *Nature Friend*, *Skipping Stones*, and *The Seed of Truth* magazines. K. A. Davis is a member of Mystery Writers of America and Sisters in Crime.